continued . . .

A
SINFUL SAFARI

MICHAEL KILIAN

BERKLEY PRIME CRIME, NEW YORK

A SINFUL SAFARI

A Berkley Prime Crime Book / published by arrangement with the author

PRINTING HISTORY
Berkley Prime Crime mass-market edition / July 2003

ISBN: 0-425-19108-7

Berkley Prime Crime Books are published
by The Berkley Publishing Group,
a division of Penguin Group (USA) Inc.,
375 Hudson Street, New York, New York 10014.
The name BERKLEY PRIME CRIME and
the BERKLEY PRIME CRIME design
are trademarks belonging to Penguin Group (USA) Inc.

PRINTED IN THE UNITED STATES OF AMERICA

10 9 8 7 6 5 4 3 2 1

For Kristie Miller,
and for Lara Weber,
Africa Hands

BEDFORD, I'd like you to teach me to shoot a gun."

It had been a busy and most pleasant Saturday afternoon at Bedford Green's Eighth Street art gallery in Greenwich Village. He and his famously beautiful assistant Sloane Smith had between them sold seven paintings, including an Andre Derain Fauvist harbor scene and a George Varian landscape, bringing in more profit in a single day than the little business had often enjoyed in a month.

Bedford was of a mind to close early and take Sloane out for a celebratory dinner at the Carousel, their favorite French restaurant. Firearms were not among the subjects of conversation he'd been contemplating.

"Gun?" he said, as though it were a foreign word.

"Yes," said Sloane. "Gun. A hunting rifle."

He was at his desk, near the front door, looking through the half-dozen checks that had been made out to him and thinking that President Coolidge, so fond of proclaiming that the business of America was business, would be proud of him.

Bedford had certainly given him little such occasion in

the past. If the economic boom of the 1920s was finally reaching his little enterprise, many of his customers had in truth been steered his way by his friend and Eighth Street neighbor, Gertrude Vanderbilt Whitney, in gratitude for a past service to her family.

"Why don't I teach you fly-fishing instead?" he said.

"But you don't know anything about fly-fishing."

"True. But you can't get so badly hurt fly-fishing."

Sloane had been standing at the front window, the late afternoon sun agreeably bright on the contours of her pale green dress—if dress it could be called. A "new woman," Sloane was as dangerously avant garde in fashion as she was in her political ideas. She stood six feet tall—Bedford's exact height—and her immodest hemlines seemed even shorter on her long legs. He could only hope fashions would turn more conservative by winter.

She turned to face him, hands on hips. Her gray-green eyes, framed by sleek dark hair worn in a chic bob, widened once, and then narrowed. Not a good sign.

"I do not intend to hurt myself, Bedford Green. I need to learn how to shoot so I won't look the fool when I go on safari."

Bedford simply stared, then attempted to mask his surprise and displeasure by brushing bits of dust from his blue blazer and gray flannel trousers. "And where are you going on safari? New Jersey?"

Sloane, though herself a Midwesterner, always talked of New Jersey as if it were a strange, exotic land where a Henry Stanley might look for a Doctor Livingston.

She did not appreciate such a lame attempt at humor. "I'm going to Kenya, Bedford. It's in British East Africa, not Hudson County."

Bedford gathered up the checks and placed them in an envelope, putting that in a desk drawer and locking it. "Africa is at a far remove. Traveling there would require no small absence from one's place of employment—a matter of some interest to one's employer."

She came up to his desk and sat upon it, crossing her extraordinary legs. " 'One's employer' appears to be upset."

"A trifle."

"I meant to tell you sooner, Bedford, but I wasn't sure I wanted to go." She gestured at the empty places on the gallery wall. "Now, we've done so well—it shouldn't be so much of a problem my being away for a few weeks."

He felt a sudden sadness—and a sense of utter abandonment. He swallowed, looking out toward the street, where a junk dealer's horse and cart had pulled up in front of a Pierce Arrow touring car parked at the curb.

"Perhaps not."

Sloane reached and put her hand on his, leaning near. "Don't be unhappy, Bedford. You owe me a vacation. And this is important to me."

"How can killing animals be important to you?"

"I don't intend to kill any animals. That's why I want you to teach me to shoot. So I'll know how to miss without looking like I did it on purpose. And when I miss, I want to make sure I miss."

Bedford shook his head. "I'm not your man for rifles. Wasn't in the infantry in the war, remember? I flew airplanes—Nieuports and SE-5s. Lewis guns. Hotchkiss machine guns. I hope big game hunting hasn't come to that."

"You know how to shoot pistols. You have one."

His 1912 Savage .32 automatic was in one of the other desk drawers. He took it out, and handed it to her. She took it unhappily, looked at it, then set it down.

"Tell me why it's important for you to go on safari," he asked.

"My Uncle Dixon invited me."

"The merchant prince?"

"He owns a store in Chicago."

"A huge department store. And miles of real estate around it."

A slight sigh of exasperation. "Bedford, you are not a socialist—much as we've all tried to convert you. Why are you being so churlish about my Uncle Dixon's money? You have all sorts of rich friends. Your lady friend Tatty Chase has lots more money than my family does. Than most families do. Yet you don't play the Bolshevik with her."

"She doesn't use it to go off on hunting sprees."

Sloane slid off the desk and lighted a cigarette, commencing a slow walk around their front display room. Reaching a painting by John Sloan, one of Bedford's favorites, she whirled around to face him.

"I could quit, you know. This very moment."

He permitted himself a slight sigh of exasperation. "How long will this safari take?"

"With the voyage to England, and then to Africa, perhaps two months."

"Sloane . . ."

"You are not my master, sir. White slavery is illegal in the State of New York."

He stood up, spreading his hands in a gesture of peace and supplication. "I would not for a moment suggest that I was your master. Most of the time, it's quite the other way around. You're the one who really runs this gallery. And you do a much better job at it than I ever have. That's not a small part of my concern. We've been doing so well. If you go—"

"Is that how you think of me? An instrument of commerce?"

He went to the window. The driver of the Pierce Arrow was engaged in a vigorous exchange with the junk dealer. It wasn't clear to Bedford why the dealer had stopped his cart there.

"Go on safari," he said. "With my blessing. I'll find someone to help out until you come back."

"Some sweet young thing out of the Pratt Institute? Maybe I won't go."

"Please tell me why this is important. The whole story."

She looked at her wristwatch. "Let's go to Chumley's."

THEIR favorite speakeasy, near both her apartment and his, Chumley's was the haunt of some of the best minds and most flamboyant reputations in the Village. Edmund Wilson and Edna St. Vincent Millay were regulars, though neither was in evidence so early in the day. They went to Sloane's favorite table, which was in a corner by the fireplace. It offered privacy, but also provided a view of every other table in the smoky, dimly lit, Old English room.

Privacy seemed to be uppermost on her mind. Once they'd been served their gins, she lowered her voice.

"My Uncle Dixon has a new wife," she said.

"Is there no other convenient way to meet her? Or have you been banned from Lake Forest for your radical ideas?"

A sharp, dark look warned him that continued flippancy would swiftly terminate the conversation.

"I didn't go to their wedding," she said. "I was very fond of my Aunt Kate, whom he divorced to marry this— to marry Georgia."

"Is she Southern?"

"Not at all. She's from Kansas. Came to Chicago, and worked her way up the social ladder."

"How many rungs were involved?"

"Two other husbands. The last one was actually in the Social Register, but he hadn't any money. Now it's Uncle Dixon, who does."

"Do I detect snobbery here?"

A darker, sharper look. "You're the one from the 'old

family,' Bedford—even if you have been stone broke most of your life. My great-grandfather was a fur trapper, remember?" She sat back, staring fixedly at her drink. "Anyway, Georgia may have been a five-and-ten cent store clerk once, but she's not a social embarrassment. She's a fast learner. My cousin Molly says she subscribes to all the right magazines—*Town and Country, Vanity Fair.* She's just so—predatory. For all I know, my Uncle Dixon is merely a step up on the way to something grander. In the meantime, my Aunt Kate has had to endure this humiliation."

"He divorced her?"

"She was compelled to divorce him. The aggrieved party and all. But it doesn't make it any easier for her at the Casino Club. Titters, you know. Whispers. And Georgia goes there now, if you can imagine that."

Ring Lardner was coming down the entrance stairs, singing a song about a dog.

"Somehow," Bedford said, "I fail to comprehend how spending weeks in the jungle with this pair is something you'd drop everything to do."

"It's not the jungle. Kenya is mostly highlands, or so I'm told. The point is, Bedford, it's an opportunity to help out my family."

"Uncle Dixon or Aunt Kate?"

"Both. There are some other interesting aspects as well."

"You've never seen a hippopotamus?"

She gave him an odd little smile. "The Prince of Wales."

"He looks nothing like a hippopotamus."

"He's going on some grand tour of the colonies and is supposed to have a stop in British East Africa. I think that's why Georgia's so keen on going."

"You once told me you wouldn't get off a barstool to see the king of England."

"The prince seems a pretty good egg—for a royal. Visited coal miners' families during Britain's General Strike. Went to the front during the war—just like you."

As an aviator in the service of the French, and later the British, Bedford had been to the front, with all its Hun ack-ack, as often as four or five times a day, flying weather permitting. The Prince of Wales, as far as he could recall, had been there all of once.

"So you want to go to Africa to protect the heir to the British throne from a fortune-hunting dime-store clerk from Kansas?"

"I don't think there's much danger of a future king of England marrying an America commoner—especially a divorcee like Georgia. I'm just not sure she's aware of that."

Lardner was walking across the room with the slow deliberation of a man with too many whiskies in his tank. Bedford quickly looked away from him and back to Sloane. He admired Lardner enormously but didn't want recognition to grow into conversation—not on this occasion.

"You said 'aspects,' " he said. "Plural."

"There's my friend Alice," she said.

Bedford could think of no "Alices." Certainly not in Kenya.

"Alice Silverthorne. Now Alice de Janze'."

She spoke the name as though it was as well known as Mary Pickford's or Louise Brooks's. Bedford could respond only with blankness.

"We grew up together in Chicago. Her father was in manufacturing of some sort. Her mother was Armour meat money."

"Ah, meat money."

"Stop it, Bedford. You're supposed to be heartbroken that I'm going away."

"I am. I'm masking it with these lame attempts at mirth."

"You should listen. Alice is someone who would interest you. Interest any writer."

"Newspaperman. And I'm not that anymore."

"Interest any newspaperman. Former or current. Alice and I came out together."

"As in debut? I thought you were against all that, Sloane."

She glanced to either side, then leaned forward. "If you tell a soul in this place, or any place, I shall be very happy to shoot you, Bedford Green. Once you've taught me how."

"But I haven't yet. You might miss and hit Lardner, there. Though I doubt he'd notice." He waved to the gentlemanly Filipino bartender for two more gins. "Back to Alice. There you were, coming out."

"She was the wildest deb there ever was in Chicago. There's nothing anyone's done in Greenwich Village that she hadn't done or tried by the time she was eighteen. But she was always like that. Her mother died when she was five. Her father—well, there was an unhealthy relationship. He was a rummy. Bad sort all around. Her uncle was made her legal guardian, but her father was allowed to take her on vacation once a year and he'd drag her off to Nice and such places. Dressed her like a courtesan, took her to nightclubs, gave her a pet black leopard—when she was all of fourteen."

"You were friends?"

"She was much in my life—for a while." Sloane dabbed at her eye. The drinks came and she accepted hers with much gratitude. "She was married a few years ago—in Chicago—but to a Frenchman she'd met in Paris. *Le Comte de Janze'*."

"*Comte?* That's even better than meat money."

"Stop it!"

"I'm sorry. It's just that I'm in such a good mood today. Or was."

"It was an improbable match—and I gather it's a horrible marriage. Especially for him. A very quiet, serious man." She drank. "I almost fell in love with him myself."

"Was he a writer?"

"Of a sort."

"Aha."

"I don't know what attracted her to him. But they married. They have two children. She gave them to her husband's sister in Normandy. I guess she sees them when she's in France. Or used to."

"Used to?"

"She and de Janze' moved to Kenya. She fell in love with another man there—an English remittance man named Raymond de Trafford. She followed him back to Paris last year, begging him to marry her if she'd divorce de Janze'. He's Catholic, and wouldn't do it. Said his family would stop his allowance. She went with him to the *Gare de Nord* to say good-bye when he was going back to London, but instead of saying good-bye, she shot him. And shot herself. They were horribly wounded, but they survived."

"And now?"

"She's back in Kenya. So is he."

"Sounds like I should teach you to shoot just so you can survive the dinner parties down there."

Sloane took his hand and held it in hers—something she almost never did. "I have a better idea, Bedford."

"Staying here with me?"

"Bringing you with me."

"Sloane . . ."

"You've never been to Africa."

"I'd rather go to New Jersey."

"You can afford to close the gallery for a while. You've

enough money to get you through the rest of the year. And Gertrude will keep an eye on things. She owes you."

They sat without speaking for the longest while, Sloane still holding his hand. It struck Bedford that they must look like lovers, though that perception would have been miles from the truth.

"I don't want to go on safari."

"Just come to Africa with me. Please, Bedford. I really need you there. The English people there—the men—they're a lot of them titled, but they're rough customers. And not much on morals, I'm told."

"Sloane . . ."

"I went to Newport with you when you asked me to. Got me mixed up with all those Vanderbilts, not to mention the Hungarians."

"There's a difference of a few thousand miles. And not so many guns."

"All right. If you won't come, I won't be coming back to the gallery."

"You can't mean that."

"Yes I can."

"But I can't afford the passage to Kenya."

"I'll pay."

"I can't accept that."

"You can earn it. Be my white hunter."

"No thank you."

"Gun bearer, then. Traveling companion."

"Paid traveling companion? How high I've risen in the world."

"You've done work for hire for friends before. Inquiries and such."

"I was compensated for my expenses. And those people were in trouble."

"My Uncle Dixon is in trouble. I'm sure Alice is in trouble. She always was. I'll pay your expenses if you'll come with me and find out what can be done about it. You did as much for Gertrude's brother, and accepted his money."

She removed her hands from his.

"How soon?" he asked.

"I sail Wednesday — on the *Carpathia*."

He was on the verge of saying "yes."

"Let me think upon it tonight. We can talk tomorrow."

Sloane's eyes sought his, as if she might find a better answer in them. Then, without finishing her drink or saying another word, she rose and left the barroom.

FEELING flush, Bedford hailed a taxicab at Sheridan Square, directing the slothful-looking driver to Gramercy Park. Alighting before a brownstone town house of four stories, he hurried up the stairs, hoping to find the owner of the residence at home.

But Dayton Crosby, his old friend, mentor, and foster father, did not respond to several rings of the bell. He was likely at one of his several clubs.

A rumpled, wheezy old gentleman in his seventies, Crosby had been Bedford's parents' lawyer, and now performed the same service for him — though happily almost never for any charge. Descended from one of New York's ancient Knickerbocker families, the old fellow had been managing partner of one of the city's most established law firms, but had retired in middle age to devote his time to more interesting pursuits, including chess, the authorship of a series of amusing histories and biographies, and an animal welfare charity he had founded.

Bedford looked in at the Masters Chess Club, the Harvard Club, the University Club, the Knickerbocker, and finally the Coffee House Club, a somewhat raffish but patrician bohemian retreat founded by *Vanity Fair* publisher Frank Crowninshield. It was Crosby's favorite. If

Bedford could have afforded a club, it would have been his favorite, too.

The old man was in the upstairs bar, talking about eighteenth-century English dog paintings with one of the trustees of the Metropolitan Museum of Art. He politely excused himself, taking note of Bedford's undisguised urgency.

"Is something amiss?" he asked, after leading Bedford to comfortable chairs by a window overlooking the street.

"Yes. I find myself possibly going on a safari."

Crosby studied Bedford for a long moment, as though searching for visible signs of madness. "You mean with guns? Shooting animals?"

"I'm afraid so. Though I certainly don't intend to kill anything." He went on to explain what Sloane intended. Crosby was incurably smitten with Sloane, and was happy to indulge her in most everything—though not, of course, to the extent of hunting trips.

Bedford waited for what he presumed would be one of Crosby's rare but always spectacular eruptions of outrage. Of all the many things of which he disapproved, the killing of animals for sport was at the top of the list.

Spiritous liquors could be had at the Coffee House Club, if one was discreet. Crosby sent for two whiskeys. Waiting for them to come, he stared down at the wooden floor, pondering the matter as though it was a complicated question of statecraft.

The scotch arrived. In a moment, he would doubtless lash out at Bedford as a cretinous clod for even considering such a lapse into barbarism. With any luck, his reproach might be so vehement as to not only justify Bedford's unwillingness to participate in this African misadventure but cause Sloane to reconsider her decision to go.

Crosby sipped his whiskey, then peered mischievously at Bedford over the rim of the glass.

"Upon full reflection, young man," he said, "I think you should go."

Beford gave a start, setting his own drink down to avoid spilling it.

"Would you mind repeating that?" he asked.

"I think you should go to Africa and accompany those overly moneyed miscreants on their bloodthirsty trek."

"Dayton, you can't mean that. You'd be drummed out of your own charity if your board members heard you say that."

"On the contrary. I know you. I know the formidable Miss Smith. I think having the both of you on this safari will prove so disruptive it could be considered an act of sabotage."

"Dayton, these people will be toting real guns. Elephant guns. Someone's bound to be hurt."

"Yes. I know. Did I ever tell you about my campaign on behalf of the right to arm bears?"

CHAPTER 2

THE African coast appeared late on a hot morning as a gray-green smudge along the southwestern horizon, warped and muddied in the steamy haze. Bedford had stationed himself at the rail near the bow to gain a first glimpse of Mombasa, but the hot sun proved too much, and at length he sought the refuge of a deck chair set in the shade.

It had been unbearable below—almost ever since Suez. The ventilator system wasn't working properly and his cabin had been barely habitable. Sloane's was not much better. She had suggested they spend the remainder of the voyage sitting naked atop the bridge. They hadn't gone that far, but had spent much of their time on deck. What breeze there was came mostly from the steamer's forward motion, and now, as they slowed approaching the coast, that was diminishing.

When the steward came by, Bedford ordered a gin. He felt as distant from the island of Manhattan as he did from the moon. Were some disaster to befall his little art gallery in his absence, it would be weeks before he'd hear about it.

The nearer they'd come to the Kenyan coast, the more he'd felt the weight of a strange foreboding. Awaiting them was a land acrawl with reasons why they should not come. He felt like one of the Greek soldiers bearing Iphigenia to the Trojan wars.

With a sigh, Sloane settled into the chair next to him.

"Good morning," she said, wiping her pretty brow with a damp handkerchief. "Are we here?"

"That's Africa," Bedford replied, gesturing toward the western horizon with his glass. "Though I've no idea when we'll actually get there. We keep slowing down. I think the captain wants to paddle in. Save on coal or something."

Sloane looked down at her long legs. "I hope you don't mind. I'm not wearing stockings."

Her dress was of a thin material, and long for her.

"That's a coincidence, neither am I," said Bedford.

"Am I being inappropriate?"

"In this climate, no."

"I'll confide something else."

"You're not wearing any, er, unmentionables."

She smiled. "Don't mention it."

"I won't. But I'll think about it."

"There can't be a heat like this anywhere else on the planet."

"You're just spoiled by all those brisk winters growing up on Lake Michigan."

A small craft that Bedford took to be the pilot boat was approaching, though at a speed almost as slow as the ship's.

"Your interesting uncle and his bride will be waiting for us on the dock?"

"I don't think so. Aunt Kate would be there, certainly, but I fear Uncle Dixon may be distracted by his new wife. They may have gone on to Nairobi without us. I gather he's really anxious to start hunting."

"Why?"

"So he can bring back loads of trophies to Chicago. I think he's only doing this because Marshall Field went on a safari."

"Marshall Field?"

"He owns another department store."

"I know. Competitive fellows, these merchant princes."

"It's Georgia more than Uncle Dixon, I think. He wants to prove his manhood to her."

"By shooting an animal."

"As many as possible. Bring back more than Mister Field."

"I don't understand how shooting a gun proves manhood. Now, if they wrestled the wild beasts to death with their bare hands, that'd be more like it."

The steward came by and Sloane ordered a gin for herself. "Are we drinking too early?"

"Not for here."

She crossed her legs and tilted back her head, half closing her eyes against the glare. She was perspiring, and her clumpy garment ill-suited her, but she had never looked more beautiful.

"Marry me," he said.

There had been something between them almost from the first moment they had met at a party in Patchin Place. He had never quite determined what that something was— let alone whether it was good or bad or dangerous or a complete waste of time. But he sensed it now.

"What did you say?"

"We can take the next steamer back. Go to the south of France. Forget Uncle Dixon."

"Bedford, the heat is getting to you."

"I'm serious."

"No. It's the heat."

She rose and went to the rail.

The pilot's arrival aboard had stirred the captain to life. There was a shuddering rumble below and the ship began to increase its speed, the wide bow shoving the waters aside with a great swoosh.

As they came closer, the city of Mombasa began to reveal itself—crude dwellings and splotches of bright color sprawling over an island between two large bays. There was a fort prominent along the shoreline—an old, unused relic whose stone walls dripped with vines. Small figures crawled and darted over the ramparts.

Sloane squinted. "Are those soldiers?"

"Apes, I think," said Bedford. "Monkeys."

She looked down the deck. Her drink had not yet come.

"What's wrong?" Bedford asked.

"Nothing."

THERE was no one to meet them at the dock. They waited until nearly all the passengers from their ship had departed, then finally surrendered to reality, counting themselves lucky when they were able to find a taxicab after they had cleared through customs. Sloane had overpacked. The driver was compelled to tie two of her suitcases onto the roof of the automobile.

"Do you remember the name of the hotel?" Bedford asked, before getting in.

Sloane went to the other side of the cab. "No. But it will occur to me."

It did not. They sat there awhile, then finally moved on when Bedford, taking a guess, told the driver to go to the most expensive hotel in Mombasa.

The little city was aswarm and asweat with humanity—of every variety and hue. English ladies and gentlemen, looking bored and unhappy; natives in aboriginal garb, some of them barefoot and carrying staffs that might as well have been spears; a few actually carrying spears. There were turbaned Hindus, Sikhs, and Muslims; Portuguese traders; Germans from Tanganyika, their former colony in East Africa; Chinese and Malays; and, here and there, most obvious of all, a few Americans, presumably rich.

Beggars were as numerous as the peddlers and market women—and the flies that buzzed about everything. Numerous also were the unfortunate children—scrawny, wide-eyed, and nearly naked—some darting along the street, others sitting in the dirt, gazing vacantly as though at worlds only they could see. The animal life was as abundant as on the upland plains, only different—cattle, goats, pigs, skittering vermin.

"This has to be it!" said Sloane, as they pulled up in front of the most elegant building they'd yet seen. "I remember now."

"It's only what I'd expect of a merchant prince. I'll bet Marshall Field stayed here, too."

She registered them both in adjoining rooms. The desk clerk, taking a while to be satisfied with her signature, finally produced an envelope bearing Sloane's name.

It was from her uncle. She read it quickly. "He's out buying guns," she said.

"Let's have lunch."

"All right. And then a bath."

"And then?"

"Then I'm going to spend the rest of this hellish afternoon in my room lying naked on my bed until the heat goes away."

"I don't think this heat does go away."

"I'll give it a try. If you decide to go strolling on our mutual balcony, do respect a girl's privacy."

"Of course."

He did, spending the afternoon in much the same way she said she was going to, dozing in the faint breeze from the open doors to the balcony. He was so enervated he scarcely stirred when some small furry tree creature entered and scratched around a corner of his room for several minutes before departing in search of quarters with more likelihood of provender. Bedford was beginning to gain real respect for Henry Stanley and Doctor Livingston.

Sunset found them both on the hotel's wide, shaded veranda, freshly bathed again and changed. Some men in the hotel were in black tie, but Bedford made do with a tan traveling suit.

He ordered pink gins for them both—a concoction he hadn't enjoyed since his time flying with the British in the war.

"Gosh," said Sloane. "Here she comes."

He turned to see a red-haired woman standing just at the door to the veranda. She was dressed entirely in white, which became her, but her skirt was much too short for what appeared to be Kenyan colonial standards and she wore entirely too much jewelry, including several long strands of pearls and large gold bracelets on both wrists.

"Sloane?" she called.

"She sees us," said Sloane.

"Isn't that why we've come?"

"Shhh." Sloane gave a slight wave, rising. The woman in white rushed forward, spreading her arms. Bedford could see Sloane stiffen.

"I'm your Aunt Georgia," the woman said, brushing a kiss across Sloane's cheek as she flung her arms around her. She gave a sort of squeal, and then stepped back, her mouth forced into a wide smile, her eyes speculative.

Georgia Smith was a compellingly attractive woman, but more sensual than beautiful. Her features were a trifle outsized, like her bosom, and there was a suggestion of coarseness about her. Her eyes went from Sloane to Bedford, and she thrust her hand out to him.

"You're Bedford Green—right? Dixon said Sloane was bringing you. I'm sure we have lots and lots of friends in common—in New York, I mean. You *are* the Bedford Green who writes the society column for that paper."

"The *New York Day*, yes. But I left that newspaper job some time ago. Now I sell art."

"Oh yes. In Greenwich Village. You and Sloane. How bohemian. I think it's just wonderful. We've nothing like that in Chicago. Greenwich Village, I mean. We have art. We have the Art Institute."

"Where is Uncle Dixon?" asked Sloane, her voice as cool as the weather was not.

"Upstairs," said Georgia. "He'll be down in a jiffy. We've been shopping for guns."

"Isn't your safari party providing those?" Sloane asked.

"Oh yes. *Le tout ensemble*. But Dixon wants some gun he heard about in Chicago." She looked about the lobby, as though there was someone or something there she had forgotten. After another calculation, she looked again to Bedford, who had pulled out a chair for her. "I think I'll have a drink."

SLOANE'S uncle, explaining he had gotten lost, joined them nearly an hour after the dining room opened. He was an unusually tall man, mostly bald, unhandsome despite his resemblance to Sloane and given to a weak, nervous smile. Hardly the look of the great white hunter. Or a robber baron.

From the moment he took his chair, Georgia was all but on his lap.

"Art," he said to Bedford.

"Sir?"

"You're in art." Uncle Dixon might just as easily have said steel, wheat, or farm implements.

"Yes, that's my, er, game," Bedford said.

"Our clients include the Vanderbilts," said Sloane—not at all a boast she would have made among their socialist New York friends.

Georgia's eyes widened at that. Then, inexplicably, she gave a nervous laugh, as though the remark had been vastly amusing.

"Do you know the Vanderbilts?" she asked.

Just then, a loud British voice boomed across the room. "Hallo there!"

Bedford turned to see a man in a tan suit with a white shirt and a partially undone black tie striding toward them. He had a bluff, tanned face and thinning hair. And, he was carrying a large-bore rifle.

"I'm Owen, Captain Jack Owen," he said, extending his hand to Bedford. "Are you Mr. Smith?"

"I am," said Uncle Dixon, seeming a trifle offended. "Are you Owen, our guide?"

"Your white hunter," Owen replied, pulling up a chair. He set the rifle on the floor behind him. "Sorry about this. Didn't want to leave it in the car."

Dixon Smith had apparently been of the mind that hunting guides were the same as servants, and not people to have at the table.

"What can we do for you?" Dixon said.

"Tonight? Absolutely nothing. But tomorrow be in the lobby ready to leave at eight in the morning. The train departs a bit shy of nine." He signaled to a waiter to bring a drink. He appeared to be well enough known for the man to be aware of his customary tipple.

It proved to be gin and quinine.

"A touch of malaria," Owen said. "Got it fighting von Lettow-Vorbeck down south in the war. Anyone here in the war?"

Bedford nodded.

"France?"

Bedford nodded again.

"Trenches?"

"Airplanes."

"Bloody Hell." Owen took a healthy sip of gin. "May take flying up myself. Trip down to here from Nairobi takes too damned long."

Georgia had perked up at the talk of war. Her expression became all the more twinkly when a remarkably attractive golden-haired couple entered the room.

The man was in a khaki British military uniform, but wore an Ascot scarf instead of a tie. The pips on his shoulders indicated the rank of major. He was a strikingly handsome, fair-haired fellow, with a tanned, bony face and blazing smile. His eyes were a bright, translucent blue. They quickly settled on Sloane.

His companion appeared to be slightly older than he— but so blue-eyed and blonde she might have been his sister. She was dressed very fashionably, in a dress of silk and linen. She would have been the most chic woman in the restaurant, were it not for Sloane, who might have come into the place directly from Fifth Avenue.

They came swiftly toward them. "Dickie Ralls," the man said, mostly to Sloane. "This is my wife Victoria."

"Lord and Lady Ralls," Owen elaborated, as they seated themselves at the next table, after moving it close. Owen nodded to the Americans, introducing each in turn, though mistakenly referring to Sloane as Bedford's wife.

"We're not married," Sloane said. "We're business associates."

Lord Ralls seemed taken aback, shifting his attention to Georgia. "But you are married, are you not, Mr. and Mrs. Smith?"

"Oh yes," said Georgia, fluttering her hands.

"Business?" pronounced Lady Ralls, solemnly. "And what is that?"

"What is 'business?'" Sloane looked offended.

Lady Ralls laughed. "Oh, no. I mean, what is your trade? We're all in business now. Aren't we, Dickie? Ours has something to do with coffee."

"Something about too low a price for coffee," her husband said, signaling vigorously for the waiter and drinks. "Actually, I do believe we may no longer be in business."

"What is your business?" Lady Ralls leaned near Bedford, smiling radiantly and putting her hand on his arm. She seemed slightly drunk.

"An art gallery in New York," Bedford said.

"Art. How lovely." She turned to Sloane, as did her husband. "Do you paint the pictures, or does you husband?"

"'Associate,' not 'husband,'" said Sloane, smiling unsweetly. "John Sloan, Andre Derain, Joseph Stella, and Egon Schiele paint the pictures, among others."

"'Stella,' 'Schiele,'" said Lady Ralls, as though the names were exotic places. "And you, Mr. Smith, are you in business, too?"

"He owns one of the largest department stores in Chicago," said Georgia.

"'Chicago,'" said Lady Ralls, making it sound the most exotic of all.

A waiter arrived with glasses and a bottle of Scotch whiskey. Lord Ralls poured, generously.

"There are three of you named Smith," he said.

"Sloane is my niece," Uncle Dixon said.

"'Niece,'" said Lady Ralls. "How nice."

Bedford had had evenings like this before, when he'd been trapped at seaside resorts with people who had become bored with summer and had turned to gin and backbiting for sport.

Dixon appeared uncomfortable with the situation, but

Georgia seemed pleased. She moved her chair closer to Lord Ralls.

"We were going to have dinner," Sloane said. "Would anyone care to join us."

Uncle Dixon looked to Georgia, who paid the invitation no mind. Owen poured himself another drink. The Rallses extended their own glasses.

"If you'll excuse us, then," Bedford said.

THEY ate quickly, lest they be joined. Afterwards, they went directly to their rooms.

They paused outside Sloane's.

"Do you suppose everyone down here is like that?"

"I've no doubt," said Bedford. "Maybe it's the heat."

"Or the gin."

"Do you want to go home?"

She hesitated, but not for long. "No."

CHAPTER 3

THE train climbed steadily through the Chyulu Hills, seemingly as bent on reaching the cooler highlands as its passengers. Bedford and Sloane rode in her compartment, but when she became tired and distracted, he left her to sleep and wandered the cars in search of Captain Owen, finding him in a capacious first-class compartment forward.

With him was an elegantly dressed woman Owen introduced as the Baroness Karen Blixen. She had bright, perceptive eyes, beautiful hands, and a pronounced accent. At first, Bedford thought she might be German; then realized the flavor in her speech was Scandinavian.

She invited him to sit down, which he did on the seat opposite.

"Captain Owen has been telling me about you and your friend Sloane," she said. "It is rare for us to have artists here."

Bedford smiled. "I am an art dealer, Baroness. Sloane is my assistant."

She laughed. "We haven't many art dealers here, either.

We haven't, alas, much art. Are you here to provide us with some?"

"No ma'am. We're here on safari."

The baroness fanned herself with her hand. "Of that we have more than sufficient quantity."

"Do you disapprove of hunting?"

She looked to the window of the railway carriage. "My husband is a hunter. A white hunter, like Captain Owen here."

It seemed neither answer nor explanation. "And you, madame?"

"I have a farm."

"The baroness owns the highest coffee plantation in the highlands," Owen said. "It is considered a local miracle that it thrives as it does."

"Not 'thrives,' Captain. 'Survives.'"

The door to the compartment slid open with a bang. Lord and Lady Ralls stood there, smiling, then entered, dropping into seats—she next to Bedford, he next to the baroness. Bedford hadn't realized they'd be on the train.

"Hello, Karen," Dickie Ralls said. "Where's Blor?"

"That is a question I stopped answering some time ago, Major Ralls. But I believe he is down in the Rift Valley, shooting animals—or assisting people like Mr. Green here in that pursuit."

"I'm not here to kill animals," Bedford said. Owen, who'd been staring idly out the window, gave a start.

"Sorry?" said the Englishman. "You're not coming with us?"

"On the contrary. But as Miss Smith's traveling companion. I didn't have in mind any shooting."

Owen snorted—good naturedly, but with emphasis. "You'll change your mind once we're out in the bush. Mr. Smith is going after elephant."

Lady Ralls leaned close. She smelled of expensive scent—and gin.

"You were a flyer in the war, though," she said, her arm pressing against his. "You didn't mind hunting then. Do you prefer killing Huns to elephants?"

"I did mind it. Two of my Germans went down in flames. The third leapt out of his aircraft rather than be burned to death. It was before they introduced parachutes."

"How ghastly."

"Then there was the strafing."

"There was nothing like that down in Tanganyika, was there, Owen?"

"I don't believe I saw a single aeroplane," he said. "Not very many Germans, either. Mostly Askaris. Thousands of 'em. Don't know why they were so bloody loyal to Kaiser Billy."

"They weren't," said Lord Ralls. "They were loyal to von Lettow-Vorbeck. An excellent fellow. Should have been an Englishman."

"You flew for the king," said Lady Ralls to Bedford. "Why was that?"

"First for the French. When the U.S. entered the war, we were supposed to transfer to the American Hat in the Ring squadron. But they wouldn't take a friend of mine— Eugene Bullard—even though he had kills and was a veteran pilot. I went with the British after Gene had an altercation with our French commanding officer and got us both in trouble."

"Why wouldn't the Americans take him?"

"He was black. Still is, actually. Owns a very popular nightclub in Paris."

All fell silent. Lady Ralls looked to her husband, who stared at Bedford as though he had just confessed to some heinous crime. Owen coughed. Only Baroness Blixen held her composure.

"That is a very interesting story, Mr. Green," she said. "Does it have an ending?"

"I don't suppose it does. Not yet, anyhow."

Dickie Ralls rose and excused himself. His wife followed. In their absence, Owen stretched and propped a boot up on the edge of the opposite seat.

"It's hard now, with the blacks," he said. "They've been restive ever since they put the railway in, because it brought in so many settlers. How many whites have we now, Baroness?"

"I think more than nine thousand now. And it seems sometimes they all turn out for the dances at the Muthaiga Club."

"The Kikuyu complain we've taken their grazing land. Hell, they took it from someone else. Same with the Masai. Both tribes came here from somewhere else. The Kikuyu from West Africa. The Masai from up in the Sudan."

"That was a thousand years ago, Captain Owen," the baroness said.

"It's all the same. History of mankind. Nothing less permanent than a map. Even one of the British Empire, on which the sun never sets."

The baroness assumed the pose of a disapproving schoolteacher. "Captain Owen. You know very well why the Africans are restive. They've been that way ever since 1922, when their leader Harry Thuku was arrested and that crowd—"

"Mob," corrected Owen.

"Gathered outside the Central Police Station in Nairobi to protest and were shot down. A hundred killed."

"The official count was twenty-one."

"Nevertheless, it was a massacre."

"Are you suggesting that Nairobi is a dangerous place to be?" Bedford asked.

"Not at all," said Owen.

Before he could speak another word, three things happened almost simultaneously. There was the muffled report of a gunshot outside the train, a large round hole with cracks spreading from it appeared in the compartment window between Owen and the baroness, and a bullet struck the polished wood paneling at the other end of the compartment with a loud "Thwunk!", sending splinters into the air.

Baroness Blixen gave a cry, then quickly restored herself, looking to the others. Owen flattened himself against the seat back. Bedford simply froze in place.

Another gunshot followed, but no bullet came their way. After a momentary hesitation, Owen got to his feet and lowered the compartment window enough to stick his head out.

"Whoever it was, they're way behind us now," he said, withdrawing back inside. "Doubtless some fool amateur trying for big game on his own—or with a white hunter who shouldn't be in business." He returned to his seat, eyeing the small crater in the paneling. "Large-bore rifle. If His Lordship were still sitting there, would have taken his head off."

The baroness made a face. She had a few crumbs of fractured glass on her skirt, which she carefully brushed off. "It's a dangerous country at times," she said.

Bedford stood up. "I think I'd best check on Miss Smith."

"Of course," said the baroness.

"Don't get your knickers in a knot, old boy," Owen said. "Always a bit of bother like that out here."

B EDFORD made his way back to Sloane's compartment without encountering any sign of damage caused by the second shot. There was none upon or about her compartment door. He knocked, gently.

"Yes?"

"It's Bedford."

"Are you all right?"

"Yes. Are you?"

"Yes. Come in."

He opened the door. Sloane was sitting just where he had left her, looking a bit wan and discomfitted. On the seat opposite was Lord Ralls, who grinned. Next to him was Georgia Smith, who seemed ecstatic.

"Someone shot at the train," Bedford said.

Georgia's happiness turned to confusion. Lord Ralls's grin vanished. "What in blazes are you talking about?" he said.

"I wish I knew."

CHAPTER 4

THEY chuffed into Nairobi the following morning. There'd been drinking late into the night—entirely too much of it. Bedford and Sloane had been as circumspect as possible, and had retired early, but both still felt bleary, and the bright, hot morning sun was not particularly welcome.

Sloane had come into his compartment, accompanied by a porter bearing a tray with teapot and two cups. She thanked him sweetly. When he departed, she leaned back against the seat and groaned.

"I don't think I'm going to survive this adventure," she said.

"Someone knocked on my door last night," Bedford said. "Was that you?"

"No. Someone knocked on mine. I thought it was you."

"And you didn't answer?"

"I also thought it might be Georgia. Or that devil-may-care Lord Ralls."

"Or both."

"A ghastly thought." She took a sip of tea. "In a country that grows so much coffee, why does this railroad have only tea?"

"Be grateful for it." He leaned to look out the window at the city. He had expected something far grander than this collection of wood and mud-walled one-story buildings with corrugated iron roofs. Here and there were some substantial houses, but, for the most part, Nairobi seemed less a colonial capital than a frontier town.

"I wonder why they come here?" Sloane asked.

"Who?"

"People like the Rallses."

"Tired of England, I suppose."

"A man who's tired of England is tired of life."

"You have that quote wrong. It's London." She sipped her tea. "And I don't think His Lordship is tired of life yet."

OWEN had railway porters create a sort of encampment at the station entrance with their luggage, placing Uncle Dixon's newly acquired Rigby rifle on top in its case. The white hunter then asked Bedford and the Smiths to stand guard over everything while he went for transport.

As they stood there—Sloane brazenly smoking in the street—the Baroness Blixen came by on the arm of a tall, engaging-looking fellow Bedford assumed was her husband, the Baron Blixen. But she introduced him as Denys Finch-Hatton, describing him as the best white hunter in Kenya.

They moved on quickly, replaced by an Englishman in tan jacket and pants and dusty boots who was accompanied by two African constables who wore police uniforms but no footgear of any kind.

"Are you the Americans on the train?" he asked.

"Yes," said Bedford. "Are you looking for Captain Owen?"

"No, I'm looking for you. I'm Inspector Jellicoe of the Kenya police."

"Have we done something wrong? We've only just arrived."

The inspector wore a look of permanent exasperation on his face, but he seemed a pleasant sort, with a habit of smiling after speaking. His face was very flushed, though Bedford found the day to be cool—at least compared to Mombasa.

"No, no," said the inspector, taking a notebook from his pocket. "I'm just inquiring of the passengers about a gunshot report I received. Someone shooting at the train."

"Captain Owen thinks it was an accident. There seems to be a lot of shooting out here."

"What do you think it was, sir?"

"The bullet that struck the compartment I was in came through the window. It was amazing that it didn't strike anyone."

"You saw no one who might have fired it?"

"No. It took us all quite by surprise. There was a second shot, but I don't know what it hit."

"The outside of the next carriage, apparently." He closed the notebook. "Thank you. Doubt we'll need to bother you further." He closed his notebook. "Probably some inexperienced hunter." Another punctuating smile. "Possibly one of you Americans."

As the inspector departed, the baroness and her friend Finch-Hatton reappeared, driving past in an open touring car whose passengers included a tall native and two gigantic dogs. A cream-colored auto pulled up in the Blixen car's wake, but Owen was not aboard. The driver, a black soldier in a sergeant's uniform, dismounted and went into the station, emerging a few minutes later with Lord and

Lady Ralls. Bedford wasn't sure whether to describe them as already drunk or still drunk.

Waving gaily, Lady Ralls got into the back of the vehicle, while her husband, leering at Sloane, sat up front next to the driver, whom he proceeded to berate as they drove off.

"Bugatti," Bedford said.

"What?" asked Sloane.

"That car—it's a Bugatti. An Italian machine, very rare and very expensive."

THE four Americans continued to be abandoned—except by beggars, peddlers, and a busy assortment of insects. Georgia seemed a bit bewildered, but put on a brave face. Her husband, like his niece, appeared fretful.

"Can't wait to get out into the bush," he said to Bedford.

"Right," Bedford replied, knowing that the insects out there would doubtless be even more numerous. To think he had been bothered by the occasional cockroach that turned up in his Greenwich Village flat.

"Have you ever seen a lion close up?" Dixon asked.

"Just the ones in front of the New York Public Library."

"We have them in Chicago, too," injected Georgia.

"Lions?"

"Lion statues. In front of the Art Institute. I'm so very fond of art. Are you?"

Bedford could have sworn he heard Sloane growl. He hoped they wouldn't be invited to too many dinner parties here. "I'm very fond of art. But it's not very fond of me."

She had no idea what he meant. "Well, Dixon is very fond of it. We have several rare paintings."

Uncle Dixon appeared uncomfortable with the subject—or, perhaps, all subjects.

Owen happily arrived just then in a two-vehicle caravan—another open touring car and a sort of truck, from
which two Africans jumped down and headed for the pile
of luggage. There was a third black man, wearing native
dress and holding a spear, who remained standing ramrod
straight in the back of the truck.

"I've arranged quarters for you all at the Muthaiga
Club," Owen said to Dixon. "You're there as my guests,
but it will be put on the bill."

"Of course." Dixon appeared well used to having things
put on the bill.

"We're not staying at a hotel?" Georgia asked.

"You'll be happier at the Muthaiga," said Owen. "It's
quite the center of things in Nairobi. And I'm told that our
fellow guests just now will include members of the royal
entourage."

"Royal?" said Georgia.

"Yes. His Royal Highness, the Prince of Wales. He's
just now in British East Africa. He's staying at the governor's residence, but the rest of his party is at the Muthaiga,
and I expect he'll make a showing there."

Georgia flushed, and not simply from the heat.

THERE were military everywhere on the expansive
grounds of the club, mostly African soldiers in fezzes,
blue tunics, and khaki shorts. A few English officers in
stuffy white dress uniforms were in view as well, as were
ladies in elegant but somewhat dated finery. A line of
Rolls-Royce automobiles were parked along the drive.

Black servants appeared without summons to take their
luggage, as Owen led the group into the Muthaiga.

It was a sprawling structure, divided into wings to catch
the breezes, with many inviting verandas. Owen himself
escorted them to their rooms, which he had procured with

some difficulty, as many of the planters had come into town for the royal visit.

To their dismay, Bedford and Sloane were accorded a room together, presenting an awkward moment.

"Sorry," Owen said. "My fault. I suppose I failed to get across to them that you two aren't married. I'm afraid there's nothing else here at the club. They're quite full up."

"That's all right," Bedford said. "I'll go to a hotel."

"There are really only two I'd recommend—the Stanley, and the Norfolk," said the white hunter. "But I expect they'll be full up."

"We'll work it out," Sloane said. "Thanks for everything." She held the door open, anxious to close it behind Owen.

The man didn't budge. "Perhaps I can find one of the local gentleman who'd be glad to double up. Or I can arrange a billet for Mr. Green with the military."

"Captain Green and I will share this one," Sloane pronounced. "We've had to make do in this manner before. Unless you think it will offend local sensibilities."

"Quite the contrary," Owen said. "It rather conforms to local sensibilities."

"But your uncle," said Bedford, uncomfortably.

"My uncle be damned. His sleeping arrangements are far less chaste than ours. Just because he's married his mistress doesn't elevate her to respectability. He certainly has no right to be disapproving."

Owen fidgeted, as though apprehensive that his safari was going to be rendered disagreeable by this unforeseen discord in the Smith family.

"Well then," he said, moving to the door.

"Wait," said Sloane. "Which way to the bar?"

"Actually, it's directly off the lobby, but I'm afraid it's gentlemen only."

"This isn't New York," Bedford observed, rather foolishly.

Sloane gave him a dark look, and turned to begin unpacking. "Ladies are not allowed to mingle with gentlemen in the bar, but they're allowed in the rooms of gentlemen to whom they're not married?"

Owen stepped into the hallway, then paused. "Ladies are served on the veranda," he said. "At any hour."

Bedford surveyed their chamber, which was large and airy, but had no carpeting.

"All right," he said. "I'll sleep on the floor."

Sloane had opened one of her suitcases and picked up a pair of silk stockings. She set them down again. "Let's go to the veranda."

THERE were a number of well-dressed people seated around the tables. Sloane and Bedford took two large chairs by the railing, ordering pink gins and observing the other guests. Some of the women's hats were quite elaborate—a few ridiculously so.

"You'd think they were at Ascot," Bedford said.

Sloane looked in the direction of one such woman, but her mind appeared to be elsewhere.

Just as their drinks arrived, a lady in white stepped out into the sunlight from the club's interior. She was dark-haired, very slender, and remarkably beautiful—the equal even of Sloane. Two British army officers accompanied her, in some evidently subservient capacity. One of them began introducing her to some of the people at the tables. When she turned Bedford's way, she shaded her eyes, peering, then came toward him.

"Bedford? Bedford Green?"

Sloane groaned. "Wherever we go."

"It's Thelma Furness," said Bedford, quietly. "She used to be Thelma Morgan. Gloria Morgan Vanderbilt's sister."

He rose. Thelma stood waiting for him, not moving an inch further in his direction. Very royal of her.

As he had chronicled in his newspaper society column, back in the days when he had one, the "fabulous Morgan sisters" had taken New York by storm while still in their teens. Gloria was the only one to have married into very big money, with her husband Reggie Vanderbilt, an aging alcoholic, conveniently dying after only a year of wedded bliss.

Sisters Thelma and Consuelo had settled for titled Englishmen—in Thelma's case, a viscount.

Bedford had done her a favor or two in his newspaper days. He'd never asked for anything in return, but resented this standoffish reception.

He began to realize there was reason for it—and nothing to do with him. The two army officers were hanging back, but kept their eyes on her, as though they were dogs and she was about to throw them something to fetch.

As he came up to her, Thelma at last extended her hand—not to be kissed, as she had liked in the past, but to be shaken, formally.

"Whatever are you doing out here in Africa, Bedford?" she asked, smiling brightly, as if to assure him that this forced formality was an inadvertent but inescapable annoyance they had to endure, and that, notwithstanding this, she was really glad to see him.

"I'm on safari," he said.

She looked as though she were barely restraining a guffaw. "In the old days, the only thing you hunted was gossip."

It always disconcerted Bedford to hear someone so young talk about "the old days."

"Actually," he said, "I'm just tagging along with a friend."

"Me, too," she said. "My friend is as beautiful as yours, but I daresay of infinitely higher social standing."

"Not in Chicago," said Bedford, somewhat defensively. "She's a former debutante from Lake Forest who moved to New York to live the bohemian life and embrace socialism."

"Well, my friend is English—and a boy. Looks one, at any rate. And he's about as far as you can get from a Bolshevik." She paused, waiting for Bedford to ask the desired question. When he did not, she frowned and then jabbed him amicably in the ribs.

"Bedford," she proclaimed, "my 'friend' is the Prince of Wales."

That revelation was the sort of gossip Bedford's former society scribe colleagues would have stood him a year's worth of drinks to obtain.

"Truly?"

"Most absolutely and wonderfully truly."

"And the viscount?"

She stepped back, warily, but with a bit of mischief in her eyes. "My husband, sir, is a very loyal British subject."

"I'm overwhelmed."

"So was I."

The subject needed to be changed. "May I introduce my friend?"

"Actually, Bedford, I think I met her once at Newport. You two were on one of the Vanderbilt boats. But I've got to run. I'm supposed to meet HRH at the racetrack. He's awarding a trophy to the winner."

DID you have a nice little Vanderbilt chat?" Sloane asked upon his return. "Something about the servant problem? Though I must say—certainly no servant problem here." She took a sip of her gin.

"We talked of something else," he said, taking up his

own drink. "I do believe Thelma has become mistress to the Prince of Wales."

"*Quelles frissons.*"

"They have a croquet lawn here. Let's play."

CHAPTER 5

SLOANE had brought an evening gown with her to Africa—but only the one. Bedford had packed his white dinner jacket, but had neglected to bring more than one formal shirt, which he'd had to have laundered every day on the ship. He hoped there would not be so many black tie occasions in the wilds, though with the British, one never knew.

At least perspiration would not be so great a problem. To his surprise, the temperature had moderated in the late afternoon, and there was a hint of coolness by evening.

They'd been invited to a reception and late supper at the club that night. Bedford was unsure whether Captain Owen was responsible or if they had Thelma to thank for this. No matter who was responsible, it appeared that all Nairobi—white Nairobi—had been invited as well. They probably could have crashed the soiree without much problem.

The Prince of Wales, of course, was the guest of honor. Sloane, in proper socialist fashion, professed to despise the royals and the rigid British class system their existence supported, though many Americans with her background spent much of their lives trying to ape that very thing.

Despising the Crown or no, Sloane appeared very nervous at the prospect of royal company. Smoking compulsively, she kept them both a good hour in their room until the convivial noise from the party indicated a crowd large enough for her entrance not to be noticed.

"If we wait much longer, you will be noticed for your tardiness," Bedford said.

She stubbed out her cigarette. "All right. Tally ho."

"Tally ho ho ho."

ENTERING the club's main lounge, they were greeted by dance music coming from a gramophone and a swarming throng of finely dressed people so thick there was no room to dance.

Sloane lingered at the entranceway, searching the faces. Bedford thought she was looking for her uncle and his wife, but she took small note of that neglected-looking couple upon sighting them standing off to the side with Owen. Instead, Sloane headed in a different direction, dragging Bedford along with her and drawing up before a sleek, dark-haired woman with enormous eyes. She wore a mauve satin evening gown that seemed more negligee than dress and sat upon a bartop, talking to two gentlemen Bedford took to be colonials. She rather reminded Bedford of Thelma, except for her extraordinary eyes, which put him in mind of some gentle forest creature.

Sloane introduced them. This was the notorious Alice de Janze'—in no way striking him as a lady who could ever have been "the wildest debutante in Chicago"—let alone one who might have shot a lover in a Paris railroad station.

Alice fell upon Sloane in an almost desperate embrace.

"Smithie," she said, in a soft voice that was almost drowned by the gramophone music. "Dear God, Smithie, what has prompted you to come out here?"

"I'm with my Uncle Dixon," said Sloane. "We're going on safari."

Alice looked alarmed. "You won't kill anything? No lions?"

Sloane blinked. "No. Of course not."

They continued their peculiar conversation, still half clinging to each other. They made an odd match, as Alice was six or eight inches below Sloane's six feet.

The enormous eyes were now focused on Bedford. "Is this Mr. Smithie?"

Sloane laughed as though Alice had said something hilarious.

"This is Bedford Green. He's an art dealer friend of mine."

Alice honored him with a slight curtsey. After a moment's hesitation—not knowing what this strange woman might do next—he bowed.

He had just straightened when he felt a tap on his shoulder. A well-tailored man with a commanding air stood there.

"Lady Furness would like to speak to you, sir." The fellow was exceedingly polite but in no way friendly.

It occurred to Bedford what this might be about. "Mrs. de Janze'," he said to Alice, "would you excuse us a moment? There's someone I'd like Sloane to meet."

"That's not necessary," said Sloane.

Alice looked stricken, then smiled. "Of course. Do you know who Lady Furness is?"

"An old friend."

"Really not necessary," said Sloane.

"Only take a minute."

Beford had guessed correctly. Thelma stood chatting

with some older Brits, and a small, perfectly dressed and groomed young man of unusual handsomeness—familiar from myriad magazine and newspaper photographs.

The British upper classes were given to strange rituals. Thelma first introduced them to the older British couple—a Lord and Lady Delamere—and they in turn presented Bedford and Sloane to His Royal Highness, the Prince of Wales.

Sloane stood dumbstruck, then awkwardly extended her hand to be shaken. As Bedford recalled from his society columnist days, something different was called for. As circumspectly as possible, he brought his right knee up to the back of her left, and gently pushed until it began to buckle. The debutante in her returned, and she accorded the prince a reluctant sort of curtsey. Only then did His Highness reach to shake her hand.

He lighted a cigarette, grinned, and all formality vanished.

"So nice to find Americans out here," he said. "I'm absolutely mad for Americans. I've even been to Hollywood, you know. Simply wizard place. Got to know Doug Fairbanks and his wife. Are you enjoying Africa?"

"I've only just arrived," Sloane said.

Royal protocol required a "sir," but the prince ignored the lack. "You must have a good long chat with Lord Delamere, then. He knows deuced more about Africa than the Hottentots do, I daresay. He's rather the king of British East Africa, don't you know. He rules. I merely visit."

"Not often enough, sir," said Delamere, a short man with gray hair worn down to his shoulders, which were as muscular as a prizefighter's.

"Hallo the prince." The voice was familiar.

"Dickie!" said the royal. "I was hoping I'd see you."

Lord and Lady Ralls swept forward, brushing past Sloane and Bedford. Victoria Ralls gave His Highness a kiss upon the cheek, then stepped back, smiling wickedly.

The ensuing conversation quite clearly did not include Bedford and Sloane. Thelma picked up on the situation and took the two Americans by the arm, steering them away.

"So many people he has to meet," she said. "It's all so very boring."

"The prince and the Rallses seem well acquainted," Bedford said.

"Oh, they were in Mayfair a lot together—when Dickie was in London. Poor fellow. I hear he's stony broke. They've been all through Victoria's money. At the moment, he's living on his army pay—and the generosity of friends."

"The poor little dear," said Sloane.

"Many of his friends are wealthy women. He'll survive."

Thelma had taken them halfway across the room— much the same socially as taking them some distance out to sea. Giving Bedford a kiss upon the cheek, she took a step back toward the prince.

"I'll leave you now," she said. "We're off on safari tomorrow. Beastly, beastly bore. I do hope to see you again, Bedford dear. Perhaps in New York. So nice to meet you, Miss Smith."

Her last words were uttered as she slipped into the crowd. Sloane and Bedford stood there awkwardly, Sloane looking a bit stunned.

"Do you know the song, 'I danced with a man, who danced with a girl, who danced with the Prince of Wales?'" Bedford asked. "Now that can be you."

"Not quite."

"You can tell all your Bolshevik friends at Chumley's."

"Not on your life." She looked about the floor. The crowd had thinned sufficiently—people going off who knew where—for a few couples to dance. "Why don't you get us drinks, while I go find Alice?"

"What would you like?"

"Anything. And a lot of it."

BEDFORD accepted two pink gins from the African bartender, then stepped aside to let a tall blonde woman who'd been waiting behind him move up. Instead, she followed him.

"Excuse me, sir, are you Mr. Green? Captain Green?"

"No longer captain."

"Here, captains are captains forever." She shook his hand. "I'm Beryl Markham."

If not quite as tall as Sloane, she was of unusual height. A better word for her, he thought, was "long." Her legs, arms, hands, and fingers were long, as was her graceful neck. Her very straight nose was long.

Bedford was struck most by her eyes, which were of a blue more brilliant than any he had seen thus far in Kenya except for the Rallses, though blue eyes among the white colonials here were so common as to seem a tribal trait. He found he had to avert his own eyes while talking to her, because hers were so distracting.

"How did you know my name?" he asked.

"Owen told me. I've put word out I wanted to meet any aviator coming through Nairobi, and so he alerted me to you almost as soon as you arrived from Mombasa."

There was something else about her—something animal, something wild—though she was exceedingly well mannered.

"I'm not an aviator. I haven't flown since the war."

"Ah, but you did fly in the war. I expect there's not a trick to flying that you don't know."

Bedford recalled a German he'd been pursuing at about seven thousand feet near Yprès once. The Hun had managed to escape him by pulling halfway through a loop, rolling upright, and diving steeply in the opposite direction before Bedford could turn and get on his tail. "Why are you so interested in aviators' tricks?" he asked

She grinned. "Because I'm a flyer myself. Or rather, I'm learning to become one. I've had lessons but I'm more or less teaching myself to fly. I have a Gypsy Moth. A lovely airplane. We've flown in it to the end of the Rift Valley and back—but I have lots to learn."

"I'd be delighted to help you, but aside from combat tactics, I'm not sure what I could teach you." He looked for Sloane, discovering to his great amazement that she was dancing—with the prince! He glanced down at the two gins he was holding, then offered the one in his left hand to the Markham woman. "Would you care for a drink? It's pink gin."

She seemed doubtful, but wished to be friendly. "Thank you. People here drink mostly champagne or whiskey in the evening, but this will be lovely. Thank you."

Bedford's eyes returned to the odd couple on the dance floor. Sloane was in no way awkward or self-conscious about her height, and moved with considerable grace. But she must have had a sense of how comical their disparity made the prince appear. His Highness apparently did not, and chattered on amiably as they circled in a fox trot.

"Are you impressed by the prince?" Beryl Markham asked.

"He's dancing with the lady I accompanied to Africa."

"She'll have something to talk about when she gets back home."

Bedford smiled, without explaining why. "Would you like to dance?"

"Well, thank you very much." She accepted his hand and accompanied him to the floor, moving lightly. "I'm not a whiz at this, I'm afraid. Rather a bush girl."

"You don't look like a native."

"I'm neither Kikuyu or Masai." When he failed to understand, she added, "I grew up on my father's farm near the Ngong Hills."

As people were keeping out of the prince's way, there was not much room elsewhere. Bedford had to hold Miss Markham close, and confine their steps to a small area.

"Do you think you might be able to come out to the airfield tomorrow?" she asked. "It's not far. There's someone I'd like you to meet. He's also teaching himself to fly, though he's much farther along than I am."

"Is he here?"

"Heavens no. He hates this sort of thing. Not antisocial, mind. Just not much for this kind of gaiety. He's a white hunter. Denys Finch-Hatton is his name. He's taking the prince's party out on their hunt. He's very, very good."

"We met briefly, at the railway station. You've managed not to crash, teaching yourselves to fly?"

"No. Not yet."

"I have. Three times. It's a very instructive part of learning to fly."

"Learning to crash?"

"Learning how not to."

She pulled back a moment to study his face, as she might some puzzle, then came close again. "Denys would love it if you could come by in the morning. He has the prince's party to attend to but not until later. If then. The prince was talking about lingering here an extra day or two. I can't imagine why."

Bedford considered how far out of her element Thelma was on this outing. "Perhaps some in his party are reluctant to go into the wild."

"That would be short-sighted of them. So will you come?"

"I'm afraid I can't. Our bunch is off on safari tomorrow."

"If the prince doesn't go, you won't go."

"Why is that?"

"Because the Prince of Wales is to be given first shot at the game. Can't have interlopers making off with the prize beast."

"Why don't the other safaris just go off in a different direction?"

"You remember your Lewis Carroll. All the directions here are the prince's."

She laughed, warmly. He liked her, and hoped she was right about the delay of his safari. His good spirits were soon dashed, however.

Because of the press of the crowd, they had twice bumped into other dancers. Now another couple collided with them—a large, older man with a balding head and outsized moustache and a pretty young woman perhaps a third his age. It was the older man's fault. He had backed into Beryl, jarring her severely. Trying to regain his balance, he fell against Bedford, who politely held him up.

The man was furious. "Hands off me, you!"

Bedford drew himself up, staying calm though his impulse was to sock the fellow. "I'm sorry, sir. Perhaps we've all been celebrating too much this evening."

The man tried to give Bedford a shove, but lacked a proper footing. He tottered a bit, then pulled back. His beefy face was crimson. "You don't belong here," he said, finally. "Go back to wherever it is you bloody damn come from."

He moved away, pulling the young woman after him.

"Who in hell is that?" Bedford asked. "Another 'lord' no doubt."

"No title on that one," Beryl said. "He's simply George Sim, the banker—one of the richest men in Kenya. At least, he was, until he married Molly. She's extravagant."

"The lady with whom he was dancing?"

"If you want to call that dancing. They make clumsy me feel a member of the *Ballet Russe de Monte Carlo*."

Someone touched his shoulder. Fearing it was the old

drunk again, he ignored the intrusion. Then he heard his name called.

"Bedford. Please."

"Sloane?" he said, turning. "I thought you were dancing with . . ."

She smiled, a trifle weirdly. "I've been replaced. It's mortifying. She just barreled up to him and took him over. Like some floozy picking up a man in a speakeasy. The Prince of Wales! Look!"

He did so. Georgia and His Highness were still in cavort. Bedford couldn't tell if or how much they had been drinking, but all protocol seemed to have been abandoned.

"And there stands my gape-jawed uncle. It's pathetic."

"Why don't you go comfort him?"

"No. He married her. He has this coming."

The noise being generated by the gramophone and merrymaking had decidedly increased in volume. Bedford had difficulty hearing Beryl when she leaned close to say good-bye.

"Sorry?" Bedford said.

"I said, if you're not off on safari tomorrow, I'll expect you at the airfield. We'll be there at eight-thirty."

"We shall see."

She gave him a nod, then Sloane a curious look, and moved off, waving to one of what Bedford was sure were numerous friends.

"Would you like to leave?" he asked Sloane.

"Where can we go? We're staying here."

"We could go for a walk."

"We might be devoured by something. If not an animal, one of these mad colonials."

"Why don't you go to the room. I'll fetch some refreshment, and see if I can find Owen and check on the plans for tomorrow. Someone was saying the safari might be postponed."

"Why?"

"Something to do with the prince. No one else can go on safari until he does."

He put his arm around her and steered her toward the outer lobby. "You go ahead. I'll be along directly with marching orders and gin."

He returned to their room a half hour later. Sloane had taken to the bed, her face and figure seeming almost an apparition behind the mosquito netting. He'd have none of that sleeping in his chair.

Bedford lifted the netting to hand Sloane her glass and sit down on the bed. She was not wearing much—possibly nothing at all—and kept the sheet pulled up to her bare shoulders.

"Thank you," she said, after a sip. "What are the marching orders?"

"It's true. We'll be here another day and night at least, depending on when the prince feels up to his trek. I think some people here will be glad to see him go."

"Why is that?"

"He broke all the gramophone records in the club. I gather they're hard to come by in East Africa."

Sloane sat still, listening. The din had largely ceased. "Broke them how?"

"Threw them out onto the veranda. No one seems to be sure whether he enjoyed sailing them through the air or had become bored with the dancing."

"Gawd."

"He had help."

"Oh no."

"I'm afraid so. Your Aunt Georgia."

CHAPTER 6

BEDFORD quickly but quietly dressed in some of the safari clothes he'd acquired—stout shoes, knee stockings, khaki shorts, khaki shirt, khaki jacket—discarding the silly pith helmet so ubiquitous in this strange colony.

He left Sloane still asleep beneath her gauzy canopy. She'd had entirely too much to drink, and would have a disagreeable awakening.

His own had not been particularly joyous, but he hoped the fresh air at the airfield would restore him. He had little other reason to look forward to this aerial outing.

In another clime, he might have been able to count on miserable weather to prevent this ordeal, but the day was brilliant—as perhaps they always were here in this season.

The attendant at the desk said he would summon a taxicab, adding he was uncertain how long this might take to accomplish. Bedford replied that he would wait, and found a nearby armchair in which to do so. A native servant in a long white robe came by and inquired as to whether he would like some fruit juice. When Bedford said he would, the man asked if he would like gin in it. Bedford hesitated, then nodded, saying thank you. The fellow was obviously used to the white man's ways—especially those of this particular set of white men.

He was served very quickly. Only then did he notice the gentleman in khaki clothes and riding boots seated in a nearby chair. Only then did the gentleman speak.

"Good morning, Mr. Green."

He had thinning hair, an agreeable smile, a charming air, and the look of a man who had passed the night pleasantly.

"Baron Blixen," the other continued. "You made the acquaintance of my wife—my former wife—on the train from Mombasa."

"I thought I saw you at the railroad station, but it was someone else."

The baron glanced away then back, "Well, now we have met. I heard you say you needed a ride to the airfield. I should be happy to drive you. But, please, finish your drink."

THE baron owned an American car—a Buick—which he drove with a minimum of attention to the way ahead, turning his head toward Bedford whenever he spoke.

"You're best away from the club this morning, at all events," he said. "After last night, people will be gunning for you."

The remark brought Bedford to greater wakefulness. "Because of my encounter with Mr. Sim?"

Blixen glanced ahead, steering around a sort of rickshaw with a fat Arab in the passenger seat. "I'm not aware of your encounter."

"I bumped into him on the dance floor, and he treated it as a declaration of war."

The other frowned. "Steer clear of that one. He's invariably trouble. But, no—banker Sim has nothing to do with this. It's gramophone records."

"I had nothing to do with that."

"You're being blamed, nonetheless."

"Me?"

"All of you in the Dixon Smith party. The ladies and gentlemen of British East Africa are furious. It'll be weeks before they can get more gramophone records sent out from England and America. They'll have to dance to this odd little African string band we have."

"A great misfortune. But this was the prince's doing, not mine."

"The prince, as you apparently have not yet discovered, can do no wrong. They're blaming Mrs. Smith—and her entire American party. That includes you."

"Well, I suppose I've been accused of worse."

"The real problem is that Mrs. Smith monopolized the prince so much that many ladies and gentleman were denied the pleasure of meeting and mingling with him. In the case of the ladies, especially mingling."

"I expect we'll be out of here tomorrow and into the bush."

"Just be prepared today for some social rough stuff."

"There's already been some rough stuff coming our way. On the train from Mombasa, someone fired a bullet into our compartment. Your wife's compartment, actually. Owen and I were just visiting."

"Did she flinch?"

"The baroness?"

"Yes."

"No. It might have been a fly."

"She's in love with Africa," he said, "though I suspect it will get her in the end."

"Almost did."

"Nothing bothers her." The baron told of her crossing some two hundred miles of rough country during the war

to bring a herd of beef cattle and a mountain of supplies to
the baron and the colonial regiment that had been raised to
fight the Germans to the south.

"All she had with her was a few servants," he said.
"Some of us call her 'the best man in Africa.'"

THEY rolled onto the grassy grounds of the aerodrome,
but Blixen stopped behind a shed well short of the field.

"There you are, my friend. Good luck to you."

"Thank you, Baron."

"I shall probably see you tonight. There's a dinner
party."

"Dinner party? You said 'rough stuff.'"

"The playing field, old man. They're inviting you onto
it. Then they'll rough you up."

"Can we decline this party? Or is this a royal command?"

"Nothing to do with the prince. But should be fun for all
of that."

Walking onto the field, Bedford paused to look back
and was surprised to see Blixen's Buick still there—and
the baron standing very close to the shed, watching him.

Or perhaps not him. There were five biplanes lined up
along the edge of the greensward and a small cluster of
people were gathered around one of them. Bedford recognized Beryl Markham by her height and blonde hair. Coming nearer, he took note of two other women—the
Baroness Blixen, wearing a long skirt; and, in baggy
trousers and a loose shirt, Alice de Janze'. There was also
a man, dressed in khaki.

Beryl strode up and took Bedford by the hand, leading
him back. "The pride of the Royal Flying Corps," she said.
"You've met Alice, I believe."

"Oh yes." He smiled. She simply observed him nervously.

"This is Denys Finch-Hatton."

"Yes. You were at the railroad station. Meeting the baroness."

Clear eyes. Somewhat pointy ears, but handsome, aristocratic features. A very firm handshake. The man removed his hat, revealing a remarkably bald head. "A pleasure, Mr. Green."

"I wasn't the pride of the Royal Flying Corps."

"We're told you shot down three Germans."

"There was a German who shot down eighty of us—Manfred von Richthofen. He was a superb shot, but a terrible pilot. Anyway, there were many, many better than I. My main accomplishment was surviving the war."

"Then there's a lot you can teach us."

"Beryl says you're teaching yourselves."

She smiled. "An exaggeration. Tom Wilson—he owns Wilson Airways—he's helping me. Wouldn't have gotten my 'A' license without him. But now I want my 'B.' Want to take others up with me."

"And I want to fly a loop," Finch-Hatton said.

"Why do you want to do a combat maneuver?"

The clear eyes narrowed a bit, but there came a grin. "I'm told it's the ultimate aerial maneuver."

"That's the outside loop. I've never done that. But I suppose I can manage an inside one." He actually had no such confidence.

Markham laughed. "I don't want to do any kind of loop. I just want to fly with you for a bit."

Neither had any idea what they were asking. Bedford had last flown an aircraft in 1918. His SE-5 had been shot up by machine-gun fire from the ground after he'd made three butchering strafing runs on a retreating German column. He'd barely kept the crate in the air on his return to base and had smashed it up on landing. He'd walked away vowing never to get in an airplane again. He'd flown so many patrols, and the war had been so close to ending, that his C.O. had indulged him in this.

Now he was on an airfield again.

Beryl's Gypsy Moth was a nearly brand-new aircraft, a sporty-looking biplane with a high upper wing, four stout struts, and a boxy engine mounted above the propellor shaft. It was painted yellow. Finch-Hatton had an older aircraft, also one of the DeHavilland Moth series.

"You want me to fly with you?" Bedford asked.

"Yes. If you don't mind. Is it all right?"

The mere thought of it was making him sweat, though the morning was still very cool. Bedford felt as jumpy and full of dread as he had on the days of the worst combat and weather of the war. On many such mornings, only brandy had sufficed to get him into his cockpit.

He reminded himself he'd just had a drink.

Markham was eyeing him curiously now, not understanding his reluctance. It occurred to him he might lastingly regret making such a formidable lady think small of him.

T'was ever thus with the male gender, he supposed.

"All right," he said.

"If you don't mind," said Finch-Hatton. "If you could please first show me the loop."

Bedford went up to Finch-Hatton's plane, taking note of the four-cylinder DeHavilland engine. It seemed small compared to the big radial motors on the ships he'd piloted at the end of the war. He wondered if its power would suffice.

"A hundred horsepower," said Finch-Hatton, as though intercepting the thought.

"To perform a loop," Bedford said, "you go into a power dive, throttle back as you pull up, then push it to the wall as you climb over on your back. A lot of stress on the wings as you come out of the dive and a lot of stress on the engine in the climb. Flying inverted, even briefly, could stop the engine."

"Then we'll need some altitude."

They'd need more than that. Bedford felt his fingers beginning to tremble and stuck his hands in his pockets. "I'll take the rear seat. You go up front. Don't touch the controls but watch how I move them."

"I'll pull the prop through," Finch-Hatton said.

"No, let me do it," said Beryl.

Bedford had seen strong men get their arms broken in this effort, but it occurred to him she must do this all the time. He climbed into the cockpit, pulling on a borrowed helmet. He said to himself what he had said to himself in mission after mission. Do it and be done with it. Get it behind you. There was no other way out.

Finch-Hatton, almost gaily, clambered into the front seat, looking back as he pulled on his own helmet.

"Why are you trusting me with your airplane?" Bedford asked. "I haven't flown for years. I haven't a license. You don't know me."

"Beryl trusts you. She's a jolly good judge of character."

BOUNCING along over the hard ground, Bedford held the stick centered and let the airplane fly itself into the air, finally pulling into a slow, circling climb. It was a nimble aircraft, managing the ascent without much labor. There was nothing else in the sky. Holding the controls in place, he leaned his head back, looking up, wondering how much of that vast emptiness above he would need to get beneath him before attempting this foolishness.

He held out his hand before him. The trembling had ceased.

Looking down, he saw the three women staring up at

him fixedly, Beryl waving. Beyond the shed, the grass was empty where Baron Blixen's car had been.

An updraft generated by a patch of open earth warming in the sun helped lift them to four thousand feet. The humming engine took them higher. When he reached six thousand feet, Bedford looked over the side again, gauging the amount of altitude he might consume in the initial dive. He decided for safety's sake to climb to eight thousand. When he reached it, he flew straight and level for a while. Finch-Hatton looked back, expectantly.

Do it and be done with it.

Feeling a little annoyed with the man for having gotten him up to this unwelcome place, Bedford gave no signal. He pushed the stick forward, shoving in the throttle at the same time.

The airplane nosed down and tore through the air for the ground in a roar of engine noise and wind rushing through the struts and wires. The field below grew only imperceptibly larger but the airspeed was rapidly increasing. Passing a hundred miles an hour, he waited until the indicator showed a hundred twenty, then began easing back on the throttle and pulling back ever so slightly on the stick, making the airplane describe a rapid but perfect curve in the air.

As though of its own accord, the nose lifted inexorably. The struts and wires gradually ceased their screaming. He shoved the throttle back to the firewall. Abruptly, the horizon vanished, and they were looking at only sky.

He closed his eyes, imagining how they must look from the ground—imagining Sloane watching him with both amazement and horror, presuming she'd risen from her bed.

They were hanging upside down now. He was held only by his leather seat belt, blood rushing to his head.

And they were slowing, seemed almost to be stopped, an infinite moment of suspension in space. If the aircraft stalled now, only halfway through its circle, it would plunge straight down, possibly falling into a spin. He might tear off the wings trying to recover, if recovery was possible. He knew nothing about the strengths and weaknesses of this aircraft.

He opened his eyes again. The nose was dropping toward the earth once more, their speed increasing, blood going back where it belonged, but leaving him a little dizzy. Putting more back pressure on the stick as they went into a steep, overhead dive, he gently brought the machine back to level flight, completing his circle in the air.

All this had consumed three thousand feet, but they were still directly above the field.

Finch-Hatton was pounding the fuselage with happiness, looking at him as might a child on his birthday. Bedford decreased the throttle now, banking into a right turn and commencing a slow, careful spiral that would bring them down for a landing. If no one else, he'd amazed himself.

He'd been in an almost dreamlike state through this entire maneuver. Looking over the side, his vision suddenly filled with an immense flash of red, the sound of the Moth's engine joined by another's as a rush of prop wash rocked the wings from below.

Wide awake now, he sat up stiffly straight, yanking the stick to the left and jamming his foot against the left rudder pedal. The other aircraft had missed them by no more than ten or twenty feet. His hands were trembling again.

As the other plane receded, he could see the pilot shaking his fist at him. Finch-Hatton was staring straight ahead, as though he hadn't noticed—though he surely must have.

Checking behind him, Bedford made another slow circle, then pushed down the Moth's nose and steered for a landing, coming in just behind the red-painted aircraft. He taxied slowly toward Beryl and the others, rolling to a stop beside Markham's plane.

He lifted himself from the cockpit slowly, fearing Finch-Hatton would now lash out at him. But the man merely nodded pleasantly as he jumped off the wing, going immediately to the baroness.

"That was an absolutely thrilling thing to watch," she said, taking Finch-Hatton's hands in hers.

"You should have been up there."

"I'm sorry," said Bedford, walking up to them. "I should have seen the other plane. In the war, we got to where we could spot aircraft miles away. Our lives depended on it. I've no excuse."

"He should have seen you," said Beryl. "I watched it all. He came dead on paying no mind to anything. He must have been looking at the field, planning his landing. He . . ."

She stopped. Bedford turned to see the other pilot striding toward them, head down and fists clenched. He went straight for Finch-Hatton.

"Goddamn you, Finch-Hatton," he said, in a thick Dutch accent. "You almost killed me. You trying to put me out of business? Yes? Out of business for good?"

"Don't be a boor," Finch-Hatton replied, smiling good-naturedly. "It was an inadvertence. We're fortunate it wasn't worse."

The Dutchman shoved him, rudely, provocatively. "Goddamn you, Finch-Hatton," he repeated, having nothing else to say.

Bedford intervened, stepping between them. "Direct your 'Goddamn you's' to me, if you would, sir. I was flying the machine."

"And who the hell are you?"

Bedford wondered if the man had been drinking, for his face was very florid. "My name is Bedford Green. I'm just a visitor here."

The other pilot looked over Bedford as though seeking

a good place to insert a knife. "You're one of those god-damned Americans in Owen's party, aren't you?"

"Yes I am."

"Well, stay the goddam hell out of my way—up there, and on the ground!"

He turned on his heel and strode away in much the same manner he had trudged up to them, pulling off his helmet and slapping it against his leg.

"Who was that?" Bedford asked, when the man was out of earshot.

"That's just Van Gelder," said Beryl. "Don't let him bother you. He's a South African, and doesn't care much for English people."

Bedford then realized that Finch-Hatton had made a pun. Van Gelder was a Boer; may even have been a fighter in England's nasty little Boer War against the South African Dutch.

"He's a white hunter—like me and Owen," said Finch-Hatton, "though not like us at all."

"He flies his clients out in that plane to the hunting spots—out and back in a single day, so they can spend their nights here in the comforts of Nairobi," said Beryl. "Supposedly, he lands his aircraft and takes his people up on foot for the shoot, but I think there's some gunnery done from the air."

"Terribly unsporting," said the baroness, putting her arm in Finch-Hatton's.

"Beastly practice," Finch-Hatton said. "Beastly kills. Van Gelder hasn't a lot of respect around here."

Alice was tugging on Bedford's sleeve, her large eyes imploring him like those of an unhappy child. "I want to go up in the sky, Bedford. I want you to do what you did with Denys—only with me." Now she smiled, beguilingly. "Please?"

"I think I've done all the flying I'm up to today," Bedford said, returning his hands to his pockets. "I'm sorry."

"I'll take you up," said Finch-Hatton. "Come along."

"I want to do the loop," Alice said.

"And so you shall."

Bedford watched them walk to the other plane, dread mingling with guilt. If something happened to Alice in this, Sloane would never forgive him. Would leave him and the art gallery, never to return.

Beryl went over to help with the propeller. When the engine was restarted and Finch-Hatton's Moth was taxiing away, she returned.

"I don't think I want to watch this," Bedford said. "I feel responsible for it."

"Oh no. No one's responsible for Denys. He wouldn't dream of allowing that." She nudged him. "Are you quite certain you've done all the flying you want to today?"

"All the piloting, surely."

She took his hand, leading him toward her own aircraft. "Come up with me then. If I don't wreck us, I'll show you some things."

SHE took off very smoothly a few minutes after Finch-Hatton's ship had lifted into the air. Bedford found it uncomfortable in the front seat—perhaps because, in that arrangement, he was the watched rather than the watcher.

Gaining only a thousand feet of altitude, Beryl leveled off, flying away from the field. Both looked up in search of Finch-Hatton and Alice, with Bedford spotting them perhaps two thousand feet higher, circling for altitude but moving away from the airfield in a different direction. He turned and pointed upward, receiving a happy nod from Beryl in return. But she kept on her divergent course to the south, and shortly the other DeHavilland was lost to view.

Keeping to her low altitude, she steered the Gypsy Moth south by southwest, heading toward a very far-off mountain. In the haze, in the nearer distance, Bedford could see a town of sorts.

Otherwise, the country was open and rolling, here and there a few plantation houses and farm buildings, but mostly a wide savanna interrupted by the occasional stream and clump of forest.

The habitations grew sparse and then vanished entirely. What Bedford began to see in their place were masses of animals—extraordinary, fanciful, amazing animals— some of them looking huge even from their height.

Near one group of trees, he saw a family of giraffes. Sweeping over a low ridge, Beryl flew along a wide, shallow-looking lake dotted with myriad pink flamingos. They passed on over a thickly green forest and then, reaching a dusty plain, encountered a herd of elephants. He hadn't seen one of those creatures since passing by a circus parade in New York a few years before. Now he was gliding over thirty or forty of them, all of them wild.

Banking to the left, Beryl soared back over the trees, slipping closer to the earth and turning toward the west. They skirted a high rocky hill, then, in the wide valley beyond, approached a running herd of antelope—dozens of them darting and bounding over the grass. Bedford thought at first it was the airplane that had frightened them, then saw the yellow shape streaking along behind, shifting with the movements of a smaller zebra at the rear of the fleeing herd.

Gradually, the distance between the hunter and hunted decreased. For a moment, they ran along in tandem, the lion's forepaws reaching almost to the hoofed animal's rear legs, but never quite far enough.

Then the antelope lurched, a momentary hesitation, and it was doomed. The big cat gathered its energy for a single, concluding bound, and sprung, digging its claws into the other animal's hindquarters and fixing its jaws onto the animal's haunch. Both tumbled and rolled, the lion never losing its purchase.

Beryl banked the plane away, this time heading for another swath of trees. She throttled back a little, dropping lower, until it almost seemed possible to reach down and snatch up a handful of leaves.

A moment later, Bedford found himself looking down into a dozen or more upturned faces as they swept over an encampment of tents and tables and large, parked automobiles.

Bedford looked back over the fuselage to the woman in the seat behind him. Beryl gave him a very vigorous nod this time, and a grin. Then she shoved in the throttle and bent forward to the serious business of piloting, as the airplane, gathering speed, began to ascend.

SLOANE was awake, but still in bed. Bedford sat down on the edge of it, taking her hand.

"What a dreadful night," she said.

"But I've had a lovely morning. Beryl Markham took me flying. We went down toward Mount Kilimanjaro and visited all manner of wild animals. We also passed over His Royal Highness's safari camp."

"You sound like a happy little boy. Did you pass over His Royal Highness?"

"He's not there yet. They're setting up camp now so he won't be inconvenienced having to wait tomorrow."

She sat up, then rubbed her eyes. "What about our safari."

"I spoke to Owen in the lobby. We're off tomorrow morning. Today we have free. Tonight, we're to attend a dinner party."

"With the prince?"

"Happily, no. It's a local couple. Josslyn and Idina

Hay—or if you will, Lord and Lady Erroll, as they've recently become. It's at some place called Clouds."

"Do we fly there?" A poor jest.

"No. It's a house outside of town. Our dear friends Lord and Lady Ralls will be there."

"*Quels frissons.* And Alice?"

"I'm not sure. When I left her this morning she had put her life in the hands of a madman."

"You saw her this morning?"

"At the aerodrome."

"The madman wasn't you?"

"No. I'm insufficiently mad for this place."

CHAPTER 7

OWEN arranged a car for the four of them, and a driver they'd not before encountered. An Indian, who spoke with a singsong British accent, he was well acquainted with their lordships and, as they rolled out of Nairobi into the very last light of day, proved happy to speak about them. By the time they turned into the main driveway of "Clouds," Bedford had learned that Idina Hay had been married two times before and was some eight years older than her titled husband, Lord Erroll.

"She has many friends, many friends," he said. "But here, not in England. It is said she cannot go back to England."

"Why is that?" Sloane asked, as Bedford wished she hadn't. There was no telling what faux pas Georgia would commit with that kind of information.

"Sin," said the driver.

"Sin?"

"Yes," the driver nodded somberly, then added, "I am a Christian."

THERE were cars parked everywhere on the grounds of Clouds when they arrived about dusk. The name had put Bedford to mind of a tall house, reaching skywards, but this mansion was lateral in its reach, built in wings, like the Muthaiga, with a high, thatched roof. It looked perfectly African, and yet, at the same time, splendidly British.

As they got out of their sedan, Bedford took note of an engine sound altogether different from that of a motor car. As he listened to it, the sound abruptly stopped. Looking in its direction, he was surprised to see an airplane, painted a bright light blue, which had pulled up on the lawn. A house servant ran up to the cockpit, taking possession of two large, full, cloth bags, then hurried back to the house. The pilot sat a moment, then lifted himself from the seat and jumped to the ground. A moment later, he had vanished.

"Let's go in," said Georgia. "I'm just dying to meet these people."

There were stylishly dressed guests in the entrance hall, and everywhere else Bedford looked. Sloane was wearing the same evening gown as the night before, and muttered something about hoping no one they'd met the previous night would be there, though there seemed little chance of that.

Indeed, they'd hardly stepped inside when Alice de Janze' rushed to Sloane, embracing her warmly. Then she took note of Bedford, and marched up before him.

"You hurt Denys's airplane," she said. "You almost killed us."

"I'm sorry," Bedford replied, a little confused. "What did I do?"

"We were going to do the loop the loop. But Denys noticed that the fabric on the upper wing was torn. He set us down to have a look at it and discovered that two pieces of wood had broken. It must now be repaired. Not only did you nearly get us killed, but now I can't do the loop the loop." She leaned close, so much so that her breast came against his arm. "Will you take me up and do that again?"

"I fear no one will trust me with their aircraft, now that I've damaged Mr. Finch-Hatton's. Is he here?"

"No. Of course not. He's at Karen's."

"Baroness Blixen's?"

"Yes. Of course. She's giving a party tonight for the Prince of Wales and Denys is going because he lives with the baroness and he's the prince's white hunter on this safari. Beryl is going because she more or less lives there, too, and because her husband was invited."

"Husband?"

"Yes. Mr. Markham. Mansfield Markham. Her second husband. She's expecting a child. Didn't you know?"

"She flies airplanes in that condition?"

"It's not a condition. She's pregnant. And she's going to the baroness's tonight. You weren't invited, were you? You're stuck here, with the rest of us. Well, we'll have more fun. Won't we, Smithie?"

Sloane had a quizzical look on her face.

"The real reason you two aren't invited is because your aunt's not invited," Alice continued. "And that's because she broke all the gramophone records at the Muthaiga Club."

"But the prince broke most of them," Bedford said.

"Yes, but he's the prince." Alice pressed nearer. "I don't know whom I'm to be with tonight. Don't be unhappy. I've asked for you."

"Be with?"

Sloane took her friend by the hand and led her away before she could properly—or possibly improperly—answer. Bedford watched them depart, then looked about him.

Dixon and bride were standing awkwardly to one side,

as usual, having not a clue as to what was expected of them. As Bedford thought upon it, he hadn't much of one, either.

"Do you know what I discovered today?" Dixon Smith asked, as Bedford came up to them.

Bedford waited, but nothing more was forthcoming. Uncle Dixon was expecting him to guess. "A mongoose in your bathroom," he said, finally.

"No. I discovered we've got the wrong damned white hunter."

"He seems to think he's the right one. And he's a nice enough fellow."

"Nice be damned. He's not the one Marshall Field had. Some guy named Pinch Haddon. He's probably the best in Africa, and I'm stuck with Owen."

"Finch-Hatton," Bedford corrected. "And he couldn't possibly be your white hunter because he's taking the Prince of Wales on safari this week."

"We should have waited until we could get him. And not taken second-rate."

"How can you say Owen is second-rate? You haven't fired a shot yet." Bedford hoped he wasn't sounding impudent. Uncle Dixon, after all, was paying the bills.

"Well, the Prince of Wales didn't hire him," Dixon grumbled.

"Why couldn't we go along with their hunting party?" Georgia asked.

"Invitation only, I'm afraid. Anyway, you've had your night of royal fun." Offering his arm to Georgia, he led them further within, seeking the host and hostess or, lacking them, someone who might be willing to talk to them. Turning the corner, he found precisely such a person.

"Good evening, Lady Ralls," he said.

He hoped he might draw her into conversation with the Smiths, but she instead drew him away, leaving them to stand awkwardly again.

"I've asked for you," she whispered. There was something very intense about her extraordinary blue eyes. Recalling the airplane he'd seen outside and its surreptitious pilot and mysterious cargo, Bedford had a glimmering idea of what it might be.

"Well, here I am."

"Don't be silly." She moved them further down the hall. "I think others have asked for you as well. Tonight you are *le dernier cri*. Half of Nairobi saw you perform that magnificent airplane stunt this morning—and the other half has heard about it. You're the only man in British East Africa to have done something more daring than Denys Finch-Hatton."

"But he was with me. And I damaged his aircraft. Almost got him killed when he went up again."

"Alice, too," she said. "That would have been a truly extraordinary event. Makes you all the more interesting." She had her arm in his now, and commenced to drag him along. "You must meet Idina."

Sinful the lady of the house certainly looked, wearing a silk gown cut so low in the back she came near to having décolletage in two places. She was a striking blonde, and would have been as beautiful as Victoria Ralls had she not such a miniscule chin.

She eyed Bedford as she might an object she was about to buy for a great deal of money and was doubtful as to its worth.

"How do you do," she said, coolly, shaking his hand. "You're with Sloane Smith, the tall young lady?"

"Yes."

"You're the art dealer who was with the Royal Flying Corps."

"Yes."

"And you're with those other Smiths—the lady who broke the gramophone records?"

If Georgia had hoped to make a name for herself, it appeared this was going to be it. "Yes again. Though I had nothing to do with it."

Without warning, Idina came forward and kissed him, slowly and langorously, her lips as cool as her demeanor. "We shall have an amusing evening," she said, and traipsed away.

"You should have arrived a bit earlier, old boy," said an older man standing nearby. "She invited some of us in to watch her bathe. Does this all the time, apparently. Everyone watches but her husband."

"Is it worth getting here so early?"

"The first time it is," said the man, then someone called to him, and he moved away.

Sloane had disappeared. African servants bearing trays of cocktails were moving through the crowd, seemingly as numerous as the guests. Tables had been set in several rooms and there were candles lit upon them, but nothing in the way of food. A few of the guests who appeared in an unusually excited state would from time to time emerge from a door off the side hall.

Failing to find her elsewhere, Bedford went to this mystery portal, opening it carefully and poking his head in. The light was dim, but he took note of a low table, surrounded by chairs, with a large bowl of what might have been sugar. He knew it was not. Sloane was not present.

He accepted another drink. Now the other Smiths had gone missing. He was about to embark on another search of the house for them, when Victoria Ralls came up and took him by the hand, leading him toward a small sitting room with three tables set for dinner in it. At last, food was being served.

"Come now and seat yourself, Captain Green. I think you'll be pleased with your dinner partner."

"And who would that be?"

"Me," she said, leading him to the table.

Victoria took the seat to his right. An American woman

named Mimi Chisholm was on his left. A gentleman opposite who had obviously been one of the early arrivers attempted to seat himself but crashed to the floor. Everyone
else at the table ignored him as he climbed to his feet.

"You're the American who flew Denys's airplane upside down today," said the Chisholm woman, after Bedford introduced himself.

"Yes." Bedford didn't want to go into this again. "Does
Lord Erroll fly? I noticed a blue biplane when we were
driving up."

"That's not among His Lordship's many skills," said
Victoria Ralls.

"The plane is mine," said Mimi Chisholm. She made
this sound a royal declaration.

"Are you a pilot?" Bedford was beginning to think all
the women down here were.

"Certainly not. I have one in my employ."

"He keeps us supplied," giggled Victoria, "with supplies."

The sacks. The "sugar" bowl. The giggle.

"Isn't that illegal?" Bedford asked. Mimi Chisholm
went stony cold, but Victoria merely smiled.

"After a fashion," Victoria said, "but that regulation is
enforced by my husband's military section." Another giggle. "I don't think he's overly concerned."

The Chisholm woman's harsh expression gentled. Bedford tried to find a mutually acceptable subject of conversation, and turned to art. It quickly proved a failure.

THERE was meat and fish, but mostly the meal seemed to
be fruit—mangoes, papaya, passion fruit, guava, something called custard apples, three kinds of bananas, and co-
conut. Gin and wine continued to be served in a steady

flow. At one point, Bedford asked for water, but was brought more gin.

A woman at the next table began to whoop with laughter—and then simply to whoop. The man beside her stuck his hand within the bodice of the gown of the woman on his other side. Victoria chattered amiably. After Bedford revealed that he had once been a newspaper society columnist, her conversation turned exclusively to London West End gossip, some of it doubtless months old. Bedford tried talking to Mimi Chisholm for a bit, but she was conversing mostly with herself—in grunts.

At last dinner was over. The sound of automobile engines could be heard outside. Bedford wasn't certain he could make it to the car. As he stood, wondering where he'd ever find Sloane, he held tightly to the back of his chair.

"A delightful evening, Lady Ralls," he said. "I enjoyed your company very much."

She put her hand on his. "And you shall have more of it." A wicked grin.

"Yes, but on another occasion. I must find my friends."

"Soon enough."

"I believe we're leaving." He could see headlamps outside the window.

"No, you're staying the night."

He gestured to the window. "But we're leaving. Hear the motors? Time to go."

She clung to him, looking up at him, her odd grin still in place. "No, no. Some are leaving. The dullards. They're off. Idina is having the rest of us stay the night. A select group, don't you know. You're included, as are your friends. An introduction to our local customs."

"But our car . . ."

"It's been dismissed. Sent back to Nairobi. Be back in the morning. Come now. We're to assemble in the library."

The invitation offered the prospect of seeing Sloane

again—and of being permitted to sit down again. He let Victoria take his hand and lead him down the corridor.

She cast him loose just short of the doorway, going to her husband, who was standing by the bookshelves on the opposite side of the room. Bedford was put in mind of George Bernard Shaw's *Arms and the Man,* a play set in Bulgaria in a manor house whose library possessed one book. The Hays hadn't done that much better. Bedford doubted there were two dozen volumes in their collection—most of them presumably having to do with horses and peerage.

Lord Erroll was present, sitting smugly on a couch between two bored and very drunk-looking women. Idina was elsewhere. Sloane was sitting off by herself in a far corner, and had not taken note of Bedford's arrival. He went to her and put a reassuring hand on her shoulder. She looked up at him as though she were drowning and he was a rope.

"They won't let us go home," she whispered.

"Yes they will," he replied, as softly, "but it's a long walk."

"Let's do it anyway."

Bedford felt so woozy he doubted he could have walked to the front door. "Wild beasts out there. We'd never make it."

Dixon and Georgia, for some reason, were seated on a piano bench that had been turned sideways away from the piano, and looking very prim—as though about to hear a lecture on horticulture. Bedford doubted they were in store for anything at all like that.

They certainly were not. Idina joined them carrying a wicker basket, and wearing nothing at all. Bedford could hear Dixon's gulp all the way across the room. Sloane stared down at the floor, muttering.

Bedford leaned close to hear.

"It's not my fault," she said. "Not my fault."

He squeezed her shoulder in pointless reassurance, as Idina strode to the center of the room. "We shall be serving cordials on the veranda," she said. "But first, it's time to distribute the bedroom keys. If you'd rather go straight on to bed, you're most welcome to do so."

She concluded with the sweetest of smiles, and then proceeded with her mission, pausing before each guest to search carefully through the keys for the precise match. Bedford had passed country weekends in some of the grandest houses in America, but could not recall ever being given his own bedroom key. They were left in the doors.

Lady Erroll already had his in hand when she came before him. Bedford had to struggle to keep his eyes on her face.

"Good evening, Captain Green."

"Uh, yes. Good evening, Your Ladyship."

"This is yours," she said, placing the key in the palm of his hand and wrapping his fingers around it. "Do try not to lose it."

"Thank you," he said, as she gave another to Sloane. He watched her move on, then held his key up close. There was a number on the leather tag.

"Eleven," he said.

"Nine," said Sloane, examining hers.

"Is this a hotel?"

"If it is," said Sloane, "it's the kind they have in New Orleans."

"I don't think I want to go out onto the veranda."

"Please walk me to my room, Bedford. I want to get away from these people."

They took a few wrong turns, but finally found the corridor with the numbered doors. She tried her key carefully. It worked. Carefully, she eased the door open and turned on the light. To their relief—and surprise—they were alone.

"Well then . . ." he began, yawning, thinking of the bed down the hall that awaited him.

"No, please wait. Until I'm safe in bed."

"As you wish, mademoiselle." He slumped into a chintz-covered armchair, watching as she walked into the bath. Then his eyes closed.

He awoke to her shaking him. She was wearing a pegnoir and a loose dressing gown. "Thank you, Bedford."

"Of course." He struggled to rise, yawning again.

She followed him to the door, preparing to lock it after him. He lingered a moment, searching for something positive to say about the next day's events. "Maybe it won't be so bad tomorrow."

Sloane kissed him—lightly, on the cheek—then pushed him out the door. "Go now, Bedford. Good night."

The door closed behind him and he heard the turn of the key. Taking his own in hand, he went on down the corridor to his room. It was dark, and he had to fumble for his light switch. It proved to turn on only one small and rather dim lamp, but the light sufficed to illuminate the room and the woman sitting up in his bed.

"Where have you been?" said Victoria Ralls, stretching out her arms.

Bedford froze at the door. "Sorry. I must have made a mistake."

"No mistake, darling. All arranged."

"But not with me."

"Is there something you do not understand?"

"I understand that my friend Sloane is next door."

She threw back the sheet. "But Bedford, that's not at all how it works. Have you never been to an English country weekend?"

On that social note, he retreated back into the hall, assisted in his rationale for this by a scream coming from Sloane's room.

Her door was open. Standing before her bed was, of all

unpleasant people, George Sim. He was attempting to show her his room key.

"It's to this room!" he thundered. "Don't you see? It's to this room!"

Bedford grabbed him by the shoulders and flung him toward the door. "You'll have to leave now. The lady is going to get dressed."

"But, but . . ." The man was sputtering. "You're breaking the rules."

"We're Americans," Bedford said. "Terribly sorry." He propelled Sim the rest of the way out of the room.

The fellow thereupon recognized him. "You imbecile."

"Good night." Bedford closed the door. "Please, Sloane. Get dressed. We're getting out of this upper-class bordello."

She sat on the edge of the bed. "I don't feel well."

"You could be feeling a lot worse."

"What will we do?"

"I'll think of something."

He had no chance to. Just as Sloane was putting on her shoes, there was a scream out in the hall, followed by another, and then another. Bedford could hear running feet.

Cautiously, he opened the door a few inches. People were in the hall. Investigating further, he saw Alice in the midst of them, highly agitated.

"They're going to kill each other!" she cried. "You must help!"

Lady Ralls had come to her door as well. "What's happening?" Bedford asked.

"De Janze' and de Trafford are very drunk and are going to duel," she said. She had put on a dressing gown.

Bedford contemplated the possibilities of a duel at a house that was full of elephant guns. "Sloane, come with me," he said.

She did, but so did Victoria Ralls, and a number of others in various stages of dress and undress. No one was in the main room or the library, but there was cursing coming from the principal veranda. Going onto it, Bedford saw Alice's former lover and present husband on the lawn— one keeping erect only by holding fast to a tree; the other, lacking such amenity, swaying back and forth on his own.

In de Trafford's hand was a large military revolver. Bedford had once had one like it. As he came up behind the man, he noted that the fellow had failed to cock the hammer.

It was easily managed. Bedford put a foot to the back of the man's knee and shoved hard, causing him to crumple and snatching up the revolver as he went down. He then went to the other and pulled him from the tree, pushing him forward. Down he went to his knees.

There was now a large crowd on the veranda. Bedford noticed Uncle Dixon, seated glumly at the far end. It occurred to him that Smith had probably been there for some time.

Sloane was standing nearby, utterly bewildered.

"Fetch your uncle there and come with me," Bedford said.

"What will you do?"

"Find a car with the key in it and drive back to the Muthaiga."

"And leave Georgia here?"

"I think trying to do otherwise at this point would complicate things badly."

She started toward Dixon. Both the would-be combatants were struggling to rise, and not succeeding. Alice was standing between them, uncertain whom to aid. Victoria was staring darkly at Bedford.

"You've made a muck of things," she said.

WITH Uncle Dixon in tow, he and Sloane moved off into the shadows. They found several cars, but not the means to start them. Finally, he opened the rear of one of the sedans.

"You get in back," he said. "We'll sleep up front."

"Sleep?"

"Best thing, don't you think?"

"What if they come for us?"

"We'll hold them off with this revolver."

CHAPTER 8

"D**ID** you enjoy yourselves at Lady Idina's dinner party, sir?" asked their Indian driver, as they thumped along the dusty track that was the Ngong Road.

"Not as much as Her Ladyship would have liked," Bedford replied.

"Her hospitality was not to your taste?"

"A bit too much sin, as you put it."

"You are also Christian, sir?"

"After a fashion," Bedford said.

"Fashion?"

"We're Greenwich Village Christians," Sloane said. "It's a different sect."

"I can't believe any of this," grumbled Uncle Dixon.

"Uncle Dixon belongs to the Fourth Presbyterian Church," Sloane explained.

"What about the first, second, and third?" Bedford asked.

"The Fourth's the grandest Presbyterian Church in Chicago—right on Michigan Avenue," Sloane continued. "Uncle Dixon also belongs to the grandest club—the

Chicago Club—where they don't hand out numbered latchkeys to other guests."

Dixon put his hand over his eyes. "We shouldn't have left Georgia there."

"We couldn't find her, Uncle. Remember?"

"We should have looked more than we did."

"I think we looked as far as we dared," Bedford said.

Uncle Dixon retreated into himself again. He was spending much of his time there. Bedford wondered if he might now be talked out of his safari, but got nowhere with the suggestion. The man was determined that he would not return home without his full allotment of dead animals to show off.

SLEEP came easily even with the sun well advanced in the sky. What seemed only minutes after Bedford had closed his eyes, a rapping at the door of their room in the Muthaiga Club compelled him to rise stiffly from his chair and answer it, finding the white hunter there, looking impatient. It was now afternoon.

"Ready for the hunt?" Owen asked.

"About as ready as I am for a trip to the South Pole."

"Come now, Captain Green. We've dallied too long as it is. We'll have a spot of lunch and then be off. All the gear's been loaded. All we need is yourselves and whatever you're bringing along."

Sloane groaned. Owen looked past Bedford toward the bed. "I gather you were enjoying a bit of Kenyan hospitality last night."

"I don't know how you people managed to beat the Germans down here."

"We didn't, old boy. Von Lettow-Vorbeck had us whipped start to finish. He only surrendered because all the Huns in Europe had already done so."

"Have you apprised Mr. and Mrs. Smith of your plans for departure?"

"It's the other way around," Owen said. "These are the Smiths' plans. They are, at all events, Mrs. Smith's plans."

"She's returned?"

"Perhaps an hour ago. And now she's keen to be off. So if you're coming with us, best to make haste."

Bedford thanked him, and closed the door. "Are we coming?" he asked the heap of legs and sheets on the bed.

"I truly do not feel like it," Sloane said, "but we have no choice."

"Yes we do," he quickly responded. "Just as we did last night."

Sloane sat up. Had Bedford been able to take a photograph of her at that moment, he'd be able to make her do his bidding for life simply on the threat of showing it around.

"No," Sloane grumbled. "She's up to something. No doubt about it. I can't leave him to her devices. Did I tell you how she parted from her last husband?"

"If you did, I don't recall."

"If I had, you would. It was a 'hunting accident.' Shotgun."

Her words came as a bolt between the eyes. Bedford now realized why he'd been brought along. "Was there an inquiry?"

"Oh yes. She was never charged with anything. The ultimate weeping widow, she was—until she married Uncle Dixon."

"Why have you kept this bit of news from me until now?"

"I didn't want you to fret."

THEIR caravan of one automobile and a high-wheeled truck left the Muthaiga Club's grounds at a little past two. Bedford sat in the front seat of the car, next to Owen, who was driving. Sloane and her uncle rode in back. Georgia had insisted on riding in the truck, saying she felt safer.

She quickly found herself dustier. Everything the tires of the automobile churned up hung in the air behind it.

"How far is it?" Sloane asked.

"Not far," Owen said. "We should be able to set up camp by sundown."

Bedford looked to the sun, which was high but easing into the western sky. "We're heading southwest. You had said something about Lake Naivasha."

"Know your Kenya, do you? Change of plan. But it doesn't matter. Plenty of game whichever way we go."

THERE'D been no advance party to set up their camp—as had been so pleasantly arranged for the prince's party. But Owen's native assistants were able to have their tents and tables up and in place within an hour. There were four of the Africans. Three of them were dressed in approximations of British colonial garb, though they had no shoes. One exceedingly tall African wore his traditional Masai cloak and carried a spear. Owen said the man was named Mzizi and was one of the best trackers in British East Africa. He spoke no English, but Owen was able to communicate with him in Swahili. Owen's chief lieutenant, a weathered former British army sergeant named Grubb, spoke the language as well.

They were provided with chairs and whiskey to occupy them while the camp was being established, but Dixon was not content. He fidgeted, rose from his chair, paced awhile, seated himself again, then was back on his feet. Instead of calming him, the whiskey seemed to add to his fret.

"What the hell's the matter, Uncle Dixon?" Sloane asked.

Bedford assumed the man was once again worried about his wife. Georgia had gone off somewhere almost immediately upon arriving at this place, a clearing on a hilltop that overlooked a wide, rolling plain.

"I want to go hunting," Dixon said. "They're taking too long. The sun's going down. I want to shoot something."

"Please, Uncle. Have a drink. Calm down."

Shaking his head, Dixon went to the wooden cases holding the hunting rifles, removing the weapon he had purchased in Mombasa—a Rigby .416 double-barreled big game rifle.

"Mr. Smith," Bedford ventured. "That's an elephant gun. It's a bit late to mount that kind of shoot, don't you think?"

Sloane glanced from one to the other of them, annoyed with her uncle for his bloody-minded compulsive behavior and with Bedford for patronizing him.

Owen entered upon the scene, disapproving of Dixon's wish. "I've already made arrangements for the morning, Mr. Smith. Please, relax and enjoy the evening. I promised you an elephant, a lion, and a Cape buffalo and I assure you, you'll have them. But not tonight. That's just impossible."

"To hell with you, Owen. If you won't take me, I'll go out there myself."

Sloane looked stricken at the prospect of her uncle wandering about in the wilds with a weapon large enough to bring down a house. Bedford was suspicious as to Dixon's real intent. His wife was out there somewhere.

Smith stood in place, temper and resolve mounting. Finally, he started out of the camp, heading toward sunset. It occurred to Bedford he might find himself in a nasty encounter with British soldiery. The Prince of Wales's safari camp was in that general direction—and apparently not far.

"Please, wait!" cried Owen. He looked for his assistant. "Grubb. Take Mr. Smith on down to the plain and see if you can't stir up something for him to shoot. But don't dally."

The former sergeant grunted. Slinging his own rifle over his shoulder, he caught up with Dixon, leading him down a different path that led south, rather than west. Two of the Africans rose without a word and followed.

"We should go with them," Sloane said, stepping to Bedford's side.

"No. He's in good hands. We should be worrying about Georgia."

"I am."

THEIR camp had been fully set up and Bedford and Sloane on their second whiskies by the time they heard the gunshots. There were two reports, at some distance but sounding like cannon, and then a third, much quieter one.

The little party returned not long after—Grubb looking grim, Dixon appearing triumphant, the two Africans behind him carrying a very small antelope tied to a pole. Reaching the fire, they laid Dixon's kill beside it, then hurried off. Grubb seated himself and poured a large whiskey.

"Bushbuck," he pronounced, offering no other comment.

"Look!" said Dixon, holding up the slain animal's head.

There was less of that than there should have been. It was missing half its left horn and portions of its skull on that side.

"Did you do that?" Sloane asked.

Dixon was beaming. "Yes! It was my shot. And it was almost dark."

"What about the other shot?" Bedford asked.

"It missed."

"And the third?"

Grubb drank. "I finished the animal off. A formality. It's something of a rare kill. They're shy and solitary. Mr. Smith was lucky to have stumbled right on it."

Sloane looked away. Bedford stared at the butchered creature. In life, it must have been a lithe and graceful thing, a beauty.

"What do you think?" Dixon asked.

"Not much good as a trophy, shot up like that," Grubb said. "Camp meat."

"You're going to *eat* it?" Sloane asked.

"Think of it as beef," Grubb observed.

This daft colloquy was ended by the sound of an approaching motor vehicle. The headlamp beams flitted and bounced among the trees, then leveled as the auto pulled into their clearing. At the wheel was Lord Ralls. Beside him, standing in her excitement, was Georgia.

"We're invited to dinner everyone!" she cried. "The prince has invited us to dinner!"

HIS Highness's party was surprisingly small—His Royal Highness, Thelma Furness, Finch-Hatton, the prince's equerry, some lesser retainers, and the Rallses. Lady Ralls was at Bedford's side in half a trice, taking him by the arm and drawing him aside.

"I simply loathe your friend Georgia," she whispered, "but I'm grateful to her for bringing us all together again."

"She's crashed your party, has she?" Bedford said.

"Out here in Africa that doesn't matter the way it would at Windsor. I don't quite know what he finds so attractive about a lowly born, middle-aged, foul-mouthed, divorced American woman, but there it is, isn't it?"

"What is?"

"Let's go to dinner." She put her arm in his. Her husband paid them absolutely no attention as they walked in that manner directly past him.

FINCH-HATTON had put four camp tables together to create a single long one, placing himself at one end and Owen at the other. The prince, at his own request, was seated in the middle, with Thelma on his right and Georgia on his left. Bedford found himself opposite the heir to the throne, with Victoria Ralls to one side and Sloane to the other.

The prince was feeling chatty and provided much of the talk, though he was careful to engage everyone else in the general run of conversation. Owen, who bore the primary responsibility for this intrusion, remained circumspectly silent. Dixon mostly stared glumly at his plate and drank whiskey instead of wine. No one was paying him any attention.

Thelma appeared little happier, but did her bit—contributing some West End gossip as garnish for the prince's only slightly amusing stories. She laughed in all the right places, but Georgia proved less adroit, giggling in the middle of one of his anecdotes and interrupting him twice. Perhaps intending compensation, she launched into a series of quite raunchy jokes and ribald stories of her own. One of them made Thelma laugh despite herself.

Finally, Finch-Hatton mercifully intervened. "May I offer you a nightcap, sir? Or would you like to get some sleep? We'll be starting early tomorrow."

"What do you think, Joey?" the prince asked his equerry. "Actually, this is the part of safari I enjoy the most." He leaned back and looked up through the trees at the stars. "It's the shooting that's a bore."

"I'm sorry, sir. I thought . . ."

"No, no. Denys. Of course we shall go shooting tomorrow. My father would never let me back into England if I should fail to kill something. But if you can manage it, I should like a glass of port before retiring."

He had several. Then, to the carefully restrained dismay of his English companions, he repaired to his tent, promising to be right back. After a moment, the most horrible wailing noise commenced and His Highness emerged with a musical instrument beneath his arm.

"Oh no," Bedford heard Lord Ralls mutter. "The infernal pipes."

"The eternal infernal pipes," said his wife.

The prince, of course, could not hear the Rallses—or doubtless much of anything. Resolutely enjoying himself, he commenced a bagpipe-playing march around the camp in a parade of one.

When the din at length ceased, everyone applauded.

Finally, it came time to leave. Victoria Ralls again clung to Bedford's arm, but reluctantly relinquished him when Thelma came up and demanded that he speak with her.

"Bedford, I want that horrid woman gone from here," she said, having led him into the darkness to the side of one of the tents. "If you're truly my friend, you will see to it."

He liked Thelma. "I'll do my best, but she seems to do whatever she wants."

"I'm serious, Bedford. She's going to cause him some terrible embarrassment. There'll be consequences."

"I'll make every effort. Are you enjoying yourself otherwise?"

"The honest answer is no, but as you once wrote of me, I'm a game girl."

"If it's any consolation, my friend Sloane is just as unhappy with Mrs. Smith as you are."

"It's no consolation at all, unless she has plans to shoot her. Good night, Bedford. We must get together in New York. I miss those little lunches we used to have."

"No guns."

"No guns. Indeed."

Lord Ralls suddenly appeared before them. "Are you coming? His Highness is asking."

OWEN had offered Bedford a tent of his own but Sloane insisted he share hers—making clear she meant as protector rather than swain. Every beast in the jungle seemed to be giving voice this night, and the myriad insect life were producing a near din with their nocturnal choruses.

"Next time we shall go to the desert," she said, from beneath her mosquito netting.

He laughed. "I'm glad you've got your humor back."

"I haven't."

"Just as well. There are flies in the desert. Even snakes."

"Perhaps the North Pole, then."

"Polar bears."

Silence, except for the insects.

"Can she possibly think she has a future socially with these people?" Sloane asked.

"Seems to." He waited, then added, "Wouldn't that be to the good, though, if she left him to take up with the English?"

"I don't think she'll leave Dixon. Not any time soon."

"Why is that?"

"I don't think you realize just how much money my uncle has. It isn't only that department store. He must own half Chicago's North Side lakeshore."

"She seems to have forgotten that—the way she's carrying on."

"No she hasn't. She never forgets that." They listened to the night sounds some more. "Thank you, Bedford."

"I haven't solved your problem."

"No, but you will." He heard her turn over on her cot.

CHAPTER 9

BEDFORD awoke to the sound of a scream. Sloane was crouching fearfully atop her cot, the mosquito netting wound about her torso like the veils of Salome.

"There's a snake!" she cried.

He shook his head and got slowly to his feet. "Where?"

"It was on my bed. It woke me up."

With her unusual height, Sloane was compelled to totter on her cot in a painful sort of crouch, clinging with one hand to the tent pole. She was close to bringing everything down.

Bedford rubbed his eyes, then sat down again on his cot to pull on his boots.

"What are you doing?" she bellowed. "There's a snake!"

"I'm just trying to avoid having my ankle bit." In his haste, he was having trouble getting his foot where it belonged. *"Scheiss!"*

"What did you say?"

"*'Scheiss.'* It means—"

"I know what it means. You never use words like that."

"I did in the war."

"Damn it! Come get this snake! *Scheiss,* indeed!"

Before he could finish getting his boots on, the tent flap opened and a tall dark African stepped in, short spear in hand. It was Mzizi. He looked at neither of them, going to the other end of Sloane's cot as though he knew precisely what was there. He paused, waiting for something, then jabbed—only once. Then he looked to Bedford.

"Wo ist das Scheiss?" he asked.

"What? *Was sprechen sie?"*

Mzizi stepped back. There was a limp, multicolored reptile neatly skewered on his sword blade. Mzizi looked at Bedford, keeping his eyes averted from Sloane, and said, *"Schlange."* Then he was gone as swiftly and noiselessly as he had come.

"What did he say?" Sloane asked, stepping down from her cot.

"Schlange."

"I heard that. What does it mean?"

"Snake."

"I told you," Sloane seated herself, pulling her knees up and the mosquito netting tighter about her body.

There was light, but not much, as the sun was just coming up. Bedford briefly embraced the happy thought of returning to his slumbers, dismissing it as it occurred to him that Sloane had been frightened wide awake and would prefer him conscious.

Bedford finished pulling on his boots. "Well, that's one small antelope and a snake dispatched. Perhaps if we can manage a goat and some kind of pussycat, your uncle's blood lust will be satisfied."

"Don't make this any more horrible than it already is with your crude attempt at wit."

"Do you want to go back to Nairobi?"

She bit her lip. "Let's give it another day or two."

He rose. "I'm not sure I can continue to resist Lady Ralls for two more days."

Sloane looked down at her feet. "You could do worse, Bedford."

"What are you suggesting?"

"That if this was Greenwich Village and she walked into Chumley's, you and Bunny Wilson would be falling over one another trying to make her acquaintance."

"I'll let you get dressed." He went out into the very young day.

T**HE** morning was still cool, but warming, as a veil of thin clouds moved off to the north, clearing the sky behind it as though with the sweep of a broom. Grubb was by the truck, supervising the cleaning of rifles.

"Your tracker speaks German."

"Mzizi, you mean? He knows a word or two. Picked it up in the war."

"He was one of your scouts?"

"One of their scouts. Damn good one. Responsible for a bloody lot of ambushes, probably."

"Why is he working for you?"

"Germans all went away."

Bedford picked up the Rigby. "You're not letting Mr. Smith have this again, are you?"

"If that's what he wants. It's his rifle. He's paying for the bloody safari."

Bedford picked up a slightly smaller weapon. "What are you giving us to use?"

"That's a .375 Merkel you've got. Hell of a gun. It's yours if you want it. Bit of a kick, though."

Bedford hefted and aimed it, then carefully set it back down. "Maybe. And Miss Smith?"

"She's a sturdy lady." Grubb handed him a shorter-barreled rifle. "It's a Remington .303. Don't worry. With the Holland and Holland cartridges we have, it'll stop the big ones."

Bedford had taken Sloane up to his farm in Cross River, New York, for an afternoon of shooting lessons. She had a brilliant mind, as she had often demonstrated, but it had been of little use. She'd been unable to master even a light .22 rifle. The "big ones" doubtless would be safe.

"And Mrs. Smith?"

"A .375 Lyon and Lyon. She requested it."

"She did?"

"First thing this morning."

"Is she a good shot?"

"Reckon so."

"Where is she?"

"Over at the prince's camp. We'll be hunting with them later in the day, but we're starting out this morning on our own."

WHEN they'd concluded their hasty breakfast, Owen gathered them around the back of the truck and explained how the morning would proceed.

"The object here is to get Mr. Smith one of the trophy animals he's after. Elephant will be hard. They like to stay in the forest and bagging one usually involves a lot of tracking, but maybe we'll be lucky."

"Meaning the elephant won't," said Sloane.

Owen ignored her. "Lacking that good fortune, we should certainly come onto some lion, so the day won't be a loss, at any rate." He picked up the Remington and handed it to Sloane. "This is your uncle's hunt but we don't want you to have a dull time of it. Is there anything you'd like to shoot?"

The distraught look that had been with her for the last

two days disappeared from Sloane's face, replaced by a
mischievous grin. "I'll just wait and see what comes along.
You say we're near the prince's party?"

"We'll be steering clear of them this morning. How
about you, Captain Green? What would you like to shoot?"
He thrust the Merkel into Bedford's hands.

"I'll just wait and see what turns up," he said.

"We'd best get moving," Owen said. "The animals are
at their most active early in the morning—and then not
again until late afternoon."

"Let's go everyone," said Uncle Dixon. He picked up
the Rigby and strode to the car.

"You don't want to wait for Mrs. Smith?" Grubb asked.

"No. I want to get out there."

"What about Mrs. Smith?"

"She's not hunting. Not with me."

SMITH, Sloane, and Bedford rode with Owen in the car.
Grubb and the natives followed in the truck. The
Africans appeared very pleased and excited, except for
Mzizi, who stood looking forward with an implacable
calm.

There was a small lake at the bottom of the hill and
progress around it was difficult. Lacking any sort of road
or track to follow, the vehicles bumped and swayed over
the rough ground. Several times they had to ford streams,
and for a time Owen plowed through a thickness of trees
whose low-hanging branches slapped at them from seemingly all sides.

Finally, he pulled to a stop in the lee of a small, treeless
rise on the other side of the water. The truck pulled up
alongside. Both engines stopped about the same time. In
the quiet that followed, they at first heard nothing, then

everything. The creatures seemed in great stir, especially the birds.

"We'll reconnoiter from up there," Owen said. "If we spot anything, we'll move downwind and see if there's a shot."

Dixon nodded, as though every inch the veteran hunter.

Owen and Mzizi led the way, with Dixon and Grubb following. The other Africans, two of them bearing rifles, spread out to the side like military flankers, but kept to the rear. Bedford and Sloane stayed close behind Grubb. Bedford sensed that she was frightened, though it was not clear whether the cause was the wild animals or something altogether different.

"Chin up," he said. "This will all be over soon."

"I just wish she were here where we could keep watch on her."

"I'm sure she and the prince are off engaging in harmless fun—breaking camp furniture or something."

Owen, who had reached the top of the rise, raised his hand. Quickening their trudge through the high grass, they joined him.

Dixon was beaming. On the plain below, moving at an amble, were perhaps thirty or forty elephants, including several babies.

"Thank you, Owen," he said, and raised the rifle to his shoulder. Owen put his hand on the barrel, pushing it down.

"We're much too far away," he said.

"I might hit something," said Dixon.

"The object is to hit what we're aiming at."

"Then let's get closer." Dixon started forward, but Owen took hold of his shoulder.

"It's too late," the white hunter said. "They've had their morning drink and now they're heading back for the forest. We'll never be able to catch up with them."

"Damn it, Owen. You promised me an elephant. Marshall Field got an elephant. He's had the whole damned thing shipped back."

"You'll get your elephant, Mr. Smith, but not today. Maybe tomorrow, if we get going earlier." He pointed to a swath of field close to the lake, where a herd of zebra were grazing. "Let's get near that lot. You never know what might be stalking them."

Slinging his own rifle over his shoulder, he started down the slope.

THEY approached the zebra herd obliquely through the grass. Owen motioned to them to stay to his rear, then he and Mzizi crept forward at a crouch. Reaching a clump of high brush, they crept into it, all but disappearing.

"What fun," said Sloane, unhappily. "Crawling around in the bushes."

"Sloane," chided Dixon. "Please. I begin to wish you hadn't come along."

She fell silent, but made an unpleasant face.

Owen rose slightly, then looked back to Dixon and signaled him to come forward. The zebras were stirring nervously, though Bedford was unable to spot the cause.

Dixon hurried to join the white hunter and Mzizi. Together, they crept forward, until they were at the edge of the brush. Owen pointed off to the right at some trees, then crouched down.

The breeze had stopped and the heat was rising in the still air. Bedford wiped his brow with the rolled-up sleeve of his khaki shirt, then rested the butt of his rifle on the ground, content to be a spectator. Sloane was holding her weapon, but awkwardly, her eyes fixed on her uncle.

"I can't believe we're here," she said.

Bedford slapped at a large, black insect that had drawn blood. "I can."

The movement to the right was sudden and swift. A lioness Bedford certainly had not seen exploded from the grass and charged at the zebra herd, aiming herself like a projectile at one of the smaller animals. The colt dodged and darted, as best it could, but was young and perhaps not experienced with lions. The predator closed the ground fast, moving in bounds.

Dixon rose, raising his rifle to his shoulder, but Owen shook his head and politely pushed it back down.

The lioness hadn't noticed. Two more bounds and she was within inches of her prey. Another bound and she caught it on the haunches with both front paws. The force of her strike knocked the zebra over, and they both went down in a great cloud of dust. The lioness lost her grip, rolling, but regained her purchase and turned back to the hoofed animal, which was struggling to its feet.

"I can't watch this," Sloane said, turning.

"It's real life. It's what happens here."

"Whoever said that was anything marvelous?"

The lioness had got her jaws around the zebra's neck. Her victim struggled, twice trying to lift its head and thrashing out in one last futile effort with its rear legs. Then it went still.

From the trees to the right came more movement, only slower and more deliberate—a procession of two smaller lionesses and a great, dark-maned lion, who plodded toward the kill as complaisantly as a gentleman entering his club.

"You might want to give this your full attention," Bedford said.

"No. It's too ghastly."

"There are more lions coming. And I believe your manly uncle intends to kill them all."

Dixon was standing, aiming his rifle in preparation for a shot, but waiting. Owen had his hand up, demanding delay. Obviously, they were going to hold fire until all four cats were feeding, then go for the male.

"If I gave a shout," said Sloane, watching now, "would the lions run away?"

"I don't know, but I think your uncle would probably shoot you."

"Damn and damn."

"You could always shoot him."

"That's not funny." She peered over her shoulder, as though she thought Georgia might be lurking in the brush with a rifle—Uncle Dixon dead in the sights.

Looking to the same place up the hill, Bedford did think he saw someone—there, and quickly gone. He thought it might be one of Owen's natives.

The females moved to the side to allow the male his pick of meat, but continued to feed themselves. Bedford supposed they were so preoccupied one could walk right up behind them and shoot them with a pistol. As it was, they were more than two hundred yards from Dixon's position. Bedford wouldn't have attempted that shot. He wondered why Owen wasn't moving closer.

The hunter began doing precisely that, waving to Dixon to follow. When he was some twenty yards out from the brush, he stopped, taking unhappy note that Dixon hadn't budged. Urging him forward with great, angry vigor, he succeeded in getting the millionaire to take a tentative step forward, then another, and finally to tiptoe all the way to Owen's side.

What conversation they had, Bedford couldn't hear, though he judged it to be terse. Owen commenced another advance, more slowly, intent on the prey.

If he assumed Dixon was following, he was in error. Sloane's uncle refused to budge a foot. He meant to accomplish his task without further ado—or risk.

The cannon-like gunshot startled everyone, including

Dixon, who tottered back a step. Owen was staring in disbelief.

Dixon had actually hit the beast—in the hindquarter. The lion turned roaring, looking for an adversary. Two of the lionesses had bolted for the place they had come from. The killer lioness remained with the partially eaten zebra, lifting her head and snarling.

"Finish him!" Owen cried.

Dixon raised the Rigby again. He had trouble aiming, as the lion was moving about, dragging his left rear leg. The second shot missed.

"Reload!" Owen remembered who was patron here. "Sir, reload quickly!"

Dixon did so, uncertain what to do next. Owen waved him forward. Together, finally, they advanced step in step, rifles at the ready. Owen was encouraging the other. Bedford heard him warn to watch for the lioness by the zebra.

All that was required to put the wounded male out of his misery and claim the desired trophy was to move up within range. But once again Dixon balked. Barely missing Owen, he fired both barrels of the Rigby at once—the recoil knocking him backward onto his seat. One of the rounds did strike the lion, inflicting another crippling—but not killing—wound. Shaking his head, Owen brought his own weapon to bear and dispatched the animal with one quick shot.

The wretched business was not yet concluded. The female at the zebra fixed her gaze on Owen, gave a roar, and then charged. The hunter's first shot missed but the second sent the lioness sprawling. He administered the coup de grace with his revolver.

"Bedford!"

He looked to Sloane, who was paying no attention to the slaughter down below. One of the smaller lionesses was crouched in the grass not twenty yards from her.

"Bedford, please! Make it go away!"

He swung the Merkel around and got off one shot without a shoulder aim just as the lioness began its leap toward Sloane. The bullet caught the poor creature in the belly but did not kill it. As Sloane screamed, her rifle dropped to the ground.

The wounded lioness landed clumsily, shook its head, then spun around and leapt again. Sloane turned away, cringing. Bedford brought his rifle up and fired truly, hitting the animal in the chest. It must have died in midair, for it fell like a pile of rags. He felt as sick as he had with that last German aviator.

Georgia had joined them. She stood at the top of the rise, a rifle of her own in hand.

"Marvelous!" she shouted.

CHAPTER 10

THEY entered the prince's camp in a procession—Owen's car, the truck, and then the Rolls-Royce Georgia had come in, each with a dead lion tied across the hood. As they roared up between the tents, Georgia sounded the Rolls's horn, bringing out their perhaps less than welcoming hosts.

The Africans were jubilant, however, feting Dixon as though he had bagged the lot with one shot. The Rallses seemed thrilled as well—if only to have an interruption of their boredom. Victoria quickly ascertained from Owen who had shot what, and rushed up to Bedford, grinning.

"What a surprise you are, sir. I hadn't thought you quite the type for this sort of thing."

"I'm not." Bedford said. "It was an unavoidable happenstance."

She looked to Sloane, who had slumped to a seat on the wide running board of the truck. Georgia began poking about the dead lion Dixon had shot. Dixon had gone to the whiskey table.

"I daresay no one has ever saved my life," said Victoria, returning her attention to Bedford.

"It's not necessarily an altogether agreeable experience."

She squeezed his arm. "I should like to find out." She sighed. "But not today. The hunting has been cancelled. His Highness has gone for a 'walk' with Lady Furness."

"A walk?"

"Yes. *À deux*. All alone. And they've been gone for some time." Her smile was no longer sweet but wicked.

"You've done no hunting at all?"

"Oh, we all went for a stroll in the bush this morning. David—the prince—killed some sort of wild pig. But he spent the rest of the time running about taking photographs. Truly tedious." She yawned, as though for emphasis. "Since he went for his walk, your Mrs. Smith has been quite beside herself—having no prince to sit beside herself. She went off in the car. We had no idea when she'd return."

"Well, she has her husband here now for company."

"More's the pity." She released Bedford's arm, walking away. "Let me know if you'd care to go for a walk."

Lord Ralls and Finch-Hatton were examining Bedford's lioness. Bedford had not gone near the animal after he'd shot it, and had no care to now, but he was curious what Finch-Hatton would have to say about it.

"Very interesting shots," said Finch-Hatton, as Bedford approached. "I assume it wasn't lying on its back. You shot it twice in the middle of a single leap?"

"Two leaps. The first shot wasn't much good. She was back on her feet quick, and jumped again."

"It was coming at you?"

"At my friend Sloane."

"Didn't she fire?"

Bedford shook his head. "She'd taken the magazine out of the rifle. No ammunition."

"Whatever for?"

"She didn't want to kill anything."

Finch-Hatton seemed bewildered by this, though he must have had his share of eccentrics on safari.

"Perhaps she'd be more comfortable back in Nairobi," Ralls said, dropping the dead lioness's paw, which he'd been holding. "I'd be happy to drive her back."

"She wants to stay with her uncle," Bedford said.

"Whatever for?" Finch-Hatton asked.

"To protect him."

Lord Ralls began to laugh. Finch-Hatton did not.

THERE was a lot of drinking, then lunch, then naps. Georgia, for want of anyone else, stayed with her husband. Bedford followed Sloane to a nearby tent.

She sprawled on a cot. "We simply have to persuade him to go home now. He has a lion. Who could ask for more?"

"He wants an elephant. Your Marshall Field got an elephant." Bedford folded back the tent flaps to admit the breeze, which had returned. He sat on the other cot. "Dayton Crosby thought it was wonderful for us to go on safari. He said that, given our chaotic natures, we'd disrupt it."

"This safari seems to be disrupting itself."

"Are you going to sleep?"

She shifted a long, beautiful leg. "Yes. I'm so weary now I haven't the energy even to get another drink, let alone back to our own camp."

"Shall I get you one?"

"No. Just keep an eye on Uncle Dixon." She closed her own eyes, then opened them. "Bedford, come here."

He came and carefully sat on the edge of her cot. "Yes?"

"Kiss me, in that sweet, gentle, prim Westchester County way of yours."

He obeyed. "I shall always love you for saving my life," she said.

"Thank you. It was—"

"But I'm going to sleep now." She turned onto her side.

U NCLE Dixon and Georgia did not return until near sundown, entering the campsite almost at the same time the prince and Thelma did. Lady Furness was not pleased to see Mrs. Smith once again intruding upon her domain. As soon as convenient, she discreetly slipped away from His Highness and took Bedford aside once more.

"I asked you, as a friend, to keep that meddlesome woman away from here, but I gather she's been here all bloody day."

"No, she came out to hunt with us for a bit."

Thelma took in the carcasses with a sweeping glance. "You killed all those lions?"

"Owen, mostly."

"Smith?"

"Part of one."

"And you?"

"All of one."

"Well, bully for you, Bedford." She came closer. "Now listen to me. The little man is becoming bored with all this. He's finished with his official functions and I think he may be leaving here tomorrow. Until then, I'd like some time with him myself."

"And this afternoon?"

"He wasn't well."

Bedford patted her shoulder. "You are indeed a game girl, Lady Furness. I'll give it another go."

"I'll be grateful. If you fail, I'll be something else."

Georgia was with the prince. As Bedford approached, he heard her ask him if he would entertain them again with his bagpipes. When he demurred, she begged—doubtless as much aware of his relish for the instrument as she was of the hatred everyone else in the camp bore it.

To Bedford's surprise, the prince declined again, more firmly. Looking to his equerry for help, he got up from the chair where Georgia had been kneeling at his side.

"Sir," said the equerry, coming on the quick. "There's some business I neglected to tell you about—a dispatch from Windsor. Shouldn't we attend to that now?"

"Yes, of course, Joey. Thank you very much." The prince went into his tent. The equerry followed. A few minutes later, so did Thelma.

Bedford went to Georgia. "Mrs. Smith, I'm afraid your husband's a bit upset about the way things went today."

"What are you talking about? You killed three lions."

"There were difficulties. At all events, I think he'd appreciate a kind word or two from you right now."

Dixon was still at the whiskey table.

"What business is this of yours, Mr. Green?"

"I'm a friend of Sloane's."

"Yes. We can see that." She got to her feet, but only to take the chair the prince had vacated. "Sloane doesn't like me and I'm not all that well disposed toward her, either. I think you'd better stay out of this, Mr. Green. As for Dixon, I think I'll just rest right here awhile. It's been a tiring day."

Shaking his head, Bedford walked away. Lord Ralls passed him going the other way, toward the prince's tent Bedford had just left, though Georgia had not.

Sloane appeared a little bewildered. "Are we invited to stay for dinner again?"

"I'm afraid I've no idea. The prince has gone off to read dispatches. Your aunt—"

"She's not my aunt."

"Georgia awaits him outside his tent, much like a faithful puppy dog."

"In either case, let's not stay."

"I'll find Owen."

"Find my uncle."

"He won't want to come."

"I think he will."

He did. Dixon even drove the car himself, arriving at their camp with only small digressions from their proper route.

Mzizi had somehow gotten there before them. Walking with his odd, loping gait, he came up to Bedford's side of the auto. *"Hungrig?"*

Hearing the man speak in that tongue still came as a startle.

"Ja," Bedford replied.

"Ich Koche."

"Danke, Mzizi."

They ate around the campfire. The night had cooled quickly and Sloane sat with a blanket draped over her shoulders. Dixon stared into the flames, raising fork to mouth distractedly. Bedford thought the man was troubled over the absence of his wife, but his surmise was incorrect.

"What's keeping Owen?" he muttered. "I'm not paying him to tend to the Prince of Wales."

"For an Englishman," Bedford offered, "it may not be so easy to escape royal company."

"It's dark, Uncle," ventured Sloane. "You can't go hunting until morning."

"I know, but I want to be ready to go first thing. I don't want to miss the elephants this time."

Sloane started to speak, then thought better of it, placing her hand over her eyes.

"The way those English drink, he might just not turn up until late tomorrow," Dixon continued. "I'll dock him, if he does that. His charges are outrageous as it is. I'll fire him—and see if I can't get someone else. Perhaps that Finch-Hatton."

"You can't have him until the prince departs," said Bedford. *If then,* he thought.

"Just get it over with, Uncle. Kill your animals and then let's go back, please. It's a long way back. And I'm not feeling well."

Dixon looked up, and then at her. "I'm sorry, Sloane. I thought you'd enjoy this. It was supposed to be a great adventure. Once in a lifetime."

She rose. "Perhaps if you had brought Aunt Kate."

His eyes became those of a whipped dog. He turned away.

Bedford had a large glass of whiskey in his hand. Sloane gently took it from him, taking a very large swallow.

"I'm going to bed. At all events, to cot. Good night, gentlemen."

Bedford drank the rest, then got up to follow. She halted him just outside the tent.

"No. Please," she said. "Not tonight."

" 'Not tonight?' There's been no previous 'night.' "

"I know. You've been the perfect gentleman, as always. I'd just like you to keep a watch on him for a while. Till Owen comes back."

"And if Georgia comes back?"

"Exactly."

She kissed his cheek, then disappeared within the tent.

Grumbling, Bedford went to refill his glass, then rejoined Dixon, who was examining the Rigby.

"Perhaps I should use a smaller-rifle," he said.

"Not for elephant," said Bedford. He cursed himself for saying that. If Dixon had a smaller bore weapon, the elephants might stand a better chance.

Dixon put two of the big .416 cartridges in the Rigby,

then got to his feet. "I'm going to get some sleep, Green. I mean to be out in the bush by sunup." He hesitated. "Would you like to come with me?"

"No thanks, Mr. Smith."

"Sure?"

"That lion is more than I could ever ask for."

Dixon seemed genuinely disappointed, and walked away without another word.

Bedford tried sitting awhile longer in the chair, but the discomfort got the better of him. He took the blanket Sloane had left behind and lay down on the ground, wrapping himself in it.

The whiskey brought sleep on quickly. He was awakened several times in the night, but never fully left his slumber. Once he was stirred by the sound of an automobile engine and then voices—people returning to the camp. Then he heard the engine again, but without voices. Later, there was a sharp but distant report. He sat up, sure it had been a gunshot, listening for it to repeat, but there was nothing but the wind and the creatures of the night. And no one else in the camp stirred.

Except for the woman beneath the blanket with him. She looked very tired and a little ill, but grinned.

"Hello, darling."

"Lady Ralls."

"Victoria, please."

"Victoria. You can't be here. Your husband . . . We're in the middle of the camp."

"Silly boy. I'm not here for amour. I just want you to hold me while I sleep. I'm badly in need of that. Just for a little."

"Just for a little." He lay back down and she moved within his arms, laying her blonde head onto his shoulder. "Mmmm."

He slept well after that. When he awakened the next

time, the sun was up and Mzizi was shaking him. Victoria was gone.

"Frau Schmidt ist tot," the African said.

Bedford sat up. Sloane's worst fears had come true. She would never forgive him for this neglect. Dixon dead.

"Herr Smith ist tot? Kaput? Ist treu?"

"Nicht Herr Schmidt. Frau Schmidt."

Bedford shook his head once, clearing his brain, then got to his feet. Sloane was standing outside her tent, wide-eyed and staring. Owen was walking toward them.

"There's the devil to pay," he said.

CHAPTER 11

THE bodies were in the center of a clearing perhaps a mile and a half from the camp, quite near the road that led back north to Nairobi though not visible from it. The man and woman lay naked, their legs entwined, their clothes lying nearby in some disarray. Georgia was sprawled facedown on the soft earth. Lord Ralls, partially beneath her, was staring upward in what appeared to be astonishment.

He had a large bullet hole in his chest. She had a smaller one in the middle of her back. There was a wide, gaping, bloody wound on one of her thighs as well, but it did not seem the work of a firearm, unless someone had used a small cannon on her.

Bedford could make no sense of this. In his newspapering days back in New York, he had often gone on murder calls with his homicide detective friend, Lieutenant Joseph d'Alessandro. He wished Joey D, as the detective was known on Broadway, were with him now.

There were flies swarming. He didn't know what to do about them.

"This is horrible," he said.

"It's bloody big trouble," Owen responded. "We don't have these very often."

"Hunting accidents, you mean."

"Mr. Green, I am certainly not about to call this a hunting accident."

Bedford studied the wound in Georgia's back. It was relatively neat and there were no powder burns. "I don't suppose anyone would have mistaken them for wild animals."

"Not if they were close enough to shoot both of them like that."

Bedford swallowed hard. He had had little to eat the night before but was not at all hungry now. "What do you suppose happened to her leg?"

Owen twisted up his face as he pondered the question—and her corpse.

"Animal," he said, finally. "Wild dog. Hyena maybe."

"Why didn't it eat more?"

"We must have scared it off."

Mzizi came forward and knelt, running his hand over the ground. He pointed to a faint depression and some other markings near Georgia's foot, then said something in Swahili.

"He thinks it was a small cat—serval, or caracal," the white hunter said.

Bedford crouched beside the African, looking at Georgia's twisted ankle. There were teeth marks, but little blood. He studied the earth around it.

"Ziehen," Bedford said. *"Ja?"*

Mzizi nodded, pointing from Georgia's foot to the leg that lay over Ralls's.

"He thinks the animal pulled the body to the side," Bedford said.

Owen exchanged a few words with his tracker in Swahili, appearing satisfied with this speculation. "She must have fallen on top of him. I suppose he was shot first—then her."

Bedford touched Mrs. Smith's shoulder, surprised by the coolness of the hardening flesh, then started to turn her over.

"I wouldn't do that, Mr. Green," Owen said. "We shouldn't move anything until Inspector Jellicoe gets here."

Owen had sent Grubb back to Nairobi as soon as Dixon had come back into camp with the chilling news. Unless he came by airplane, it would be a few hours before the policeman was on the scene.

"We can't leave them here," Bedford said.

"No we can't. The beasts would be on them for certain."

"We ought at least to cover them up. Keep off the flies."

"There's a shelter half in the trunk. I'll get it."

Bedford looked back to Owen's car, which sat on the other side of the trees. Dixon was still in the backseat, holding his rifle, as motionless as a statue.

"He said he'd been out hunting," Bedford asked. "On his own?"

"Yes. Said he fired one shot at a giraffe, though he's not sure if he hit it."

"A giraffe?"

"Said it was down at the water hole at the end of these trees."

"He doesn't know if he hit it?"

"Perhaps he was nervous. He's rather that way, I daresay."

Bedford studied the rifle Smith was holding. "He still has a round in that weapon."

"I suppose so."

"Do you think it's safe to leave it with him? He looks pretty despondent."

Owen sighed. "You're right. He shouldn't have that."

"I'll attend to it."

"Right."

Dixon held the rifle loosely by the barrel, which was pointed straight up. His eyes were rather glazed, fixed on nothing. His shoulders were slumped, his head hanging down somewhat. If one were to paint a picture of a man contemplating suicide, Dixon here would have served as a perfect model.

"Dixon," said Bedford, as he came up to him. He put his hand on the man's arm in a gesture of consolation that also served to prevent him from moving the firearm.

There was no response.

"Dixon," he repeated, reaching now for the gun barrel. "Let me take this. You could have an accident."

Smith turned his head slowly, fixing Bedford with a zombie stare. Again no reply.

He gently pulled the weapon from Dixon's grasp, lifting it carefully over the side of the car. Smith slumped back now, closing his eyes. Owen had left his own rifle in the front seat. Bedford took that, too, carrying both back to the clearing.

He broke open the Rigby. One shell had been fired.

Owen was about to spread the canvas cover over the bodies when Bedford interceded. "I'm sorry, Captain Owen. The animal's already moved her. I think we'd better look at something."

"What?"

Without answering, Bedford resolutely turned Georgia over, her arm flinging backward. Her expression was much different than Ralls's—reflecting more pain than surprise. He looked to her chest. The exit wound between her breasts was large, about the size of the entry wound in Ralls's chest. Picking up a twig, he probed it a bit, then turned to Ralls, carefully rolling him over as well. The entry and exit wounds in both bodies lined up.

"They were standing very close together, I think," Bedford said.

"Well now, that often happens when a man and a woman take off their clothes."

"Owen, they were killed with the same bullet."

"You think?"

"Yes. See how the wounds match up."

Owen leaned closer, then stood upright. "I daresay you're right, Mr. Green. You know what that means?"

"I'm not sure."

"Did you look at the Rigby?"

"Yes. One round was fired."

"One. Well, there you are."

Bedford noticed that ground between the two bodies had been scratched up as well. The wild animal that had been feeding on Georgia must have been trying to pull them both somewhere.

"I'll cover them up now," Owen said, and did so.

THEY left Mzizi and one of the African gun bearers to guard the bodies, returning to camp over a bumpier but more direct route than before. Bedford worried about Dixon every lurch and thump of the way, though the man stirred little from his trance-like state.

As they pulled up beside the truck, Sloane came running from her tent. Bedford could not imagine how she might have learned of the tragic occurrence, but she seemed well aware that something was terribly amiss. Reaching the side of the car, she looked first to her uncle, who somberly ignored her.

"He's all right?" she asked Bedford. "He's not injured?"

Bedford snapped open the door and took her aside, and then down the slope a little. He put his arm around her. "Georgia is dead. So is Lord Ralls. They've been shot. With the same bullet."

She shuddered, but not with grief. Her concern seemed solely for Dixon, to whom she looked again. "Did he . . .?"

"I don't know. Perhaps it was an accident. At all events, there are some significant questions that will have to be answered."

Sloane's mind moved quickly. "Were they . . . ?"

"*Flagrante delicto*. They were undressed, and—"

"But they hardly knew each another."

"You've observed the tribal customs here. Such niceties don't seem to matter."

She glanced about her, at everything in view, as though there lurked some new threat to her peace of mind. "Would you think me a complete rummy if I were to have a drink?"

"Not today, love."

"Good. Would you like one?"

"Not yet. It would be well if you attended to your uncle, though."

"He's just sitting there."

"Maybe so, but he's in a highly disturbed state. I had to take his rifle away."

"Good. I hope you got rid of it."

"Gave it to Owen."

"You don't think much of Uncle Dixon, do you?"

"Because he may have murdered his wife?"

"He's in trouble. I have to get word to my Aunt Kate. Is there any way to do that?"

"We're a long way from Chicago."

She wiped at her eyes. "I wish I were there now."

"Get yourself a drink and then sit with him awhile. I'll see what else needs to be done."

He watched her walk away. A moment later, Owen was at his side. "This is a balls-up, all right, Captain Green. The prince's party should be informed. This will complicate his visit."

Sloane was at the whiskey table. The remaining Africans in the camp were standing about, watching Owen and Bedford. The morning was moving on, bringing heat. The noise from the birds was diminishing. The other creatures they'd been hearing were settling down as well.

"Where is Lady Ralls?" Bedford asked.

"In her tent, I imagine." Owen fidgeted.

"I've no wish to visit the prince's camp," Bedford said.

Owen hesitated. "She likes you. That'll make telling her easier."

THERE was nothing easy about it. Bedford halted at the tent flap, calling her name before committing the intrusion. She stirred and murmured in response.

He moved inside, standing awkwardly for a moment, then sat carefully on the edge of her husband's empty cot. Her blonde hair was in disarray and her eyes opened blearily, but she was as beautiful as at any other time he had seen her, as she had been under his blanket.

Gently, he touched her shoulder. When she did not respond, he brushed his fingers across her cheek.

One bright blue eye opened. "Why, Bedford. Am I still beneath your blanket? Am I dreaming? Where am I?"

"You're back in your tent—in the prince's camp."

She opened the other eye. "Why so I am. Have you come here to be with me?"

He'd done this in the war enough. "Victoria, there's been an accident."

"An accident?"

"Your husband has been killed."

His words seemed to paralyze her. Something dangerously close to madness was in her eyes.

"I'm sorry," he continued. "It's complicated, Victoria. He was with Mrs. Smith. She's dead, too."

Lady Ralls turned away, touching the sheet, as if to make certain it was real and she was conscious.

"When did this happen?" she asked, softly.

"A short while ago. In a clearing, not far from here. Dixon Smith found their bodies and came back to tell us. Owen and I went out there." He shrugged. "There was nothing to be done."

Slowly, she swung her legs over the side of the cot and sat up, grimacing as though the movement brought pain. She was not much dressed. Hanging her head down, she stared at her bare feet.

"Someone has shot Dickie," she said. "Who could have done that?"

"We're not sure."

"You said there was an accident."

He liked her. She deserved the truth. "Possibly not."

She put her hands over her eyes, and seemed about to lose control. He went to her side, putting his arm around her. She began to cry, more in a soft mew at first, then in a full flood of uncontrollable sobbing. He held her tightly, until she was drained of her tears—though probably not sorrow.

"Don't leave me today," she said.

"I'll be here."

"Do you know something, Bedford? I am no longer a 'Lady.'"

DEATH suffered in this manner was a highly consequential event in the colony. Inspector Jellicoe arrived in a large open car accompanied by a white subordinate and four uniformed African policemen.

The inspector spoke to Owen first, the white hunter having spent as brief a time at the prince's camp as possible. Receiving a brief but apparently satisfactory report—all of it taken down on a notepad by the subordinate—a

Constable Sheridan—the inspector then called Bedford
aside.

He'd been sitting with Victoria on chairs outside her
tent, holding her hand. Her grip on him was very firm, but
otherwise she had ceased to pay him much mind. When he
excused himself to talk to the inspector, her hand fell away,
and she sank completely into her thoughts and misery as
though beneath the waves of the sea.

"Owen said you moved the bodies," Jellicoe said, un-
happiness in his tone.

"Just a little. An animal had been messing with them
before us. I was very curious about their wounds."

"Why is that, sir?"

"It was important to me to know whether it was deliberate or an accident." Reluctantly, he nodded toward
Dixon.

"Owen said your Mr. Smith claimed to have discovered
the bodies, and that one shot had been fired from his rifle."

"Yes. And as far as I can determine, one shot killed
them both."

"Too bad they weren't shot indoors. We might have recovered the bullet."

"This might have been an accident, Inspector."

"Two naked people, embracing each other in a clearing? An outraged husband?"

"It was dark. Only the faint light of morning."

"Only one round was fired. If it was an accidental dis-
charge, why this story about a giraffe?"

Bedford shrugged.

"All right, then. Let's go have a look at the bodies."

MZIZI and his comrade had protected the corpses well.
Throwing back the canvas, Bedford found them unmolested and in the same position in which he had left them.

Jellicoe approached them with an odd reluctance for a policeman, giving the wounds a cursory study. He asked one of his Africans in Swahili to turn over the bodies, which the man did as he might a hunting kill.

"Your theory seems borne out," the inspector said. "I'm not much of a policeman, mind. I'm a planter by profession—in reduced circumstances. I only took this job because my coffee crop failed too many times in a row." He made a visual reconnaissance of the surrounding woods. "If she was hit first and they fell more or less where they were shot, I'd say the bullet must have come from that direction."

It was the direction from which they had come—and that Dixon had come from when he had found them.

Jellicoe scratched at the dirt before them with the toe of his boot. "You came just in time. The beasts would have made short work of them."

He ordered the Africans to wrap the bodies in the canvas and carry them to the car, then took Bedford by the shoulder. "You're a member of Smith's party, right?"

"I accompanied his niece here."

"Well, you'd best attend to her, sir. I'm afraid I'm going to have to place him under arrest."

CHAPTER 12

J ELLICOE asked Bedford and Sloane to accompany him to the police station for what Bedford assumed would be a brief conversation in which they might offer whatever help they could.

Instead, they found themselves grilled rather harshly by Jellicoe and his man Sheridan. Lord Erroll, wearing his military uniform, observed the proceedings.

Sloane went into Jellicoe's office first, returning in tears. Bedford's role, he quickly gathered when his turn came, was to provide contradictory testimony that might render Sloane a liar, for she had obviously been defending her uncle.

It was difficult to avoid serving the authorities' purpose here, as he had no exact notion of what precisely she had said, but he stuck to the truth — at least about the circumstances of the grisly morning. Pressed about Dixon's relationship with Georgia, he said more or less nothing.

"I only just met the man — when we arrived in Mombasa," he said. "And Sloane almost never talked about him before that."

"And why is that?" asked Erroll.

"She seldom talks about her family."

"And why is that?"

"I believe they embarrass her."

"And why is that?"

"Because they're very rich."

This answer seemed to strike to the core of the man's very British class-ridden sensibilities. Unable to muster up an adequate response, he leaned back against the wall, as though he had drawn forth a very significant fact.

"Lord Ralls had little money," said Jellicoe. "Why would Mrs. Smith have been interested in him?"

"The title, I suppose," said Bedford. "But I think the line you're pursuing is irrelevant. I think that if Dixon Smith did fire the round that killed them, it was accidental."

"A naked man and woman, embracing in a clearing? What animal does that resemble?" Sheridan asked.

"It doesn't matter. I think it was accidental for the simple fact that Dixon Smith was a very bad shot. Owen will back me on that. He twice had to finish off animals Smith had hit badly or missed. He's not the man for that kind of killing shot."

"Unless he'd crept up on them, and fired close," Lord Erroll countered. He lighted a cigarette, making a face.

"But how would he have known where they were? They didn't go there from our camp. She was at the prince's."

"The lamentable fact remains," said Jellicoe, "that Mr. Smith was the only one near Lord Ralls and Mrs. Smith, they were killed with a single shot, and a single bullet was fired from Mr. Smith's Rigby rifle. I'm sorry, but he's going to have to be charged."

"Had any of the other rifles in Owen's camp been fired?"

"We haven't inquired. I assume it was his practice to

clean them every night. That's customary for professional hunters."

"And what is he to be charged with?"

"Murder. It was certainly that, wasn't it?"

"Is there a good lawyer in town?"

"A barrister's what you want," corrected Erroll. "To represent him in court. I'm afraid, though, the answer is, 'not really.'"

"There's Mr. Asif," said Sheridan. "He represents small-time criminal cases. Wogs, mostly."

"He's Indian, you know," said Erroll.

"I don't mind that he's Indian," Bedford interjected.

"Yes, but your Mr. Smith might."

"Am I free to go now?" Bedford asked Jellicoe.

The inspector nodded. "For now."

WHERE are we going?" Sloane asked, as Bedford hurried her out the door of the police station.

"First, down to that garage I saw by the railroad station," he replied. "I'm going to hire a car. Then to find a lawyer."

"Why do we need a lawyer? We're going to be leaving soon."

He turned to face her, gripping both her shoulders. "Sloane. Your uncle's going to be charged with murder. There will be a trial. If you want to leave, I certainly shouldn't blame you. But I thought you'd want to see it through."

She swallowed. "Of course I do."

"They mentioned an Indian man, named Asif."

"Do you suppose he's any good?"

"Because he's Indian?"

"No, because they recommended him."

"Let's determine that for ourselves."

They started down the road. "What about your lady friend?" Sloane asked.

"You're my lady friend."

"I mean Lady Victoria. Where has she disappeared to?"

"Idina Erroll swooped in and took her off to Clouds."

"Drown her sorrows in depravity."

"Come along, Sloane."

She did so, obediently, which was unlike her. "I've managed to send a cable to Aunt Kate."

"How do you think she'll take the news?"

"She loves him. Though I don't know why."

THE only automobile available for hire that seemed in running order was another of the seemingly ubiquitous Buicks. A touring car, it had a ragged roof and no side curtains. If caught in the rain, they'd be in for a swim, but the sun was shining for the moment.

Mr. Asif took some finding. They had to go first to a non-white quarter of the town and, once there, ask directions—not all of which were intelligible. At length they discovered his quarters, in a whitewashed stone building adjoining a pleasant courtyard. His rooms included a sort of office that doubled as a sitting room.

He greeted them in a rumpled white suit, stained white shirt, and weary-looking tie. His eyes seemed to dance around behind his spectacles, which were slightly steamed. He badly needed a haircut, and wore sandals. The man appeared to be very busy, though it was not at all clear at what.

"You would like tea?" Asif asked. "I am making tea."

"Yes. Thank you." Sloane seated herself quickly. Her skin had gone very pale.

Asif disappeared behind a doorway curtain, but continued to chatter.

"You say you were sent here by the colonial office? They gave you my name?"

"We need an attorney," said Bedford.

"A solicitor, you mean," said Asif.

"Not 'barrister'?"

"I am a barrister, yes. In the criminal law court."

"Then we have come to the right place."

ASIF returned with a tray, teapot, and teacups—his eyeglasses all the more steamy. "You have been charged with a crime?"

As the lawyer poured, Bedford began to explain. By the time he finished, they had each consumed two cups. Asif beamed. "I think, yes, we can make a very good case. Yes, we can, sir."

"How is that?" Sloane asked.

"We need only to find who wanted Lord Ralls dead."

"And my Aunt Georgia?"

"Her, too."

"But she's only been here a few days. Why would anyone want to kill her?"

"Miss Smith—you said she broke all the gramophone records in the Muthaiga Club?"

"With some help."

"Well, there you are."

BEDFORD, preoccupied with the difficulties of a right-hand drive, took the wrong road and quickly became thoroughly lost. He neglected to inform Sloane, however.

"Do you think Mr. Asif'll do us any good?" she asked, after lighting a cigarette.

"He's defended a lot of small-time criminals of every

stripe. When I was in the war, I liked to fly with pilots who'd made a lot of landings."

"My uncle is not a small-time criminal."

"You're uncle is the one who'll have to decide about Asif."

"No he isn't. I'm paying for this."

"Mr. Asif is so inexpensive I could afford to pay him."

"That's what worries me."

There was a cow in the road ahead of him. It occurred to Bedford that this also was the wrong road. He used the animal as an excuse to turn around.

"Are you worried about the effect an Indian lawyer will have on a jury?"

"They'll all be Brits, won't they? White males."

"We could ask for a bench trial."

"Could we? That might be worse."

They passed through a patch of trees and found themselves back in the town. Coming upon Nairobi's surprisingly unpretentious Government House, Bedford turned onto the correct route.

"This is taking a long time," she said.

"Things are rather spread out here."

"Bedford, speaking of long times. This may take a while. Quite a while."

"I know."

"If you want to go back . . ."

"Sloane. Of course I'll stay with you. Whatever it takes."

She dabbed at her eyes. "I have more than that to ask of you."

"Anything."

"Get my uncle out of this."

ARRIVING at the Muthaiga, they found their luggage in the lobby, along with Alice de Janze', who was seated in a nearby chair. She shakily got to her feet, then limped up to Sloane, throwing her arms around her.

"Poor Smithie," she said. "Poor, poor Smithie."

She was wearing clothes similar to those she'd had on the day they'd been flying—corduroy trousers and a loose cotton shirt.

"I'm fine," Sloane said, stepping back and looking to Alice's foot. "What happened to you?"

"I tripped. Too much to drink. Sick-making."

"Why have they packed up our baggage?"

"That wretched Owen ordered it. Your uncle's no longer his client, and he's washed his hands of you, as it were. And your uncle. But don't fret. You're staying at Karen Blixen's."

"We are?" Sloane asked.

"She insisted upon it." Alice stuck her hands in her trouser pockets, producing nothing. "She left a note, but I seem to have lost it."

"You're certain?"

"Oh yes. But I'm very upset, Smithie. Very unhappy. Do you suppose you could stay with me?"

"That's very kind of you, Alice, but . . ."

"Please?"

"All right. And Bedford?"

"No, Smithie. Just you."

BEDFORD followed the tall African servant into the baroness's house as others hastened to bring his bags from the Buick. He stood a moment in the central hall, unsure where to go or what to do next, when he heard his name called from a large room off the corridor. Stepping inside, he noticed first a blonde head.

It turned. From the couch, Beryl Markham welcomed him with her remarkably friendly eyes and another disarming smile.

"Come sit down, Captain Green. Karen's off attending to coffee matters." She lifted her head. "Where's Miss Smith?"

"At Alice de Janze's. They're old friends from Chicago, and Alice is in a state over what's happened."

"As well she might be. This must be particularly horrible for Miss Smith—her uncle and aunt and all. The poor man. I think it was a bit boorish of Jellicoe to haul him off to a dungeon like that. No one really knows what happened, isn't that so?"

"Someone knows. Perhaps we'll find out who that is." He took a chair near her. She was wearing a silk blouse and white, wide-bottomed linen trousers. While Alice de Janze' looked somewhat mannish in such garb, Beryl was stunningly elegant.

Unbidden, a servant brought in glasses and a bottle of Dutch gin on a tray, setting it on a wicker table before her and withdrawing swiftly to whatever quiet quarter of the house from which he had come.

"Yes, please," he said, in response to Beryl's pointing to a glass.

"Thirsty times," she said, pouring.

"Why should Alice be so upset?" Bedford asked.

A sharp and knowing look. "Amour, Captain Green. She and Dickie Ralls were lovers. Alice is an oddity here. She falls in love with the men she sleeps with. Must be hell on her nerves—given the men she sleeps with."

"She shot one of them."

"Shot herself, too, of course. It may well be a jolly good thing, your friend staying with her."

They were interrupted by heavy footsteps in the hall

and the sound of a burden being dropped on the floor. Then Finch-Hatton appeared, hunter's hat and rifle in hand.

"Hello the flyers," he said, crossing the room to place the rifle on a rack.

"How is it you're back?" Beryl asked. "Haven't you princely duties to attend to?"

"You haven't heard," he said, pouring himself some gin and seating himself next to Beryl. "The prince has taken ill." His eyes went to Bedford. "He and Lady Furness went off this morning to drive back to Nairobi all on their own, if you can imagine such a thing. They stopped on the plain near Ngong and he fell into a swoon. Fever of some sort. Lady Furness cannot drive an automobile, so there they were. If one of our bearers hadn't happened upon them, I fear they'd be there still."

"Put you out of business, had that happened, Denys."

"I daresay it would. They have him in hospital, and he's reviving. But he'll be back to England soon. His father is ill as well. Quite seriously, I gather. So it's an end to the safari. Just as well. He didn't seem much interested in it. More in Lady Furness."

"What happened with Mrs. Smith?" Bedford asked. "How did she come to be with Lord Ralls?"

Finch-Hatton gave a sort of shrug. "She was hanging about the camp, as you know. Quite the thing, rubbing shoulders and whatnot with royals, I suppose, especially for an American. But I think the prince had become a little weary of her. Lord Ralls felt obliged to take her off his hands."

"Going off into the bush to make love to her at the crack of dawn—as duty to his sovereign?" Bedford asked.

Beryl and Finch-Hatton laughed. "Dickie and Victoria were members in good standing of the Prince of Wales set," Beryl said. "They do look out for one another—no matter what the cost."

Two enormous dogs of a sudden came bounding into

the room, heading for Finch-Hatton. A moment later, the baroness entered—dressed in a white shirtwaist, khaki riding skirt, and boots. She was flushed and sweaty and not a little excited.

"I do believe we are going to be a success this year, Denys," she said. "A rare development on this plantation." She sobered her expression on taking note of Bedford. "So here you are, Captain Green. I am so pleased you are able to join us." She paused. "And Miss Smith?"

"She's staying with Alice," said Beryl. "Offering comfort."

The baroness proceeded into the chamber, seating herself in a wicker chair near enough to Finch-Hatton to take his hand. "Ah, yes. Her infatuation with Lord Ralls. Such an unhappy tale."

"This story needs an ending," said Finch-Hatton, "and Captain Green thinks he can provide it."

"An ending other than the hanging of Mr. Dixon Smith?" asked the baroness.

"That is my hope."

"Oh, they won't hang him," said Beryl. "They don't hang cuckolds, do they? Fifteen or twenty years in prison, I'd say."

"I would not consider that a very happy ending," said Bedford.

The baroness's eyes were twinkly. "Do murder stories have happy endings, Captain Green?"

"They can have just ones."

"From all accounts, Mr. Smith is not a very admirable man," the baroness observed. "Isn't that right, Denys?"

"Not one of Owen's favorite clients," Finch-Hatton said.

"But he's paid for his sins," Beryl interjected. "His punishment was being married to that woman."

"Then his punishment is at an end," said the baroness. "So we have our happy ending after all." She looked benignly at Bedford. "But you and Miss Smith are not happy. That we must attend to."

"I should like to learn a bit more about some of the people here," Bedford said.

The baroness rose. "I gather we shall not lack for conversation at dinner."

I T proved another late night, with much brandy and whiskey. Bedford went to bed missing Sloane but glad she was in more comforting quarters than the Muthaiga. He dreamt of her—and a weekend they had once passed together in Newport, Rhode Island.

He was awakened by the baroness's manservant, who shook him firmly. It was near enough to morning for a dim gray light to have filtered into the room.

"Someone come to see you, sir," he said. "He wait outside."

Bedford sat up, slowly, rubbing his forehead against a sudden pain. He was doubtful about a people so bent on drinking their way through their lives.

"Just a minute," he said.

Hastily pulling on shirt, pants, and boots, he followed the barefoot African out through the house onto the front lawn. There, near the veranda, stood Mzizi, robe wound around shoulder and spear in hand.

Mzizi knew at least one English word.

"Giraffe," he said.

CHAPTER 13

LEAVING Mzizi to wait on the mist-shrouded lawn, Bedford took time to attend to his morning ablutions and dress more usefully. The house servant offered him a piece of cake for breakfast, which he happily accepted and greedily wolfed down, along with a tepid cup of coffee. With some difficulty, he managed to get the Buick started. Then, with Mzizi standing up in the rear, looking much the captain on his quarterdeck, Bedford prepared to depart for the bush—halted almost immediately by the sight of Beryl Markham in a nightdress running across the lawn.

"Where are you off to, Captain?" she asked, taking note of Mzizi's presence. "What in blazes is going on here this morning?"

"I'm going to look at a dead giraffe." He kept the engine running.

"Sounds a bleak way to start one's day. Whatever for?"

"Dixon Smith said he'd fired that round from his Rigby rifle at a giraffe, not his wife. Mzizi says he has found the late giraffe and I want to see if I can find the missing bullet."

She peered over the side of the car. "Speaking of bullets, where's your rifle?"

"I don't have a rifle. I was using one Owen provided me and he took it back."

"Well, you shouldn't take a step out there without one—unless you're as adept with the short spear as our friend Mzizi here."

"Not with any kind of spear, I'm afraid."

"Well, I'll fetch you a weapon—and one for myself."

"Yourself?"

"You shouldn't take a step out there without a Beryl Markham, either."

AFTER dressing in khaki garb not much different than Bedford's, Beryl returned with a basket containing what she said would be lunch, along with two canteens and two rifles slung over her slim shoulder. "You were starting out rather under-equipped, Captain. I fear we should have found you in much the same condition as the giraffe."

"Then I'm grateful for your intervention."

"Let's hope we don't encounter anything else that will make you grateful for my presence."

She insisted on driving, arguing it was more sensible for her to steer their course herself rather than provide him with a constant stream of directions. Beryl drove very fast, even when the road gave out and they moved onto the open plain. Bedford kept looking for familiar landmarks, but there were none.

"Is this the same route Owen took?" he asked.

"No, it's a shortcut."

"Do you come out here often?"

She nodded. "Sometimes on foot. I often come out on horseback, but when I was a little girl, I used to go hunting out this way with men like Mzizi—walking barefoot.

Learned to use spears, short and long. A lion took a little bite out of me once, I will admit." She slapped the place on her leg that had suffered. "But I didn't know as much then as I do now."

"Do you suppose lions have been feeding on this giraffe I'm after?"

"Quite possibly."

"It's the bullet I need—and someone to verify how and where I found it."

"Well here I am." She saluted, in sideways British army fashion.

THEY parked under some trees, then crept forward, with Mzizi leading the way. Passing through some rather nasty thornbushes, they followed a wide stream between two small grassy hills and then left it to enter a grove of widely spaced mimosa trees.

In the shade of one, sprawled on its side, was the dead animal, its orange and white markings splotchy in the shade. There were so many flies it seemed almost to be twitching, but it was as dead a creature as Bedford had ever seen.

He started for it, but Beryl grabbed his arm, holding him back.

"No," she said. "We have visitors."

Bedford looked about them, finding nothing. She pointed with great emphasis at the giraffe. "No, there," she whispered. "Two lions, still feeding. At the belly. In the clearing beyond, there's a hyena, waiting his turn."

Bedford crouched down. Squinting a little, he could make out two tawny forms just above the line of the giraffe's midsection. He had left his rifle in the car, but Beryl had hers at the ready. She lifted its stock to her shoulder.

"You don't need to do that," Bedford protested.

"Yes I do." The crack of the gunshot that immediately followed set Bedford's ear to ringing.

One shape had vanished. The other lion bolted and was bounding away. Beryl stood and fired two more times. There was dust and gun smoke. Bedford could not tell if the animal had been brought down. There was definitely more movement.

"Why did you shoot? We could have just scared them away."

"They wouldn't have gone far and they would have come back. When that lion caught hold of me when I was a little girl? I was saved because the African man I was with came rushing up to me. The lion let me go and turned on him because it thought the man was a fellow wild creature trying to steal its food. Those two lionesses would have done the same thing if we went up to the giraffe."

"We could have waited until they had gone away."

"You wouldn't have much giraffe left. You want a good look at it, do you not? That's what we came out for, isn't it?"

"Yes, but Beryl—"

She shook off further reproach and moved forward, holding her rifle to the fore with both hands.

Mzizi got there first, prodding the lioness slumped at the giraffe's belly with his spear to make sure she was dead. Then he moved around to the carcass of the larger animal—or what was left of it. Peering closely, he lifted a large flap of skin. It still had sinew attached to it, but it came loose. Bedford turned away, feeling sick. If Dayton Crosby were to have witnessed even ten seconds of anything that had gone on out here in the Kenyan bush, he'd never speak to him or Sloane again.

"Blicken," the African said to Bedford.

Collecting himself, Bedford came up close and looked where Mzizi indicated. There was a large, round hole in the skin.

"A shoulder shot," said Beryl, from behind him. "I wouldn't have thought he'd be that good."

"He wasn't." Bedford indicated to Mzizi that he wanted to bring back the piece of hide, prompting the African to slice it off with one quick swipe of his spear blade.

Moving to where the lions had been feeding, Bedford waited for his nausea to abate before speaking. "Now we have to find the bullet."

"Well, I'm not in much of a mood to go pawing through all that bloody muck."

"Would it be in the shoulder?"

"Not a .416 H and H. It might bloody well be in Uganda."

His sense of frustration was overwhelming. He'd said a hundred times that he'd do anything for Sloane, but now he realized there were limits.

"I wonder if the police could be persuaded to come out here and look for it."

"I doubt that very much."

"Do you suppose Mzizi would consider it an imposition?"

"I'm sure he wouldn't mind. But he'll deserve some generous compensation."

"That will be no problem at all."

Beryl explained the need in Swahili and the African went readily to work. Bedford wanted nothing more than to return to the car and wait there, but felt guilty enough having shirked this grisly labor, and so stayed where he was. Beryl, however, moved out of range of the flies and smell and sat down against the trunk of a more hospitable tree.

As he might track an animal, Mzizi found the channel made by the bullet, digging it open all the way through to where the spine joined the hips. He worked awhile at that spot, then stood back, very still. *"Nichts."*

"Well, now," Beryl began, but she had nothing more to say.

"It's got to be somewhere," Bedford said. Using his boot sole, he scraped at the ground where the lions had been feeding. Mzizi joined in, and, reluctantly, so did Beryl. His affection for her at that moment was unbounded.

But they found nothing.

Mzizi turned the dead lioness over, pulling her away. There was no bullet. Bedford swore.

"Feeling a little testy this morning, are we, Captain Green?"

"I'm just now thinking that a month ago I was in New York, lunching at the Plaza Hotel."

"A month ago I was in some place much like this." She paused, placing a long slender finger to her cheek, and tapping. "We're not out of the match yet, though, Bedford."

He scratched his head, having not a clue as to where her thoughts were taking her. It proved to be to the other dead lion, which was lying some fifty yards distant.

"This one was feeding close to where the bullet stopped. They gulp their meat. You find all sorts of things in their spoor." She motioned to Mzizi, who comprehended without any instruction.

Bedford was so happy to see the battered piece of metal he accepted it from Mzizi blood and all. Beryl was smiling, too.

"Now we can go home," Bedford said. "All of us."

CHAPTER 14

I'M sorry, but I'm afraid this proves nothing," said Inspector Jellicoe, holding the spent bullet up to the light.

"But, sir," Bedford replied, dumbfounded. "Mr. Smith said he'd fired that expended round in his rifle at a giraffe. We found the giraffe right where he said."

"We dug it out ourselves," said Beryl. "A shoulder shot. Killed the poor beast instantly."

"I know, Mrs. Markham," Jellicoe said, reexamining the torn piece of hide with a bullet hole in it. "But he jolly well could have shot the giraffe, put another round in the chamber, and then shot Lord Ralls and Mrs. Smith."

They had brought Mr. Asif with them. He appeared to be wearing the same clothes he'd worn the day before.

"Inspector," Beryl intruded. "We went to a considerable amount of bother to fetch these two artifacts back from the bush. It's not very gracious of you to dismiss them out of hand."

She and Jellicoe apparently knew each other. How amicably was not so certain.

"Not dismissed, Mrs. Markham. Simply considered in the light of everything else we know about this case."

"Which is damned little." Beryl's annoyance showed.

Mr. Asif selected this moment to make his contribution. "Inspector, sir, if I might speak."

Jellicoe nodded, wearily, but not without interest.

"Inspector, sir. Mr. Smith has been charged and imprisoned because you made the presumption that the bullet that killed the unfortunate Lord Ralls and Mrs. Smith had to have come from his rifle, because he was there and there was no other apparent explanation. When he said he had shot the missing bullet at a giraffe, you presumed that he was lying—further adding to your suspicion and your presumption of guilt. Is that not so, sir?"

"Lies are a poor defense, Mr. Asif."

"But now you have three witnesses, counting the tracker Mzizi, who tell you that he was not lying. So that weight must be taken off the scale. And your presumption of probability now becomes mere possibility. Isn't that so?"

"We can't dismiss the charges just because you've brought in a bullet."

"Not dismiss, Inspector, sir. Suspend, if you please. You haven't enough certainty to keep Mr. Smith in custody. Only suspicion now. You should release him."

Jellicoe lighted his pipe, reflecting on this. "We'll consider it. That's all I can promise." He put the piece of hide and the disfigured bullet in a desk drawer, then got to his feet, looking to Beryl. "Always nice to see you, Mrs. Markham. I'm delighted you've taken an interest in this matter."

"Just trying to do my bit for king and colony—and the notion of fair play." She walked out, with Asif following. Jellicoe called Bedford back, however.

"If I could have a private word with you, Captain Green."

Bedford halted, wondering what might happen if he declined. Jellicoe went past him and shut the door, then returned to his desk and sat down on the edge of it, puffing twice on his pipe.

"There's a superintendent coming up from Mombasa," he said. "A Scotland Yard man named Haynes. A nononsense sort of chap. The Crown is taking this case very seriously. Because of Lord Ralls's family, don't you know, and because the American consulate has expressed an interest in its outcome. At all events, I'm going to have very little to say about it after he arrives."

The inspector looked to the closed door, as though he thought Beryl and Asif were listening just behind it.

"I've been making further inquires—involving other possibilities than Mr. Smith," he said. "I've talked to Lady Ralls. She says she was with you in Owen's camp when her husband was killed."

"She was there. Yes."

"You're not attending to my meaning, Mr. Green." His voice lowered still further. "She claims she passed the night with you—in an intimate manner—and was with you when the news came about the murders."

Bedford had brought her the news—after her return to the prince's camp. He couldn't understand why she would tell so false a tale—and obligate him to substantiate it.

"This is a personal matter, Inspector."

"And this is an official police inquiry. You were seen under a blanket with her. Now can you verify her statement?"

Whatever door the man thought he was opening had to be closed fast—for now.

Bedford took a deep breath. "I guess that's more or less accurate, as best I can remember. I'd had a bit to drink. Everyone had." He hesitated. "If you could be discreet about this . . ."

They stared at each other. Finally, Jellicoe broke, setting down his pipe. "Thank you, Mr. Green. We'll have another chat soon." He waited until Bedford had gotten to the door, then added: "She asked me to tell you she would like to speak with you. Out at Clouds. You know how to get there, do you?"

"Yes. I've been there before."

OUTSIDE, walking toward the Buick, they saw Sloane and Alice de Janze' coming toward them—oddly, hand in hand.

"Where have you been, Bedford?" Sloane asked. "I rang Baroness Blixen's. She said you had gone off into the jungle."

"The bush," corrected Bedford. "We found the giraffe your uncle said he'd shot. We brought the bullet back to Inspector Jellicoe."

"He discounts this new evidence," said Mr. Asif. "But I believe it has cast some doubt on his supposition."

"Will he let my uncle go now?"

"Inspector Jellicoe said he'd think about it. But he's reluctant."

"We've come to see him. Will you come into the jail with me, Bedford? I expect it's horrible in there."

Beryl seized upon the moment as an opportunity for departure. "I'm off to the racetrack then," she said. "I don't know if I told you but I'm a horse trainer by profession, and I've neglected my animals for too long." She smiled brightly, a smile one could see from Mombasa. "See you at supper." She hurried away.

Mr. Asif stepped forward. "I have not yet visited Mr. Smith. Do you still wish me to represent him?"

Sloane put her arm through Bedford's. "Yes. Of course. Please come with us."

NAIROBI'S Central Police Station was a considerable enterprise—its jail home to some one thousand prisoners, the overwhelming majority of them black, as were most of the warders. Dixon had been put into a small section reserved for whites. His cell was also small, but comparatively light and airy, though it bore the strong smell of disinfectant.

Dixon was lying on his cot, and rose unsteadily to greet his unexpected guests. His face was pasty, careworn, and ill-shaven. There was a bottle of brandy on the small table that, with its chair, was the only other furniture in the room.

"They let me buy things," Dixon said, noting the focus of Bedford's attention. "The warder gets them for me."

He offered the women their choice of the chair or the cot. Both declined. Finally, Mr. Asif pulled out the chair, seating himself at the table.

"Who is this?" Dixon demanded, looking at the Indian.

"This is your attorney—Mr. Asif," said Sloane. "He's been to the police inspector, trying to get you released from jail."

"I didn't ask for him."

"If you please, sir," said Asif, "I think we can prepare an excellent defense for you. Captain Green has—"

"I didn't ask for his involvement, either."

"Bedford found the giraffe you shot, Uncle Dixon," Sloane said, sternly. "More to the point, he found the bullet. He's turned it over to the police. Mr. Asif thinks they may now release you."

"Perhaps not right away," Asif said.

Dixon returned to his cot, slumping back against the wall. "When?"

Mr. Asif smiled and shrugged.

"I don't want this man as my lawyer," Dixon said, staring at the floor.

"Don't be petulant, Uncle," Sloane replied. "Anyway, I'm paying him."

"No. Please. Everyone please go away. I don't want a lawyer."

He poured himself a drink, appearing near tears. If the man had any redeeming qualities, Bedford could not recall noticing any. Perhaps he was generous with the collection plate at church.

"We should go, Mr. Asif," Bedford said, moving to the cell door. "We can straighten matters out later."

Dixon gulped some of the brandy, then poured more. Alice went up and took the cup from him, taking a long drink herself. Then she gave it back and joined Bedford at the door. Sloane lingered, with apparent reason.

Bedford summoned the warder.

WHAT will you do now?" Alice asked him, as they stood waiting on the lawn of the police station.

"That depends on Sloane."

"Do you want to go flying?"

"If I could fly from here back to America, I would say 'yes.' "

"I don't want to go back to Chicago. I don't even want to go back to Paris." She smoked, tapping her foot on the earth nervously. "Did you know I have two daughters?"

"No. Sloane never mentioned it."

"They're with my sister in Paris. They'll be there forever. I'm just no good at that, you know?"

"Good at what?"

"Being a mother."

"I'm sorry."

"No. I'm happy. Though today I'm sad. And scared."

"Scared?"

"That horrid person—the murderer—he's still out there."

"Unless he's Mr. Smith."

"No. You've proved he isn't." More smoking. "Who would kill people while they were making love?"

"Someone who disapproved."

She dropped her cigarette onto the grass. "So what will you do now?"

He sighed. "When Sloane's done here, I think I should go see Lady Ralls."

"Oh, you don't have to do that."

"She asked to see me."

"And so you shall. But you don't have to go now. You can go when we all go to Clouds."

"What do you mean?"

"Idina is having a sundowner, and everyone's going."

"What's a sundowner?"

"It's a sort of party. A good way to get blotto before dinner."

"Alice, can you think of anyone who disliked Lord Ralls so intensely as to want to kill him?"

"Everybody loved Dickie. I loved him."

"Someone who loved him too well, perhaps. Someone who didn't like his sleeping with another woman?"

"Captain Green, if people here started killing each other over that, we'd all soon be dead."

SLOANE remained inside another half hour, emerging at last in the company of Inspector Jellicoe. They had a brief conversation by his car, and then she rejoined her friends, speaking first to Mr. Asif.

"You're still his lawyer," she said. "Whether he likes it or not."

I**DINA** Erroll's "sundowner" was held outdoors on a long sweep of lawn facing west and overlooking a wide valley. A line of shallow, purple hills marked the horizon, darkening as the sun settled behind them. Just above them, its wings winking in the flare of sunset upon them, an airplane crawled across the sky. It was at some distance, but Bedford could hear its engine clearly.

He was standing by himself. Alice had gone to friends, dragging Sloane along with her. He was just as happy in this solitary state, though he realized there was work to do here. He was pleased when Idina, ever the gracious hostess, left the others to attend to him. A few days before, he would have run.

"Dear Captain Green," she said, holding her drink before her as though it were a staff of office. "Why are you neglecting the rest of us?"

"I'm admiring your view, Lady Erroll."

"You don't find the view of my other guests admirable?"

He eyed them. Several were drunk already. "I do now," he said, fixing his attention on her. "As I would also if Victoria Ralls were in it."

"Oh, the poor dear. She's still in bed, I'm afraid, sleeping. All day. It's been a simply awful blow, don't you know. She's taking this very, very hard. I do believe she really loved Dickie, despite everything."

"Love can bring on peculiar behavior."

Idina was in no way stupid. "Do you mean, 'violent' behavior?"

"All sorts."

"You and that Indian lawyer are working to get Mr. Smith out of this, aren't you? My husband thinks you're going to cause the Crown authorities a lot of inconvenience and bother."

"Not if I accomplish what I mean to quickly."

"You mean, getting him off."

"No, I mean, finding the killer."

She looked off toward the sunset. "I'm sure we'd all be happy to help—if you really think Mr. Smith didn't do it."

"You in particular could help a lot, Lady Erroll. I perceive that you have a unique perspective on the social life of the colony. You're probably the most knowledgeable of anyone."

"What do you mean?"

"Lady Erroll, I would like a list of the women Lord Ralls had relationships with."

This startled her, but she began to warm to the notion. "That could be half of British East Africa."

"Seriously."

She gestured to the guests at her party. "Certainly most of the women here. Except, of course, for your friend, Miss Smith. Or am I incorrect? He preferred other men's wives, but I think he fancied her."

"Please. Anyone you can think of."

"Myself included?"

"I'll leave that up to you."

"This could be rather fun." She began to move away in a traipse. "I'll draw up a list and give it to you when you leave. A sort of party favor."

This is hilarious," said Baroness Blixen. "It means that so much gossip is true."

"Unless it's just more gossip," said Beryl, snatching the piece of paper from her hostess's hand.

The two women were seated on the baroness's large and comfortable couch—Beryl barefoot and sitting in cross-legged Indian fashion, Karen Blixen reclining quite regally. Bedford and Finch-Hatton were in adjacent chairs, the white hunter looking on with polite amusement, more interested in the baroness's reaction to the list than in the names it contained.

"'Angela Keating, Lady Delamere, Alice de Janze', Molly Sim, Benita Spottswoode, Idina, herself,'" read Beryl. "Gracious. And it goes on! This isn't gossip; this is mass slander. If this were London, she'd be sued."

"None of it's surprising?"

"Oh yes. There are two men here."

"I should think that must have been back at Oxford," Finch-Hatton said.

The baroness cleared her throat. "My dear, I believe you've omitted a name."

"You mean mine?" Beryl asked. "Well?"

"I was young and impressionable. And he had a title. I used to believe that was something rather special."

"And now?"

"Except for Delamere, I think they're the worst of the lot down here."

Bedford set down his brandy glass. "What can you tell me about their husbands?"

The baroness took the list from Beryl and handed it with a grin to Finch-Hatton.

"Hmmm," he said. "The list is incomplete. She left off Joan McCardle and Penelope Witting."

"But they're dead," said Beryl.

Bedford's eyebrows rose. "Murdered?"

"They perished of local ailments," said the baroness.

"Drink, in Joan's case," explained Beryl. "Drugs in Penelope's."

"And their husbands?" Bedford asked, trying to keep this on track.

"Both back in England," Beryl said. She had Finch-Hatton return the paper.

"You needn't include Delamere as one of your suspects," she said. "They've had a very understanding marriage, and he worries far more about Kenya than petty infidelities. George Sim, however, he's a nasty sort, and Dickie Ralls owed him a lot of money."

"He owed everyone a lot of money," the baroness observed. "He even borrowed from Bror, who had to get it from me."

Beryl folded the list carefully, keeping it in her hand. "These women ought to be included as well. Every one of them but Lady Delamere is a first-rate shot."

"What about de Janze'?" Bedford asked. "Is he capable of something like this?"

Beryl shook her head. "No. Even if he was, he should have done it long ago. It's Idina's husband Alice has a yen for now."

"Why do you keep asking about the husbands?" Finch-Hatton questioned. "Do you not think a woman could have done this?"

"I was once a newspaperman," Bedford said. The baroness and Beryl were taken aback, as though he'd just said he'd once been a garbage collector, or petty criminal. He had a proud impulse to tell them his family was one of the oldest in America, but to Europeans, that would have sounded silly. "In my experience as a police reporter," he continued, "it's the men who settle these things with shooting. The women usually turn to poison."

"This is Kenya," said Beryl, with a grin. "Here, everyone shoots."

BEDFORD had been drinking so much among these jaded, self-indulgent people that his nervous system had begun to rebel, causing him to wake in the middle of the night, as it had done that night in Owen's camp.

He lay in his bed, thinking first of how much he missed Greenwich Village, and then of how much he missed

Sloane, and then how much he disliked these separate sleeping arrangements. Finally, staring at the ceiling, he realized what had prompted his wakefulness — a buzzing sound, faint at first, now quite pronounced. An airplane, flying through the night sky somewhere very near.

When it had faded, he remained motionless a long while, then abruptly sat up on the edge of the bed. A moment later, he was in his shirt and trousers.

"Bedford," whispered Beryl, looking up at him from her pillow. "What are you doing in here? I'm fond of you and all that, but I hope our discussion of that list didn't give you ideas."

"It's not that. I'm sorry for the intrusion. But I'd like to go flying."

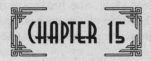

CHAPTER 15

BERYL made it quite clear she was coming to view Bedford as a lunatic, and protested that she had business that day at the racetrack. But the twin lures of flying and curiosity drew her with him to the airfield, and they were aloft as the sun was rising.

She got to what had been Owen's hunting camp handily. Bedford was more interested in how easy it might be to locate the grove of trees and clearing where the bodies had been found from the air. Riding in the forward cockpit, Bedford had a better view, but didn't recognize the site until they were directly overhead. Beryl, flying confidently from the rear seat, had taken them unerringly to it.

As he had requested before they'd climbed into the Gypsy Moth, she now put the aircraft into a tight turn—the left wing seeming to pivot on the exact center of the clearing. It didn't take Bedford too long to turn his suspicion into a firm conclusion. With one person flying, a second would have ample opportunity to work his worst on the unsuspecting and unlucky folk below.

Turning in the cockpit, Bedford pointed down several times. Beryl nodded. Shaking his head, he repeated the gesture with great vigor. She finally caught his drift, but, glancing to either side of the cockpit, could only shrug. Then, looking dead ahead, she nodded once more, opening the throttle.

The slanting rays of the early sun distorted his perception, as it had flying dawn patrols over Belgium. He saw only more watercourses, trees, and rocky hillocks. The nearest suitable landing ground appeared to be at some distance—two or three miles or more.

Beryl had seen something that appeared suitable to her at least. The stream ran straight for several hundred yards, then turned sharply to the left. Just beyond this point was a sloping field rising to a tree line. Banking sharply from side to side, she got the little plane down over the water, flying between the trees and raising the nose slightly to decrease their speed. They were only a few feet off the ground when they reached the stream's sharp turning. The slope was largely in shadow at this moment and her flying had been reduced to a lot of guesswork. But in a moment he felt the right wheel touch earth, and sensed her moving the control stick left to bring down that landing gear. Gripping the leather-covered cockpit rim as they bounced their way up the rise, he wondered if he shouldn't now just throw himself over the side and take his chances rolling off the wing.

That would not be necessary. Lurching a little to the left and right, the aircraft's bouncing gentled and it began to slow—barely rolling by the time it reached the top of the rise. The propeller was no more than twenty feet from a large tree when they finally stopped.

"I couldn't have done that," he said.

She removed her helmet and shook out her blonde hair. "I didn't know I could do it, either."

"How will we take off?"

"Don't know. I've never done this before." She took a deep breath of air and then unhooked her belt and harness. "We have a small hike back upstream now and then we're there."

Bedford's hand was shaking. He clenched his fist twice to make it stop.

LACKING Mzizi, they had a small bit of trouble finding the clearing on foot, having to double back after following the stream too far. The ground at its center had been much disturbed by wild animals who'd scented the blood and the humans who'd removed the bodies.

Bedford studied the patch, noting the claw marks and bloodstains, and trying to recall with some exactitude where the two bodies had precisely been. He figured he'd have to dig up a fair amount of earth, unless he got lucky.

First, he lay down, looking straight up, and then all around him. The trees, with their weird, twisted trunks, were tall, making the clearing seem smaller than it was. Nothing in this observation contradicted his earlier conclusion.

"Is there a reason for this or are you just feeling in need of a good lie-down?" Beryl asked, standing over him with her hands on her hips.

"There's a reason for this." She had her rifle in hand, but no other weapon. "Have you a knife of any sort?"

"I have a fairly long bush knife in my airplane."

He got to his knees. "That will do nicely."

HE used the blade to loosen the earth, and his hands to lift and sift it. The labor was more than he had anticipated, and at length Beryl knelt down and helped him. It was she who found the bullet, carefully brushing it off before handing it to Bedford.

Standing, he turned toward the light, peering closely. It was a smaller round than they had taken from the animal, and less misshapen. Unable to learn anything more from his examination, he returned it to Beryl.

"What do you think?" he asked.

"I make it out to be a .375."

"Which would make it what kind of rifle?"

"Any of a number—Winchester, Remington, Mannlicher-Schoenauer, Merkel."

"Not a Rigby?"

"I think it would take a larger cartridge."

"Hmmm." He took the bullet back, placing it carefully in a pocket.

"What will you do with it?"

"Give it to Jellicoe, of course. Get Mr. Smith out of jail and get the hell out of here."

"I'm sorry you think so ill of us."

He started toward the aircraft. "Come see me in Greenwich Village, anytime—with your husband."

BERYL scouted the other side of the ridge and found a long, narrow decline without many bushes. "If there aren't any large rocks, we should be in the air before we reached the bottom."

"And if there are?"

"A prang, I fear, but let's hope not."

THE day was fully upon the town when they got back to Nairobi. The airfield was surprisingly busy, with one aircraft taking off as they approached and two others preparing to do so. One was the red plane belonging to Van Gelder. As Beryl taxied and turned to her hangar, the Dutchman killed his motor and sat watching them. Finally, taking note of their rifles as they removed them from the Gypsy Moth, he climbed out of his cockpit and strode over to them, exhibiting much less belligerence than the time before.

"You have been out hunting, Mrs. Markham?"

"Didn't fire a shot, Mr. Van Gelder." She started walking toward Bedford's Buick.

"Where have you been?"

"Out to look at the sunrise."

"But where?"

"Down toward the Ngong hills."

"Any game?"

"Nothing special."

"The weather is good?"

"The weather hasn't changed in days, Mr. Van Gelder." Bedford started to follow Beryl.

"You, Green."

He stopped, facing the Dutchman slowly. "Yes?"

"Are you leaving Nairobi?"

Bedford touched his pocket, just to make sure the excavated bullet was still there. "Yes, I think now I am. Very soon."

"You want to fly down to Mombasa?"

Bedford shook his head. "Too much luggage. And I'll have two others with me."

"Two?"

Bedford decided to leave it at that. He couldn't remember the Flemish word for good-bye, so spoke German. *"Auf Wiedersehen."*

He didn't look back at the field until he was at his car. Van Gelder had gone back to his plane. The other aircraft was taking off. It was the blue one he had seen at Idina's the first night—the American Mrs. Chisholm's, doubtless bound for the south and another load of joy.

"I must get back to my horses," she said. "There's a race meet this afternoon."

"I'll drop you."

"Do tell me what the good inspector has to say."

"So you've been out collecting bullets again," said Inspector Jellicoe, examining the round Bedford had brought back from the clearing. "You really ought to take up a more interesting pasttime."

"I should think that very interesting indeed," Bedford replied.

Mr. Asif spoke up boldly, "It proves conclusively that the victims were not shot with my client's weapon."

"I thought he had declined to become your client."

"The uncle of my client, then," said Mr. Asif. "But there you have it, Inspector, sir. Mr. Dixon Smith is quite innocent. You must release him immediately, please."

Jellicoe gave the object one last turn before his eye, then dropped it into the same desk drawer into which he had deposited the round from Smith's Rigby.

"Of course," he said, "there's no proof that you found it where you say you did," he said.

"I have Mrs. Markham to testify to it."

"Where is she?" He looked about his office, as though she might be hiding somewhere in it.

"She went to the racetrack," Bedford said, tiring of this colloquy.

"Yes. Of course," Jellicoe said. "Does she also concur in your odd theory that the killer was firing from an airplane?"

"She concurs that he could have done that."

"All the same, it sounds quite improbable. And tell me

this, Captain Green. How would this pilot know that Lord Ralls and Mrs. Smith were going to slip off at dawn to this clearing? And be there waiting? Hovering about in the sky? And wouldn't they be disturbed by this airplane? And not just lie there motionless, waiting to be shot by a single bullet?"

"I've no idea. It may simply have been happenstance—someone out hunting from an airplane. From the air, the two might well have been mistaken for game, naked as they were. At all events, Inspector, the bullet went right through them and into the ground, and at not much of an angle."

"But who would go hunting from an airplane?"

"That Dutch hunter, Van Gelder. I'm told he sometimes has clients who do that. You should question him."

Jellicoe gave a sort of harrumphing sigh, then leaned forward, elbows on desk. "The problem, Captain Green, is that an honest evaluation of all this requires the services of a ballistics expert, of which we are rather wanting in this police service. One has been sent for—a very good chap at this sort of thing, I'm told—but he's coming from South Africa, and will be a while in arriving. We really can't be making any judgments until he does. Superintendent Haynes feels that strongly. He has imparted that sentiment to me quite strongly."

"You don't need to make judgments, Inspector, sir," said Mr. Asif. "You merely have to release Mr. Smith from jail while you're waiting for a judgment to be made."

"We undoubtedly shall—at the appropriate time," the inspector said, rising. "In the meantime, he's comfortable enough. His money has seen to that. I daresay he has everything he might want in that cell—except, of course, for gramophone records, of which we're suffering a great shortage."

He smiled, amused. Bedford wasn't. "Inspector, Mr. Smith is a very important man back in America—"

"Lord Ralls was a very important man in the colony."

Bedford shook his head in resignation. "Let us go, Mr. Asif."

The police official waved his hand. "No, please wait, Captain Green. I apologize for my sarcasm. This business has rattled a lot of us. But I do think it will all be sorted out in due course—and quite reasonably. The pressure's off now, with His Royal Highness gone."

"The Prince of Wales?"

"Yes. His fever proved to be much less serious than we feared, and he's departed for England. This obviously is not the sort of thing we would have wanted to have him involved in. But that concern is behind us now and we can proceed more normally."

"I don't understand." Actually, he did, but wanted to hear Jellicoe say it.

"We can proceed without having to take anything more into consideration than the evidence."

"Or lack of it," said Mr. Asif.

Jellicoe was not amused, but ignored the remark. "The truth is, Captain Green, that Mr. Smith is no longer charged with anything. He's simply being detained in a police inquiry. There's no need to drop charges, because there aren't any."

"Isn't there a limit as to how long you can hold him?"

"I don't know. Is there? I shall have to ask. In the meantime, this bullet shall be examined along with the other one. And we will take another statement from Mrs. Markham." He went to the door and opened it. "While you're waiting for developments, what will you do? Go on safari again?"

"No."

"Good. I gather you've bagged enough wild beasts to satisfy any man."

MR. Asif accepted a ride from Bedford to the center of town. After getting out, he lingered by the side of the Buick, resting his foot on the running board.

"I have gotten really very bad criminals off with less evidence than you have produced on behalf of Mr. Smith," he said. "I do not know why they are being so obdurate about releasing him."

"They would prefer having a suspect in jail, however innocent, to not having one at all," Bedford said. "I think they'll keep him there until some higher authority arrives to fob this case onto."

"Well, I know a judge. Many of my clients have been acquitted in his courtroom. I am going to talk to him. We will prevail, Mr. Green, rest assured."

He walked off into a crowd of Africans, the wrinkled jacket of his white suit hanging slightly askew.

THE bar at the Muthaiga was crowded—as it always seemed to be. Bedford had hoped to find Owen or Finch-Hatton, but neither was present. A gentleman made a place for him, but when Bedford ordered a pink gin, the bartender—an Arabic-looking African—simply stood formally.

"I am sorry, sir," he said. "I do not believe you are a member."

"I am the guest of a member," Bedford replied, suddenly realizing he wasn't that any longer.

"Which member, sir?"

"Captain Owen. At least I was."

Several of the men around him were staring. It occurred to Bedford that he had placed himself in a most socially awkward situation—and he a man who had dined with the Prince of Wales.

The bartender simply stood there.

"I shall be happy to pay," Bedford said.

A silence, interrupted finally by a voice behind him. "I'll stand him the drink."

It was George Sim, appearing much less bellicose.

"Thank you," Bedford said, as the bartender moved swiftly to perform the required service.

"You're still here in British East," Sim said.

"We can't leave until we have extricated Dixon Smith from his predicament."

"You think you can do that?"

"By rights, certainly." Bedford told him about the two bullets.

"Sounds a lot of rot." Sim, who was drinking whiskey, set down his glass to be refilled. "The man was cuckolded and did what he had to do. I'd do the same in his situation. Especially with that bastard Ralls."

Bedford resisted the impulse to show Sim the list of Lord Ralls's conquests in his pocket. He wondered how the man could not know that his wife, Molly, belonged in such company. This was the most gossipy place Bedford had ever encountered.

"I'm afraid Mr. Smith is not that sort of man," Bedford said.

"We're all that sort of man, when it comes down to it." Sim drank from his refreshed glass. "But is that all you've found? These two odd bullets?"

Bedford told him about his conclusion that the killing shot had been fired from the air.

"That's preposterous," Sim said, looking about quickly to see who near them might be listening.

"It wasn't during the war," Bedford replied, sipping his own drink. "I'm afraid I killed a number of Germans that way."

"Machine gun."

"If there were two people in an aircraft—one with a

rifle—and the aircraft slowly circled around a particular point. I believe it could be done quite handily. And I would remind you that Lord Ralls and Mrs. Smith were not exactly moving targets—at least not laterally."

"Rubbish."

"I'm told Van Gelder's clients often go hunting that way."

"More rubbish. Have you talked to Van Gelder?"

"Not to any satisfaction."

Sim knocked back his drink. "I must go in to lunch. Feel free to finish your gin." With that, he set down his glass and abruptly departed.

The man next to him, a older fellow in a khaki suit and old-fashioned cravat, nodded to Bedford. "You're right about that airplane hunting," he said. "That blackguard Van Gelder does it all the time."

Bedford sipped again. "Do you know any of his clients?"

"Americans mostly. Passing through. But I steer clear of him. I'd advise you to as well."

THEY'D already run one race by the time Bedford got to the racetrack, and there seemed to be some excitement in the crowd about the next. He purchased a program, but could not make equine heads or tails out of it. He regularly played the races in New York, and could not resist the compulsion here, going immediately to a man with a chalkboard who was accepting two-pound wagers. On impulse, he bet on a filly named Lady Jane Gray. With this important transaction completed, he began to wander the crowd along the rail.

He could find no one he knew, and then at once he did. Idina and Lady Ralls, both radiantly blonde and rich-looking in their straw hats and summer dresses, were standing near the starting rope with a man in uniform who proved to be Lord Erroll.

Bedford bowed to the Errolls, then to Victoria, who seemed as fresh and happy as a schoolgirl in the first days of spring.

"I see that you're feeling better, Lady Ralls," he said, formally.

She took his arm, and stood on tiptoe to kiss his cheek. "Oh yes. Much better. Chased away the black dog." She stepped back, her eyes uncertain. "Why do you call me 'Lady Ralls,' Bedford? Have I displeased you in some way?"

The Errolls were watching all this intently.

"Not at all, Victoria," he said. "I am happy to see you in such good spirits, after what you've been through."

"I just don't think of it, is all. I shall have to tomorrow. We will be having Dickie's funeral. I do hope you'll come. But he would be sad were I just to sit and wallow in melancholy. I shall never get over this. But there is life, isn't there?"

"Yes, I . . ."

"And I'm so grateful for all that you've done. And are doing."

Bedford looked to Lord Erroll, who appeared quite somber, or at least serious.

"We'll get the man responsible for this," Bedford said, producing no reaction from Erroll whatsoever. He turned back to Victoria. "May I have a quick word?"

She seemed a little flustered at this, but, clinging to his arm, followed him a ways back from the crowd.

"You told the police inspector that you and I were together that night," he said.

Her expression was innocent, though her words were not. "Yes. I thought that best."

"But we weren't."

"Yes we were."

"Not all night. Or all morning."

"You were asleep, darling. You can't really say. At all events, I was just trying to spare both of us any disagreeable questions."

"I've more or less had to tell a lie."

She put her hand to his cheek. "Thanks awfully, Bedford. You're such a dear. But now there will be no complications, and we can put this horrid police business behind us."

"Don't you care who killed your husband?"

"Under the circumstances, it's perhaps better that I don't know. We're all such friends here."

He held her by both shoulders, studying her face. "Are you quite sure you're all right, Victoria?"

"Actually, no. I'm quite close to staggering. But I couldn't just sit there at Idina's drinking and crying all the time. I'm near to tears all the time, but I try to find a way to soldier on. Being here helps. Seeing you again helps."

She came close to him. He held her a moment, becoming conscious suddenly that many in the crowd were no longer attending to the track.

"We'd best go back."

"Thank you—dear."

They returned to the Errolls just as the rope dropped, amid a fanfare of kettledrums, starting the next race. Unlike the American tracks, the British courses ran clockwise, from left round to right, giving Bedford the odd notion that they were running backward.

His horse might as well have been—finishing dead last. "You know what happened to the actual Lady Jane Gray?" Idina asked.

Bedford guessed, hitting on what he calculated on his small knowledge of British history would be the correct answer. "Beheaded?"

"Exactly!"

"You rotter!" The familiar voice was directly behind him.

"Sorry?"

Beryl came up beside him. "I heard all that. You bet against my horse."

"I'm sorry."

"You should be. We won by five lengths. I've another in the next race. 'Arthurian.'"

Victoria had her arm in his again. "I'll wish you luck," he said.

"Won't need it," Beryl said, ignoring Lady Ralls's remarkable presence. "By the by, your friend Sloane is here—somewhere—looking for you. Your lawyer told her you were here."

"Lawyer?" asked Victoria.

"Mr. Asif."

"The Indian?"

Bedford disengaged himself, reaching for his wallet. "Put this fiver on Arthurian for me," he said to Beryl, handing her the note. "I'll look for Sloane." He shook Victoria's hand. "I'll see you soon."

He found Sloane with Alice at a refreshment stand near the paddock, where Lady Jane was being led away with a slight limp.

"There you are," said Sloane. "I've got good news. My Aunt Kate is coming. She'd left Chicago for London by the time I sent my cable, but someone forwarded my message. She'll be here within a fortnight."

"Fortnight? Sloane. I should hope we'd be long gone from here within a fortnight." He recounted his discovery of the second bullet.

Sloane shook her head. "We must stay here no matter what—until Kate comes."

"But Sloane. This is a murder investigation. If we can get your uncle clear of it, we should get the hell out of this place as fast as we can get aboard a ship in Mombasa."

"Bedford, you're being a stick. My Aunt Kate is coming. To be with Uncle Dixon. It's all going to be put right."

A dark look was coming over Alice's face much like the shadow of an approaching cloud.

"I wish you would go away, Bedford Green."

Sloane cast down her eyes, but did not intervene.

"I heard about all the lions you've killed—you and Beryl," Alice said. "Four lions. Or is it five? You talk about murder."

"Alice has a pet lion," Sloane explained.

"I'm sorry," Bedford said. "It wasn't intentional. I mean, well, Sloane's life depended on it in the first case."

"I've explained that," Sloane said.

"You're a beast," said Alice. "I don't know why I live here." She walked off to join some smiling man Bedford had not seen before.

"She's in a state," Sloane said.

"Everyone here seems to be that—except Victoria Ralls."

"Were you trying to give her the air?"

"Not exactly."

"She's coming for you," Sloane said.

Bedford had no place to turn.

"Can you drive me home?" Victoria said, putting her arm in Bedford's yet once more. "I don't want to go back to Idina's. Her friends are beginning to gather again and they're working up another ghastly sex romp."

"Of course," said Bedford. The Ralls residence was the last place he wanted to be at that moment, but as he thought upon it, probably the place he most ought to be if he was going to sort things out. "I don't know where you live."

"I'll show you. It's a bit far."

"How far is that?"
"It will be dark when we get there."
"Dark?"
"Yes."

CHAPTER 16

AS they drove along the Ngong Road, Bedford caught sight of a tall African walking along the side, heading toward town. This was far from uncommon. He'd found that, even in the dead of night, peering into the darkness to the side of the roads one might well see the silent forms of dozens of blacks, moving on mysterious, silent journeys.

This particular African, though, Bedford recognized as his friend the Masai. He braked sharply, putting out his arm to keep Lady Ralls from being knocked into the dashboard.

"Mzizi?"

The tracker stood looking at them as he might one of the wild beasts he hunted for a living.

"Was ist los?" Bedford asked.

"Ict nicht langer fur Hauptmann Owen arbeiten," Mzizi said. *"Er ist argerlicht weill ich fur sie helfen."*

Lady Ralls was waiting, impatiently. "Bedford?"

"Captain Owen fired this man — because he helped me."

"There's other work."

Bedford, squinting against the afternoon sun, considered this. *"Komt, bitte. Sie will fur mich arbeiten."*

The African said nothing more. His form of acceptance of Bedford's offer of a job was simply to walk to Bedford's touring car and climb over the side into the rear seat. Victoria viewed him as she might had he climbed through a window into her boudoir.

"What are you doing, Bedford?"

"He helped me. In an important way. So I've just now hired him."

"To do what?"

Bedford looked back over his shoulder. Mzizi was standing up.

"Footman," Bedford said.

A⸻S Victoria had foretold, they arrived at her house after sunset, bumping up her long drive in a thickening dusk. Two servants wearing what appeared to be very long shirts appeared on the veranda and remained standing there as Bedford pulled to a stop.

"Well, here you are," he said.

"Here *we* are," she said. "Come in and we'll have a spot of dinner."

Bedford could in no way understand Victoria's attraction to him. Perhaps she had exhausted the supply of suitable men in Happy Valley and considered him desirable as a novelty.

If she was guilty of this misjudgment, there was little he could provide along those lines—save in conversation. But she had not been much interested in his talk of New York café society, Broadway theatricals, Prohibition bootleggers, and Greenwich Village verse libre poets. His mysterious appeal, whatever it was, lay elsewhere.

After a meal of sorts that was mostly fruits and meat,

she led him by the hand to a rear veranda longer even than that in front. Steering him to a chaise longue positioned with a view of the wide valley below, she gently pushed him onto it.

There were few lights on in the scattering of houses visible in the landscape, but the moon was nearly three-quarters full and the folds of ridge and the hills beyond were clearly discernible.

His view was suddenly filled with her loveliness, as she sat facing him and took his hand in hers, pressing it to her slender bosom. He could feel the heat of her flesh beneath the thin blouse.

"I want to make love with you," she said.

"You have made that somewhat evident," he said.

"And you?"

"I'm very flattered—and amazed."

"You're not supposed to feel flattered," she said, slipping his hand within her blouse. "You are supposed to feel desire. Do you not find me desirable?"

"Well, yes. Of course." This truth was in fact manifesting itself.

"I was drawn to you from our first meeting in Mombasa, Bedford." She now reclined beside him on the chaise, turning onto her side to avoid falling off. "After what's happened, I need desperately to go to bed with a man, and I'd so much like it to be with you."

"But your husband has just been killed. I—"

She kissed him, pulling herself on top of him. Then she lifted her head to look into his eyes. Her own seemed aglow in the soft moonlight.

"Dickie would be happy for me," she said. "If it had been the other way around, this is what he'd be doing now—probably with your friend Sloane."

Bedford wondered if the servants were looking on.

"Here?" he asked.

She pressed herself against him, her blonde hair falling onto his face.

"They know better than to disturb me when I'm entertaining a guest."

"And Mzizi?"

"We left him standing in the back of your car. I rather imagine he's still there."

"Victoria—"

"Shhh." She sat up and began unbuttoning her blouse.

LATER, as she lay snuggled and naked against him, he was able to persuade her that her bed would be more comfortable—not to speak of warm and decorous. She brought a bottle of wine to this sanctuary, and they sat talking as they drank it.

"I mean to find your husband's killer," he said.

"Of course you do. That's very sweet of you. But there really isn't any need for you to expend further effort."

"What do you mean?"

She sat quietly a moment, sipping wine. It occurred to him, finally, that she was waiting for him to acknowledge what she doubtless considered the obvious.

"You think Dixon Smith did this," he said, finally.

"Of course I do. It's all so bloody obvious. If you weren't such a good friend of his niece, it would be obvious to you, too."

"But the bullet was fired from above. I'm quite convinced it was from an airplane."

"Bedford, have you no idea how absurd that sounds?"

He made no reply, except to take her hand in his and gently stroke it.

"Bedford, I should like to have this whole horrid business behind me. Please don't go mucking about, stirring up more trouble. Please." She put her head on his shoulder.

He had a number of things he would have liked to have said at that juncture, but forbore, choosing the wiser course of putting his arm around her and holding her close.

"I'll not cause you any trouble."

She patted his knee. "Thank you." Finishing her wine, she set her glass down on the night table. "And now my sweet, let us sleep."

"Sleep."

"Yes. It shall be lovely to sleep with you. Just sleep. To have you at my side." She lay down, pulling him after her.

SHE was quite right. It was blissful to slumber there, with such a woman in one's arms. It was far from easy to keep from sleeping, yet he managed. At some hour well after midnight, he slipped from her side and sat up on the edge of the bed, listening and waiting. When at length she murmured and turned onto her side, away from him, he waited a moment more, then rose and walked silently, barefoot, from the room.

The study was just down the hall. He closed the door behind him in the darkness, then stood awhile waiting for his eyes to adjust. Making out the desk and a lamp beside it, he turned it on. Seating himself, he took note of a framed photograph of the Rallses together standing arm in arm and smiling on the same veranda where he and Victoria had so pleasantly occupied the chaise longue.

It was not without uneasiness that he sat there, naked in a dead man's chair, having just left the bed of the dead man's wife. He assuaged himself with a thought of the noble end he sought here—if anything to do with Dixon Smith could be so characterized.

Then he began opening drawers.

Lord Ralls had apparently been a neat and tidy person. Private letters, commercial correspondence, bills and statements—all were neatly bound. The man had considerable debts, and had been frequently reminded of them. He discovered one angry note from George Sim, demanding instant payment and threatening bodily harm. This he set aside, along with one he picked at random that had been written in a woman's hand.

Another drawer yielded a Wembley officer's revolver just like the one Bedford had carried as an aviator in the war. In another were stacks of agricultural records and some colonial military correspondence. In the last was a metal box. Opening it carefully, he found to his amazement that it was filled with one hundred-pound notes.

As he leaned to return it to its place, there was a sharp, percussive slap of a sound outside and a shattering of glass as a bullet crossed over his head.

CHAPTER 17

BEDFORD'S first impulse was to fling himself from the chair to the floor. Once there, he quickly raised himself back up high enough to reach the lamp and extinguish its light, just as three more shots came through the shattered window in quick succession. That provided incentive for his next idea—to remove himself from Ralls's study before Victoria or another bullet discovered him.

He ran into her in the hall, literally. He tried to hold her in his arms, but she was frantic, and pulled away. She had not taken time to put on a dressing gown. Her fear was palpable.

"Where were you?" she said. "What's happening?"

"Gunshots."

"I know! Why?"

"Whoever killed your husband apparently wasn't satisfied."

"But why? My God, why?"

She darted into another room, emerging with a rifle. Her eyes were wild, and she swung the barrel about carelessly. He reached for her, but she moved off the other way, down the hall and out a door onto the rear veranda.

"Victoria! Don't go out there!"

She ignored him, going to the edge of the veranda. Raising the rifle, she fired three shots into the darkness. "Bloody bastards!"

He went to her side. "Victoria. Give me that." She had bolted another round into the chamber and the rifle discharged into the night sky as he grabbed for it. But she did not resist as he took it from her.

Three of her servants—the two men from before and an old woman—were standing in the doorway. Mzizi appeared from around the side of the house. Somehow, their presence made Bedford feel safer—especially Mzizi's.

He motioned to the African, who came forward dutifully.

"Haben sie jemand sehen?"

Mzizi nodded, pointing to some brush off the end of the veranda.

"Gehen?"

The African looked to Victoria, then shook his head. Bedford put his arm around her. "Come inside, now. Please."

Meek now, she obeyed. One of the servants handed her a robe, which with some embarrassment she clumsily put on. No one had provided anything for Bedford.

"You must go, Bedford. It is not safe for you here."

"And you?"

"They were shooting at you. I saw it. You were in our study and they shot at you through the window."

"Victoria . . ."

She put her hands to her ears. "Just go now. Please! Go!" When he didn't move, she reached and took back the rifle. He half feared she was going to aim it at him for emphasis.

"But what about you? I can't leave you here alone."

"I'm not alone. I'll be fine. No one's after me. It's you. So you must leave." She turned and spoke a few quick words in Swahili to the younger of the two male servants. He hurried off.

"Have you a telephone? We should call Inspector Jelli-coe."

She clenched her fists, holding them tight against her sides. "Damn it! Go!"

The servant returned with Bedford's clothing. Mzizi took the bundle from him and then stood holding it in shelf-like fashion as Bedford dressed.

When he finished, she graced him with an affectionate but very quick kiss, then pointedly shoved him toward the door.

AS Bedford turned from Victoria's drive onto the road to Nairobi, Mzizi leaned forward from his station in the backseat. "Lady Ralls, she go on veranda," he said.

Startled by the English words, if not the German accent, Bedford almost put the Buick in the bordering ditch. "You speak English?"

"Yes. I live among the English a long time. I learn."

"And you don't let on that you know it?"

"I am sergeant in the army of the German Empire, so at first I do not wish to speak English. Now I find it useful to know it, but not speak it."

"But you speak it to me now."

"You are not English. And you will go away soon. Also, you are my friend."

It was true.

"So you have heard things they don't know you under-stood?"

"Yes, Captain Green. But tonight I saw something Lady Ralls does not know I saw."

"And what was that?"

"It was a woman who fired a pistol at the window of the room where you were. The pistol she throw into the bushes and then she run off."

"You mean Lady Ralls?"

"Maybe."

T**HE** baroness was at home and happy to see him when he got to her house, despite the late hour. Beryl was still in Nairobi, tending to her horses and presumably celebrating her victories. She'd had two winners.

"Mzizi is working with me now—for a time," Bedford said. "Can he camp here?"

"Of course." A friendly smile. "Have you eaten?"

"Yes, thank you. Is Denys here?"

"No. He's in Nairobi. He has a hunt to prepare for— after poor Dickie Ralls's funeral." She led him into her large sitting room. "Brandy?"

He nodded, noting her open book and half-filled glass. "I'm sorry to turn up so late."

"There is no 'late' in Happy Valley, my dear." She served him his drink and then curled up on the sofa. "I think that, among those up late this night, there are many talking about you."

"About me?"

"About you and Lady Ralls. You've become quite notorious." She sipped. "You seem surprised. Gossip travels swiftly here. I'm sure you were only comforting her, but her attentions upon you have been viewed as unseemly— even for this place."

"In truth, I was only comforting her, but now matters have become more complicated."

"Which accounts for your tardiness this evening."

"Yes."

"Fascinating."

"There's more, if I may speak in the utmost confidence."

"Of course."

He told her of the money he'd found in Lord Ralls's desk, and of the gunshots through the window. He hesitated, uncertain as to how much he wanted to share of Mzizi's revelation.

"My friend Mzizi. He says he saw a woman outside the window with a pistol. She threw it in the bushes."

"Victoria?"

"Quite possibly. Only . . ."

"Yes?"

He flushed. "I forgot to ask him if she was dressed."

The baroness shifted her position, sitting up cross-legged. "This truly is an interesting story."

"Nearly a tragic one. Why would Victoria want to kill me?"

The baroness shook her head. "If it was her, she obviously didn't. Both the Rallses are considered among the best shots in Kenya. If that was what she wanted, you'd be lying there still. No, I think this story is more interesting than that, Captain Green. I think she must have caught you in her husband's study and emphatically wanted to make you leave immediately."

"I see."

"The most interesting part of the story has to do with whatever she didn't want you to discover."

"But I did discover it. A metal box containing a great many hundred-pound notes."

She waved her hand in dismissal. "Many of the settlers keep large amounts of money about their places, including those who have substantial debts, like Lord Ralls."

"He could have paid off those debts with that money. A lot of them, anyway."

"Perhaps so, Captain Green. But the point here is that he'd hadn't wanted to."

They heard a car pull up. Not long after, Beryl walked into the room, looking exhausted, but very happy. She took something from her purse and presented it to Bedford as she might a trophy—though it was one that belonged to her.

"Your winnings, sir." She placed twenty-two pounds in his hand.

"Congratulations," he said.

"Won by four lengths going away," she said, heading for the brandy.

"Perhaps you should keep this," he said.

"It was your wager."

"I have yet another favor to ask." Her happiness faded a little. "I need to go flying again."

A coldness came over her features. "Bedford, haven't we exhausted the possibilities of aviation as concerns your problem." Drink in hand, she slumped into a chair. "I've certainly exhausted myself today."

"I want to go back to where Owen's camp was—and where the bodies were found."

"We were just there. And you can drive there, you know."

"That would take half the day. And there's Lord Ralls's funeral in the morning."

"You want to fly out there before the funeral? I simply can't."

"Perhaps if we could just go to the airfield. I want to look at the logbook they have there—departing flights and arrivals. There is such a book, isn't there?"

"Yes. We mostly make the entries ourselves—so that they'll know where we were bound in the event of trouble and a forced landing."

"Does everyone do it?"

"Religiously. It could mean your life—if you're down in the wrong place and no one knows where you are."

"And the practice is required by law?"

"Some sort of regulation."

Bedford thought a moment. "Beryl, I know I've imposed upon you a great deal in this, but I really would like to take a look at that book, and it would be helpful if you were around, so it wouldn't just be me poking around there on my own."

The baroness leaned forward. "Perhaps on the way to the funeral."

Beryl yawned. "Well, all right. Just this once." She swirled her brandy, looking speculatively at Bedford. "Are you sure you want to go to this affair? Alice is going to be there. She's in quite a state, and there could be a row. She's carrying on about all the lions that have been killed and she could make quite a scene."

"But virtually everyone she knows has killed lions," the baroness said. "You just shot two yourself."

"True enough, Karen. But she is in a state over Dickie. She's bent on a scene and a row. And I fear Bedford's going to be the target."

"Why? Aside from the fact that Alice is as mad as a hatter."

A pointed glance at Bedford. "She's a very old friend of Bedford's friend Sloane. And I think she doesn't like it much that Bedford has a new friend named Victoria Ralls." She got to her feet, returning to the decanter. "And to think that people come here for a simpler, less-complicated life."

"There is no such thing," said the baroness.

CHAPTER 18

THERE were few names on the page. One of them was Beryl's.

"You went flying that day?"

"You sound like a bloody policeman."

"Sorry."

"Yes. I took a lesson. Touch-and-go landings."

"After that last one, I'd say all of your landings are touch-and-go, Beryl."

"Too, too, amusing, Bedford."

"That's why you put down no destination?"

"Correct."

He turned the page. "Who's Nigel Holden?"

"Hell of a chap. Flies all over Africa. He was just passing through on his way to Uganda."

"And this one?"

"Ernest Truscott? He flies for Mrs. Chisholm."

"He of the interesting cargoes. He put down that he was going to Nyeri that day."

"As you might imagine, I'm sure that's a lie—but I

don't think he'd be much interested in doing in Lord Ralls. They were quite friendly."

There was one last entry. "Our friend Van Gelder went up. Said he was going to Thika."

"Rather near—but in exactly the opposite direction of Owen's camp."

He closed the book, then stepped out of the little office onto the grass. Beryl shut the door behind her. The airport manager was not on the premises.

No one was flying that hot day. There was a desultory breeze that made a half-hearted attempt to lift the wind-sock, and then abandoned it. All the aircraft Bedford remembered were in place and tied down, including Van Gelder's.

"Why is no one flying?"

"Dickie's funeral. Who'd miss it?"

Bedford started over to the red aircraft. Moving around the left wings, he went up close to the side and peered into the rear cockpit. A moment later, he boosted himself into it.

W**HAT** were you looking for?" Beryl asked, as he returned.

"Whatever might be there."

"Such as an expended rifle shell on the floor of the cockpit?"

"Unfortunately, there wasn't one. Just some cigar wrappers and a bottle of Bols gin under the seat."

"That's a dangerous thing to have lying about in turbulent air."

"He's a dangerous man."

"Let's be off, Bedford. We're going to be late for the service."

They walked back to Bedford's hired Buick. He wondered what prying eyes might be watching them, and what might be made of it.

"Beryl, that landing you made by the stream—is there any other pilot around here who could manage that?"

She nodded. "You."

"Not me. I'd have killed us trying anything like that. Anyone else?"

"Tom Black. Woody Wood. They're the best in Africa. But neither have been in Nairobi of late."

"Not Denys?"

She shook her head. "He's still learning."

"And Van Gelder?" He opened the door for her.

"He's a bit heavy-handed, but he might—if he really had to."

THERE was no formal church service, or military one. The funeral as such was held at the gravesite in a small cemetery atop a hill across the Muthare River from the Muthaiga Club. A great many automobiles were parked at the base of the hill. Except for one couple drinking from a flask at the side of a Rolls-Royce, and two African policemen standing by a small truck, their owners had all trudged to the top.

An Anglican priest was officiating. Bedford, a Presbyterian, could not tell whether he was performing a ritual or speaking from the heart. At all events, he appeared to be taking his time about it.

Victoria, wearing black for the first time, stood at the head of the open grave, flanked by Lord and Lady Erroll. Bror Blixen was nearby, with an attractive, older woman on his arm. Standing next to the clergyman were Lord and Lady Delamere, and just behind them was Inspector Jellicoe. The policeman kept glancing about the crowd, as though a criminal were lurking in it. When his eyes finally took note of Bedford, they lingered upon him. Then his attention returned to the priest.

George Sim and his wife were present, as were the baroness and Denys Finch-Hatton. A dapper and extremely well-groomed gentleman took note of their arrival and came toward them, smiling. He gave Beryl a kiss, shook Bedford's hand smoothly and firmly, and introduced himself as her husband.

"Heard about you," he said. "Having an interesting time, are you?"

"Gets more interesting every day."

"Yes, well." He took Beryl by the arm. "You're all right, m'dear?"

"Simply wizard." She pulled away from his grip, but only to take him by the hand. "Please excuse us, Bedford."

He was left alone, and felt it. People were watching him, a few leaning to whisper. Lady Delamere appeared to be pointing him out to her husband.

Ignoring them, he kept searching among the crowd for Sloane, perplexed not to find her.

But then he did. She and Alice were standing beneath a tree off to the right. He hurried toward her.

She embraced him, lingering in his arms, easing back only a little. "Poor Bedford," she said, in a half-whisper. "This hasn't been much fun for you."

"It's a funeral."

"I mean everything."

"Didn't come here for fun, did we?"

"All these hypocrites here, pretending to be sad. I have to make arrangements for poor Georgia. I've had her embalmed. Don't know whether to have her buried here or sent back to Ohio."

"Isn't that up to your Uncle Dixon?"

"Yes, of course. But he's done nothing. He just sits and stares. And drinks. He's so very sorry he came here."

An elderly couple nearby gave them a very scolding look. Sloane, predictably, ignored them.

"I'll ship her back to Ohio," Sloane said. "That's what I must do. Then I must get us all shipped home, after Kate gets here." She stepped closer. "Are you making any headway in Uncle Dixon's case?"

"Of a sort, though I'm not sure where I'm headed."

Alice had been listening intently. Finally, she marched around to Bedford's front and kicked him sharply in the right shin. Only his wartime discipline kept him from crying out. He could barely restrain a hop.

Sloane yanked Alice away. "You'd better go, Bedford."

"There's something I have to ask you."

"Later, Bedford. I'll come out there, to the baroness's."

He stepped away and retreated to a circumspect spot off to the other side of the grave, waiting patiently for the grim ritual to conclude. It did, finally, with Victoria weeping over the casket as it was lowered.

With the proceedings over, he started toward her, but a strong arm restrained him. He looked to see Inspector Jellicoe beside him.

"Captain Green, if you would come with me, please."

"Certainly, what's afoot?"

"I'll explain in a moment, sir."

Bedford followed Jellicoe over the hill and down to the little truck, where the two black policemen snapped to barefooted attention. Both had rifles, and brought them to order arms.

"What's going on?" Bedford asked.

"You shall be pleased to know that we're going to release Dixon Smith," Jellicoe said.

"That is good news. Have you found new evidence, or are you finally paying attention to what I told you?"

"A bit of both." Jellicoe nodded to the two Africans, who came forward. "I regret to inform you, Captain Green, that I must detain you in custody as we continue our inquiry into Lord Ralls's murder."

"Custody?"

"At the Central Police Station."

"I don't understand."

"The ballistics specialist has examined the round you dug up at the murder scene. It came from the rifle you were using. A Merkel."

"That certainly doesn't mean I fired it."

"And Lady Ralls has recanted her statement. She said you were not with her that morning. She doesn't know where you were."

"Then why did she say she did?"

"To protect you, she said."

"Which she no longer wants to do?"

"You shouldn't blame her. We were very insistent in our questioning."

"But Lord Ralls and Mrs. Smith were shot from an airplane. The bullet was in the ground beneath them."

"You're an aviator, Captain Green."

"But I was in camp. With her."

"Please, sir, get in the truck."

As he did so, he saw Victoria and the Errolls walking to a car. She looked his way, sadly, but not for long.

CHAPTER 19

I T was three days before anyone came to see him. His first visitor was Sloane. She appeared to be wearing traveling clothes.

"Dear, dear Bedford. I'm so sorry."

She stood, awkwardly, glancing distastefully about the cell, which was the same one her uncle had recently inhabited. It was musty and still smelled of disinfectant, but was cool and its insect population wasn't particularly overwhelming. Bedford had resided in much worse places during the war.

"Where have you been?" he asked.

"Trying to get in here to see you. The police were being difficult."

"They've been relatively pleasant to me—though I've yet to see a judge."

"What will become of you?"

"Hanging, I think," he said. "Or perhaps a firing squad."

She sat down on the cot beside him, taking his hand.

"Don't talk that way. This is all a misunderstanding that I'm sure we can clear up. Do you have a lawyer?"

"I haven't been able to talk to anyone—until now."

"Would you like to see Mr. Asif?"

He considered this. He had to assume that any British attorney here would be even more prejudiced against him than they'd been against Dixon Smith, who deserved some sympathy as the husband of an unfaithful woman. Bedford's role in this was now as Lady Ralls's lover. He was perforce a blackguard, accused of doing in the innocent and unsuspecting husband—the victim a local colonial officer and peer of the realm to boot. No matter that he had been killed in a moment of *amour impropre*.

"Mr. Asif will be fine. I should also like to see Mzizi."

"The African man?"

"Few colonials here named Mzizi. There are things he can do for me."

"You're going to need money." She took some pound notes from her purse. "Here's a hundred. I'll put another five hundred in a bank account for you."

"That's not necessary." He stared at the currency in his hand, the notes bearing the portrait of King George V.

"Of course it's necessary. You're in a terrible jam, and I'm responsible."

"Okay. Thank you." He pocketed the money. "What have you been doing with yourself—when you've not been pounding on the door to the Central Police Station?"

"I've been with Alice, who's quite lost her mind. And I've been to see the baroness, to ask what to do about you. I also had Georgia sent back to Ohio. But mostly I've been with Uncle Dixon. He's coming out of his funk."

"I'm so happy for him."

"Aunt Kate will be here soon. I think I can get them back together now."

"You think she'd still want him?"

"She wouldn't be coming here if she didn't. There are a

lot of husbands like Dixon in Chicago. But they don't marry their floozies. If he had been content to keep Georgia on the side, like other members of the Casino Club I could name, there wouldn't have been such a problem. Aunt Kate's the most tolerant person I know. She voted for Robert LaFollette in the last election."

"Sounds like a wonderful woman." He brushed away a cockroach that was marching toward him across the bed. "They never brought your uncle before a judge, either."

"Let's hope you'll fare as well."

"What did the baroness have to say?"

"She said to say hello and that she's going to look out for you."

"What does that mean?"

"I've no idea. She said you shouldn't despair."

"And Beryl Markham?"

"She's gone off with her husband somewhere."

"A rare event in British East Africa."

Sloane clutched her purse with both hands, in preparation. "Bedford, I have to go. I'm taking the train to Mombasa."

"On a one-way ticket?"

"Of course not. I'm just going down to meet Aunt Kate's ship, so she doesn't end up in Mozambique or someplace." She leaned down to kiss him. "You need a shave."

"I haven't a razor."

"We'll get you one."

"A hacksaw would be better."

"Good-bye, dear. Don't fret. We'll get you out of here." The smell of her perfume lingered.

MR. Asif did not show up until the next day. He appeared not to have changed clothes since Bedford had last seen him, though he may have merely been one of those persons incapable of neatness, no matter how fresh his shirt or new his tie. It had been said of Dayton Crosby that he always looked as though he had just stepped from the shower—with his clothes on.

"Your case is no more hopeless than Mr. Smith's," said Asif, ever smiling.

"How encouraging," Bedford said. "Who shall we get to take my place? Or shall I trade places with Dixon Smith again?"

"No need. I am preparing many legal papers. We shall have you out soon. As for Mr. Smith, I am told he is leaving soon."

"No doubt." Bedford brushed some lint from his sleeve. Sloane had sent around some toiletries and clean clothes. He was feeling more himself again. She'd also sent gin. "Would you care to join me in a drink, Mr. Asif?"

"Oh no, thank you very much. I do not drink alcohol. I am a Moslem."

"I thought you were Indian."

"Indian I am, and also Moslem. There are millions of us in India."

Bedford poured and sipped. "I see. I'm not sure how much good all your legal papers will do, Mr. Asif. I've not even been formally arraigned by a judge."

"One of my papers requests that—and soon."

A chill came over Bedford. He had no idea of the cause. "Have you been given a retainer?"

"Yes. By Miss Smith. Very generous." He seated himself at Bedford's little table and took out a small notebook and a shiny fountain pen. "What would you like me to do?"

"First of all, I'd like you to check the court records to see if there are any liens against Lord Ralls's property. And also if there were any bank attachments."

Mr. Asif paused to clean his eyeglasses on his tie, then

scribbled an entry in his notebook. "That should be easy," he said.

"Then I'd like you to check with your police friends and find out if Lord Ralls, Denys Finch-Hatton, Captain Owen, or that white hunter Van Gelder have ever had any brush with the law."

"Lord Ralls was the law, Captain Green. He was in charge of border security and caught many criminals."

"All of them African, no doubt."

"Yes, mostly."

"Anyway, ask around."

"Very well." More scribbling.

"I'm interested in learning who among the social set here might have any dealings or connections with Nairobi's criminal class."

More jotting. Asif looked up. "You did not mention Mr. Ernest Truscott?"

"Him, too."

"Anything else?"

"I'd like to know where Alice de Janze' was the morning Lord Ralls was killed. Could you make discreet inquiries? Among servants?"

"Hers?"

"Anyone's."

Asif closed the notebook.

"If you please, there's something else," said Bedford. He took a carefully folded piece of paper from his pocket. "There's an African tracker, Mzizi. He works for Captain Owens. Or did. I need to speak with him. No one's been able to find him for me, but perhaps you can. If you do, would you please give him this note?"

Asif took it, and, annoyingly, unfolded it to read. "It's not in English," he complained.

"It's in German. He'll understand it."

The lawyer rapped on the door to summon the guard. "I'll find him. I will try. Yes indeed, Captain Green."

"There's something else."

With some exasperation, Asif took out his notebook again. "Yes?"

"A copy of Burke's Peerage."

"The English nobility?"

"The very one."

HE had no visitors the next two days, though Baroness Blixen sent him several books, including a collection of stories by Somerset Maugham, as well as some wine, fruit, and English biscuits. They were small substitute for human company, but he made do. The wine, from South Africa, was particularly good—as were Maugham's stories.

THE guard rattled open the door to his cell the next morning to announce a most unexpected visitor. He gave Bedford a moment to pull on a shirt, trousers, and shoes. Bedford was still buttoning the shirt when she entered. Like all his guests, she stood uneasily in the center of the room, though he could not tell whether her anxiety was due to fear or guilt.

"Your Ladyship," he said, getting to his feet.

"Hello, Bedford," she replied, tremulously.

"Are you all right?"

"No, not really. But how are you? It must be awful being locked up here."

"I'm surviving. For now."

She took a step toward him, then thought better of it, and went to the little table, seating herself demurely, legs close together, hands folded in her lap, head hung down a little, eyes very sad. The guard had remained near the door, as he hadn't when Sloane and Mr. Asif had come.

"I'm so sorry," she said.

"Sorry?" He sat down on the cot again.

"I fear I'm responsible for your being in here. When I told the police inspector that we weren't together all that night after all, I had no idea he would seize upon that as reason to arrest you."

"He needed to arrest someone."

She observed him somewhat curiously a moment. "He made it clear to me that he'd been informed by someone at the camp that we weren't together. I was afraid I might go to jail for lying. I'd no wish to hurt you, but under the circumstance—"

"Which circumstance is that?"

Her eyes lifted. "Bedford, did you shoot Dickie?"

Her words had much the same effect on him as if she'd picked up the table and hit him over the head with it. "Why on earth do you think that?"

"I don't know. I've thought about it quite a lot. I know you care for me. I know you care for Sloane, and I know how much she disliked that woman."

"Victoria, I did not shoot your husband. I've never killed anyone, outside of Germans in the war."

"Now I'm terribly confused."

"As am I. If you harbored the slightest suspicion I might have taken your husband's life, why would you come here? Why would you have had me to your house?"

She began sniffling. "Because I care for you—as I think you do for me." She took a handkerchief from her purse.

"Didn't you love your husband?"

"Yes, of course. In the beginning, in London. Lately . . ." She wiped at her eyes. "It's hard out here, Bedford. It's so different. There are no constraints. Dickie's a wonderful fellow. He was . . . I warned him he was going too far, even for Happy Valley."

Victoria began crying in earnest. When he did not go to comfort her, she came to the cot and sat close beside him. Reflexively, he put his arm around her. She was shaking.

"You musn't . . ."

She turned and put her arms around him. "You've no idea how horrid it can be in this place. You don't know what it can do to people. We lord it over the blacks like gods. We have the most absolute freedom to do as we please. Yet there's so little money. And . . ."

He held her close, thinking of the huge sum that had been in the box in her husband's desk drawer.

"You should go back to London," he said.

"I intend to, as soon as this dreadful matter is dealt with."

"Do you believe me when I say I didn't murder your husband?"

"Of course, Bedford. Certainly. But they're going to make it hard for you. I don't know what to do."

He eased his hold on her. "You could bring me your husband's papers."

"Papers?"

"His business transactions."

"He had none. We've been living on his army pay, and my little trust fund."

"I'm sorry to have brought it up."

They sat without speaking for a long time. She was breathing deeply. He watched the rise and fall of her bosom beneath her blouse, then removed his arm from her shoulders.

"Is that what you were looking for in Dickie's study?" she asked.

"How do you know I was in the study?"

"I saw you come out. After I heard those gunshots."

"Your gunshots."

"Whatever do you mean?"

"A pistol—fired through the window. Several times in rapid succession, but aimed too high."

"I don't know what you're talking about."

"Of course you do."

She rose, shakily, her face very wan. "I'll do what I can for you."

"Thank you."

He hoped she would look back when she reached the door, but she did not.

ASIF turned up after the heat of the afternoon, bearing a bulging briefcase. "I have wonderful news."

"I'm to be released?"

"Not exactly. That is, yes—but only for brief periods of time. They are going to permit you to exercise."

"They already do that. There's this little courtyard."

"No!" Asif was beaming. "Outside! They will let you walk outside. With an escort, of course. But you can go a mile in any direction from the Central Police Station. Is that not very nice?"

"To whom am I obliged for this kindness?"

"Inspector Jellicoe—and I think Lady Ralls had something to do with it." He collapsed in the little chair, wiping his brow with his already moist handkerchief.

"She is such a dear," Bedford replied, edgily.

"Oh yes. A very lovely lady." Asif opened his briefcase, taking items out as might Santa Claus beside a Christmas tree. "Here is a copy of Burke's Peerage, which has to be returned to the library." Next came some papers. "Here is a list of the people engaged in criminal activity that you requested." He handed it to Bedford.

"You've got virtually everyone down here except Lord Delamere. "

"But it's all true. My clients may be criminals, but they do not lie to me."

Bedford reread the list. "Why didn't you write down the crimes they're supposedly involved in as well?"

"Were I to do that, and were someone to read that paper, then I would be guilty of slander."

Bedford took out a pen. "Let's have them. I'll risk the slander charge."

The infractions came in a rich variety. Truscott was a smuggler. Owen had done poaching in his time, as had his assistant, Grubb, who also had a criminal record back in England. George Sim cheated on his taxes. Van Gelder was a poacher and a smuggler. Baron Blixen had passed bad checks. Baroness Blixen apparently violated a number of laws concerning relations between whites and the colored races. Beryl Markham broke all manner of motor vehicle regulations. Idina Erroll had broken a large assortment of morals laws, and Mrs. Chisholm trafficked in drugs.

"And Lord Ralls?" Bedford asked. "Why isn't his name on this list?"

"He was an important military officer—one of the top security officials in British East Africa."

"When he was on duty."

"He was on duty when he needed to be."

Bedford refolded and pocketed the paper. "Very good, Mr. Asif. I thank you for your efforts. Did you locate Mzizi?"

"No. He has vanished."

"Then continue harassing Inspector Jellicoe with your legal motions, and let me know if he's up to anything in my case."

The lawyer gathered up his briefcase. "I will do so,

Captain Green." He paused. "Mr. Dixon Smith, he has asked about you."

"Asked what?"

"If you are going to get out of prison."

"What does he care?"

"He wants you to help him find out who killed his wife."

CHAPTER 20

THE Central Police Station was three blocks north of the railroad station and not far from City Hall and the center of town. Walking west up Nairobi Hill, however, one got into a lovely bit of countryside and, at the intersection with the Ngong Road at the top of the hill, there was an extraordinary view. This prominence became Bedford's daily destination. It was only a small distance farther than the prescribed mile and back, and his two African guards, with a small monetary inducement, were happy to indulge him.

He was just returning from his third daily visit to this pleasant place, crossing the wooden bridge over the drainage ditch that marked the western boundary of the town center, when he saw a Rolls-Royce touring car approach from the direction of the police station.

Behind the wheel was Sloane. Beside her, dressed in a large, old-fashioned hat and khaki-colored duster, was a middle-aged woman with quite handsome features and graying blonde hair. As Bedford guessed, she was introduced as Aunt Kate.

"My dear Mr. Green," she said, shaking his hand after

allowed to do so by the guards. "I'm so grateful for all that you've done for Sloane and Dixon. And I'm so sorry for the predicament in which you now find yourself."

She had a brilliant smile and a breezy, gracious, confident, upper-class manner. In sum, she was everything Georgia had not been—though, to be sure, Georgia had possessed qualities and proclivities doubtless lacking in Aunt Kate.

"You've made Sloane very happy by coming," said Bedford. "This is not everyone's favorite destination."

"I've always wanted to come here," Kate said.

"All's well that ends well, Auntie," said Sloane. She gave a sharp look to one of the Africans, who was getting fidgety. "They let you go out like this—every day?"

"I'm sure these gentlemen are excellent shots. They needn't worry about my wandering off."

"We must return soon," said the fidgety guard.

"I should be happy to contribute a pound note to the Nairobi Central Police Station Guard Contentment Fund if you would allow me to converse with these nice ladies a bit more."

The guard moved back. Bedford went to Sloane's side of the Rolls, putting a foot on the running board. She gave him a sad, sweet kiss—but on the cheek. "Poor Bedford."

"I think I may yet get free of this place."

The two Africans paid no attention to this. Sloane leaned close. "What is that?"

"I'm making a great deal of progress in learning who killed Georgia and Lord Ralls."

"But you're in jail."

"Turns out it's a wonderful place to think. I've drawn up a list of people who might have wanted to send Lord Ralls to his reward, and now I'm narrowing it down."

"What sort of people?" asked Aunt Kate.

"If you'll pardon my being so coarse—cuckolds,

spurned lovers, creditors, assorted criminals, and one or two crazy people."

"That doesn't sound very narrow to me," said Sloane.

"I trust you are not including Dixon in that pack," Kate added.

"No, I think we can safely eliminate him."

"Why do you say that?"

"He doesn't want to leave this place until the killer is found out."

His remark appeared to have dashed some high hope or fine dream of Kate's. She froze in place, as if turned to stone.

"He must leave," she said. "We've bought steamship tickets. It's all arranged."

"Well, then," said Bedford, stepping back. "Shall we say good-bye now?"

Sloane arched her brows. "Don't be a stick, Bedford. Aunt Kate and Uncle Dixon are going. I'm staying until you are free of this place, even if I must wait until I'm a withered old hag."

"That won't be necessary—if I'm given the rope."

"No, no. You're getting out. One way or another." She came close again. "Bedford, who is your best friend in Kenya?"

"I haven't been here long enough to have friends."

"Victoria Ralls certainly seemed friendly. Tell me at least who you know here that you trust."

He thought only briefly. "The Baroness Blixen. Perhaps Beryl Markham."

"Anyone else?."

"Mzizi. Especially Mzizi. I've tried to get word to him, but he's disappeared."

"We'll find him for you, then," said Sloane, restarting the automobile. "We'll do everything we can for you, Bedford."

"Everything, dear," Aunt Kate said, with another of her brilliant smiles.

"Where are you staying?" Bedford asked.

"Aunt Kate and I are at Alice's. Uncle Dixon is at the Old Stanley Hotel."

"Okay. I guess you know where to find me."

It was not permitted his extended perambulation the following day. Inspector Jellicoe had him brought to his office again for interrogation instead. The policeman asked him mostly the very same questions he had at the commencement of the investigation, and Bedford replied with generally the same answers. Then the subject turned to Lady Ralls.

"You were a visitor to the Rallses' house, after His Lordship's murder."

"As that's not pertinent to the case, I'd rather not discuss it."

"There are some who might venture to say it is pertinent."

"Fine. Are you going to get on with my case? Let me have a chat with an actual judge. Charge me with a crime anytime soon?"

"We once had a fellow here three months before he ever went to court," said Jellicoe, good naturedly. "It was a similar situation—quite a lot of evidence indicating guilt, but not quite enough to prove it."

"What is it you need in my case?"

Jellicoe didn't hesitate. "A witness would jolly well do."

"I know of none."

The policeman shrugged. "Have you been comfortable? Are you enjoying your daily walks?"

"Very much."

The other man lighted his pipe. "You rather stray the bounds, I see."

"I remain in the company of my warders—and I always return."

"Bribery is a Crown crime, did you know?"

"I'd be shocked to discover anything like that was going on in this prison."

Two puffs. "A crime is a crime, old boy." He consulted a note on his desk. "Mr. Dixon would like to have an interview with you, but does not wish to do so in this prison. He's not fond of it here."

"Somehow I find this not surprising."

"Perhaps we can make some arrangement." Here he came forward and shook Bedford's hand in farewell, as though they were parting after a friendly drink in a pub. "The chief warder has a package for you. From Miss Smith."

It proved to contain clean clothes, but they were garments for the bush—khaki shirts, shorts, and socks, and a pair of dun-colored, thick-soled walking shoes.

He wore them on his next walk up Nairobi Hill. At the top, Sloane and Aunt Kate were waiting in the Rolls-Royce.

Kate was in her duster again. Sloane looked ready for a garden party at the governor's residence. As it turned out, that's where she was bound.

"Your dear friend Lady Ralls invited us," she said. "Aunt Kate is thrilled. She's never been to such an affair."

"Only to parties at the consul general's in Chicago," replied Kate. "I'm a member of the English-Speaking Union."

He came nearer. "Your Uncle Dixon sent a message that

he wants to talk to me. Jellicoe's going to make arrangements. It could be soon."

"You must persuade him to drop all this and leave with Kate," Sloane said. "We have to get him away from here."

"I think he feels an obligation to his—to Georgia."

Kate suddenly commenced a study of the nearby mimosa trees. Sloane started the Rolls. "We'll talk later."

"Soon?"

"Soon."

CHAPTER 21

JELLICOE'S arrangement for Dixon Smith's visit was peculiar but workable. Two wooden chairs were set up in the center of a field adjoining the Central Police Station. Four guards were posted to keep watch from a distance. Bedford and Dixon were allowed a half hour for their conversation.

"This whole damned business . . ." Dixon waved his hand to include the police station, if not all British East Africa, "it's outrageous."

"A tragedy. Almost Greek. Definitely Shakespearean."

Dixon had recovered somewhat from his trance-like state. He reminded Bedford of a rummy coming off a binge—trying to bring his life back to some semblance of order.

"I'm never going near a firearm again," he said.

"If only you'd come to that decision a couple of months ago."

"You did your share of shooting."

"I never wished to. I wasn't interested in trophies when I did that. Only Sloane's life."

"I'm sorry. I'm grateful."

"Sloane and your former wife—the previous Mrs. Smith—would like you to go home."

"Can't. Can't just leave it like that." His head went into his hands.

"Sloane has sent Georgia's remains home to Ohio."

"I know."

"I believe Owen sent your lion to a taxidermist. You could fetch that and be on your way."

Dixon sat up straight again. "I don't want it. I can't think of anything that would bring me more pain."

"Toss it in a trash bin then."

They sat in silence. Bedford watched a truck full of uniformed soldiers and what looked to be prisoners—all of them African—turn off the road and come up to the prison entrance. The captives were much subdued, their captors loud and pushing. When they were all at last inside, Bedford looked to his watch. "What do you seek of me, Mr. Smith?"

"My wife's murderer."

"So I understand. But here I am in prison, accused of the crime."

"Mr. Green. Sloane says you've helped others in similar straits—including the Vanderbilts."

"Gertrude Vanderbilt Whitney is a very good friend."

"I'd like you to help me. I'll get you out of this damned jail. I'll hire the best lawyer in Nairobi. What they're doing has got to be illegal. They can't just lock you up without a trial."

"This isn't America."

"Even if I can't get you out. I'll do whatever you need me to do—spend whatever it takes. First thing I'm going to do is have a check deposited here for five thousand dollars. If you get the bastard for me, it's yours."

"Mr. Smith, I'm more than willing 'to get the bastard' for you. I'm not any more fond of this place than you are.

But I don't want your money." He thought on that. "But your help I would appreciate."

"Anything."

"First of all, is everything you said about going hunting on your own and coming upon the bodies by chance—is it the truth?"

"Yes. It was the most horrible morning of my life."

"Why did you go into that little clearing?"

"I saw a lion coming toward me. I ran for that clump of trees around the clearing. I thought maybe I could climb one."

"But then you saw the bodies."

"Yes. I didn't know they were dead at first. I thought they were just . . ."

"Describe them. How they were arranged."

Dixon did so at length, shuddering at the end.

Bedford rubbed his chin, realizing he had forgotten to shave that morning. The formerly unforgivable was becoming the commonplace. If he didn't discipline himself better, he'd soon resemble one of Sloane's Greenwich Village verse libre poets.

"You were out there very early. At first light?"

"Yes."

"Did you see me and Lady Ralls?"

"No. I just got up, got my rifle, and headed out."

"Did you hear the gunfire?"

Dixon had to think about it. "Yes, I believe I did. Hadn't thought about it, but I did. I wondered who it might be—and if the bullets were coming my way."

"Bullets?"

"There were two shots."

"You're sure?"

"Yes."

"Why didn't you tell the police?"

"I answered all their questions. They didn't ask me

about gunshots. I didn't think about it." He hesitated. "Do you want me to tell them now?"

"No. Not yet." One of the guards had edged closer. Bedford glanced again at his watch. "Did you hear an airplane?"

"What?"

"When you went out hunting, did you hear an airplane?"

"I don't know. May have."

"You can't remember?"

"Wasn't paying attention. That bush country, it gets noisy at night. The damned insects."

"Gunshots, but no airplane."

"Maybe no airplane."

The guard was coming toward them. Bedford sighed, then rose from his chair. "I've retained Mr. Asif for myself. I'll use him to send messages to you."

"All right."

"You do the same. Are you still at the Old Stanley Hotel?"

"Yes. I've booked my suite for the month."

"You're in contact with Sloane?"

"She comes by every day."

"And the former Mrs. Smith? Aunt Kate?"

"I've talked to her. She came all the way out here to help me. I think we're still friends, despite everything."

The guard was standing very near, remaining circumspect, but looking impatient. Dixon stood. "Is there anything you want me to do?"

"Talk to that aerial white hunter Van Gelder and see if he'll fly you out to where your wife was killed."

Dixon blanched. "I don't like flying in airplanes."

"You don't have to. Just see if he's willing to do it. If he's not, offer him a lot of money and then tell me what happens."

"I don't understand."

"I'm not sure I do yet, either." The guards came up all around him—one of them nodding toward the prison. Bedford started toward it, then stopped and looked back to Dixon. "Those gunshots, were they in quick succession?"

"No. There was one. And then nothing. And then finally another."

Bedford was beginning to regret turning down that five thousand dollars.

"Good-bye, Mr. Smith. Let's talk again soon."

"I'll be here."

"You're sure you don't want to leave Kenya?"

"I'll stay here as long as you do."

ON the next day's walk, he encountered Sloane and her Rolls-Royce at the bottom of Nairobi Hill. She was alone and appeared somewhat agitated.

"You're not wearing the khaki bush clothes I got you," she said, sounding like a mother scolding a child.

He had put on a white shirt he'd had laundered, a pair of gray flannel trousers, and his navy blazer. "I thought it was bad form to wear the same clothes two days in a row."

"In Africa one can make allowances." She motioned him closer. "I've bad news. They're going to arraign you within the week. The trial will follow soon."

"Mr. Asif was by last night and didn't say a thing about that."

She checked to see how closely the guards were listening. "Mr. Asif doesn't move in the same social circles as Alice's friends. You must prepare."

"I am preparing. Mr. Asif and I are working up a case."

"That's not what I mean. All of your needs will be taken care of, you may rest assured—as long as you're prepared to take advantage of opportunities." She looked as nervous as the getaway driver for a bank robbery gang.

"What's wrong, Sloane?"

"What's wrong? You're in this filthy jail. Uncle Dixon is drowning his sorrows in some wretched hotel and refusing to budge. We're stuck in Africa. That's what's wrong." She glanced furtively at the guards again. "I must go, Bedford. Kiss me."

He did so, though it was like kissing a mouse backing away from a trap.

"Soon, Bedford. Soon." She had kept the engine going. Shifting into first gear, she let loose the clutch and the Rolls leapt away.

Bedford looked at the guards and shrugged. One of them grinned, and they resumed their walk.

As the highway neared the summit of the hill and the intersection with the Ngong Road, it made a sharp turn to the right around a hedge-like thicket of bushes. Trudging by it, Bedford noticed a sudden rustling of the leaves. A moment later, an African man with a scarf wrapped around his face appeared as if magically in their midst, throwing a long wooden club. It struck one of the warders in the head and he crumpled to the dirt. Before the other could turn, the intruder scurried forth, snatched up the club, and whacked him with it. He sat down hard, still conscious, but so dazed as to be incapable of pursuit, or much of anything.

The assailant grabbed Bedford by the arm, hauling him toward the thicket. *"Kommt,"* he said.

Bedford started to resist, but then decided to accept his moment of deliverance. If nothing else, there was no other way of discovering who had arranged it, and why.

Pulled along by the man, he was quickly enveloped by the bushes. With heads lowered, they scurried over the dirt beneath the branches, Bedford twice getting scraped by thorns. Emerging at last on the other side, they came upon a car parked at the side of the road. Its engine was running. Behind the wheel was Baron Blixen.

"Quick!" he hissed. "In the back."

Bedford did as bidden, but found himself pushed into the vehicle by the now impatient assailant, who got into the backseat after him, sitting very straight.

"Guten tag, Herr Green," he said. He pulled off the scarf, revealing himself to be Mzizi, as Bedford had known from the start.

Blixen drove off with a minimum of noise, heading over the hill toward the open country beyond.

"Why are you doing this?" Bedford inquired.

"Karen asked me to," said the baron. "Please keep down."

THE baroness came out of her house as the car came up the drive, a rifle melodramatically in her hand. "Isn't this exciting?" she said, as Bror pulled on the hand brake.

"You're not planning a shoot-out with the police?" Bedford asked.

She looked down at the rifle as though she hadn't known it was there. "No. We have been having trouble with a lion. It's been after my dogs." She hefted the firearm. "I keep this with me now at all times."

"What exactly is happening here? Neither the Baron here nor Mzizi could explain."

"What's happening is that you are going to be my guest for the night. And then in the morning you are going on a journey—as I will explain at dinner. In the meantime, I would like you to stay in my toolshed."

"Baroness. Sheds are the first place police look for fugitives."

"There is a hiding place. Mzizi will show you."

THEY provided a blanket and two bales of hay, plus some pate, bread, cheese, a bottle of South African wine, and one of Portuguese brandy.

"I'll keep you company, for a while," the baroness said.

"And then?"

"Very early in the morning, Beryl will come and fly you to a place far away from here."

"To what end, Baroness?"

"To spare your life—or spare you a life's imprisonment."

"Not only are you all behaving like criminals, you've made me officially declare myself to be one."

"Once you're back in your Little Bohemia, that won't matter."

"Little Bohemia? Do you mean Greenwich Village?"

"Whatever it is that you call it. Once you are back there, you will be safe. They will not come after you. This story will have a happy ending."

"Just like all the other comic operas. Whose idea was this? Sloane's?"

"Yes. But Beryl thought it sensible."

"And a bit of adventure."

"That, too."

"But if I take it on the lam like this, it will always be assumed that I was the culprit."

"On the lam?"

"Baroness, you are the most well-behaved person I have encountered in this self-indulgent place. How can you countenance something like this?"

"I can countenance it because I do not think you will find justice here. You are a foreigner and a convenient scapegoat. These are English colonials. Some of them are my friends but theirs is a selfish system."

He sipped some wine. She watched him, then tore off a

piece of bread, added a slice of cheese, and handed it to him.

"What do you think of Lady Ralls?" he asked.

The question surprised her. "I've always liked her, though she and her husband were far too promiscuous. Even though it was said they married for love."

"Is Alice de Janze' a good pistol shot?"

"Pistol competitions are one of the amusements here. She often wins."

"And Van Gelder, does he support himself entirely as a white hunter?"

She made a shushing noise, said a word or two of remonstrance in Danish, and got to her feet. "I must do my farm accounts, Bedford. And you must get some rest. If someone comes, I'll send my manservant to warn you, but I don't think that will happen. If they have followed anyone, it will be your friend Sloane. That was her plan."

"Very well. Thank you. Thank you very much."

"Good night, then. I think you'd best turn out the lantern when you have finished eating."

"I will." She was almost out the door of the shed when he called to her. "Baroness, a favor, if I could."

"Of course, Bedford. Anything."

"Where is Mzizi? Did he go?"

"It's a long walk back to Nairobi. No, he's here. He is eating."

"I should like to speak to him before I retire."

CHAPTER 22

THE hand that shook him awake was not the baroness's, belonging to someone a bit younger. It was dark in the shed, but the blue eyes shone.

"Victoria?"

"Are you dreaming of amour, Bedford? Lady Ralls is not here. It's Beryl."

He sat up. It was indeed. "I trust you are not here for amour, Mrs. Markham, though that seems to be the way of this place."

"Not today, bucko." She slapped his leg. "We must get a move on."

"Where are we going?" He swung his legs off the hay bale, which had been as scratchy a mattress as he could remember.

"Far from Lady Ralls—and blessedly far from here. You're going to Mozambique."

"Mozambique? That's far down the coast. Are you going to fly me there?"

"No. I'm going to fly you out to a spot in the Rift Valley. Then Denys will pick you up and fly to Mozambique.

Someplace where you can get a train to Maputo—the main port. It's a Portuguese colony. No one will interfere with you."

Bedford remembered his schoolboy maps. Vast expanses of featureless wilderness. Long rivers. Mysterious place names. Darkest Africa.

"You said Denys was 'still learning' to fly."

"He can do it if anyone can. And then there's you to take over—eh, Great War flying ace?"

He stretched, aching in many places. "I wasn't an ace."

"Everything's prepared. Extra clothes. Food rations. Firearms. And Sloane's packed you a great wad of money. There's a sort of railway to the coast and from there you can take a steamer to Lisbon and then a liner to New York. You could be home in a fortnight."

How far away the bar at Chumley's seemed just then. "A fortnight."

"But we must leave now, before any of Jellicoe's constables turn up. Come on."

"What about Sloane?"

"Sloane has arranged everything. She wants desperately to rescue you from this. Now, dear boy, show your appreciation by cooperating with the general plan."

She went out the door, leaving it open. Breaks of light were visible through the trees. Bedford sat a long moment, envisioning a map of Africa—and the long, long journey that awaited him.

Perhaps not so long after all.

After a thorough washing up and a change into bush clothes, as requested, he had a quick breakfast of biscuits and tea. Then he walked with the baroness down to the open field where Beryl's Gypsy Moth awaited. Beryl had the engine cowling off, and was tinkering with some part of the machinery.

"Just climb aboard," she said. "Some creature got in here while I was waking you from your slumbers."

She quickly finished her task and put the cowling back in place. Bedford and the baroness embraced, he thanking her profusely; she expressing a strong desire to meet again. She stepped clear as Bedford made his way to the front cockpit. When comfortably seated, he commenced the starting ritual, with Beryl pulling the propeller.

The engine exploded into life with a great, chuffing cough. Bedford modulated the sound to a gentle sort of roar with the throttle, waiting for Beryl to climb into her seat and pull on her helmet and goggles. He did the same. With a thumbs-up and a waggle of the Moth's rudder, she gunned the engine and they bumped on down to the edge of the field, turning into the breeze. They exchanged waves with the baroness, who stood with her dogs at the top of the rise, then Beryl shoved the throttle to the wall. Like a gust-blown feather, they were quickly aloft.

INSTEAD of crossing the many farms and plantations that lay on this reach from Nairobi, Beryl set course due west until they were well over the Rift Valley, then she turned abruptly south.

An hour later, she began their descent. Bedford saw a small, irregular lake off to the left, with a large village on its farther shore. To the right were some small but jutting hills. Beryl steered closer to the lake. Sweeping low, she passed over a swath of trees, startling a herd of wildebeest on the other side. On the open plain beyond, Bedford took note of Finch-Hatton's aircraft.

BEDFORD waited until the prop had stopped, then left his seat and jumped off the lower wing of Beryl's plane, waiting for her to get out of her cockpit.

"You've gone to a lot of trouble," he said. "I am very grateful."

"You're a right enough chap, Bedford. We're all happy to see you out of this."

Finch-Hatton was standing by his plane. Bedford stopped about a hundred feet from it. Looking around, then south. "I'm going down there, am I?" he asked Beryl, pointing straight down the wide Rift Valley.

"As good as a highway, with plenty of landing places along the way—just in case."

The other pilot came up to them, smiling. "Right on schedule, Beryl. Are you ready to continue, Bedford?"

"Wouldn't mind a bit more to eat, and I think I'd best make prudent use of the bushes over there."

"I was going to recommend that," said Finch-Hatton.

Bedford nodded, and hefted his pack. When he returned, he found that Beryl had set out some biscuits and marmalade while the white hunter had poured out three tots of whiskey from his flask. Bedford wolfed down two biscuits, then raised his little tumbler. "To you two. May all your journeys be happy ones."

"May yours," said Finch-Hatton, raising his own vessel. Beryl did the same and they all drank.

"All right," she said. "I need to be back to Nairobi. Let's hop it."

She returned to her aircraft and climbed into her seat as Finch-Hatton went around front to attend to the propeller. While they dealt with that, Bedford moved to Finch-Hatton's airplane, stowed his gear, and climbed into the front cockpit. He'd leave it to Finch-Hatton to handle his own propeller.

Beryl's engine started, but she kept the throttle back,

sitting as she might upon a horse, waiting. Finch-Hatton
hurried back to his own aircraft, going directly to the front.

"Switch on," he said.

"Switch on," responded Bedford.

"Switch off."

"Switch off."

The engine caught, and Finch-Hatton leapt back. Bedford waiting until he was darting around the wing, then
shoved the throttle all the way forward. The Englishman
stood dumbfounded at first, then realizing what was afoot,
flung himself after the rolling airplane—but far too late.

He flew north about five miles, then set the biplane
down in a soft, pretty meadow, leaving the engine
kicking while he consulted the map Finch-Hatton kept in
a cockpit side-pocket. As he had hoped, various hunting
campsites were marked upon it, including the one where
Finch-Hatton had taken His Royal Highness. It was not
far.

He found it fairly easily and, after a couple of circuits
around it, located the stream that Beryl had used for
her landing approach and finally the little field where
she had set down her Moth. Bedford had no interest in
attempting that feat, however, or in putting the aircraft
that close to his destination. Instead, he turned to the
north, finding a sandy plain about three miles off the watercourse and setting the DeHavilland down less than
gently.

Using rocks to secure the tie-downs, and placing two
others against the landing wheels, he set off on foot.

HE reached the grove of trees about midafternoon. Setting down his pack, he went to the little clearing where the bodies had been found. All seemed as it had been when he last looked upon this disturbed earth, but he knew very well that second, third, and even fourth looks always yielded something new.

Walking slowly around the spot, he paused several times, hunching down and sighting across the ground. Completing the circle, he dug at the roughened dirt in the middle with the toe of his shoe, then walked back to his pack. Leaning against a tree, he had lunch, gazing all the while at the murder scene and munching on thoughts as much as he did his ham sandwich.

Finally, he got to work, starting with the trees closest to the clearing, then working his way out. He found what he sought about two hours later. He carried a small pocketknife in habit. This was the first time on this African trek he'd found use for it.

MZIZI did not show up until early the next morning, creeping through the trees silently in the gloomy gray light of dawn. Bedford had awakened to attend to the needs of nature and had been about to return to sleep, but fortuitously thought better of it.

He watched and waited, wondering how long it would take the African to apprehend the true situation. As it turned out, it wasn't long at all. Mzizi bent down to examine something in the clearing—doubtless one of Bedford's fresh footprints. He rose and turned slowly until he was looking directly at Bedford.

"Good morning," Bedford said.

The African swiftly came forward, short spear in hand. *"Gute Morgen, Herr Green. Warum—"*

"We needn't German now, Mzizi. Let us speak English."

The African squatted. "You ask me to come here. Why do you come here?"

"To meet you, of course. We have much to do." He reached into his pocket, displaying an object. "I have, however, already located what I wanted you to find."

CHAPTER 23

BEDFORD asked Mzizi to find someone with a reliable vehicle and hire him for a week. The result was a tall black man named Isaiah and a decrepit Ford Model T truck with American left-hand steering. The front seat was open to the elements but for the large windshield and a bit of canvas roof. The rear cargo area was completely enclosed in canvas, which could be rolled up on the sides and rear and secured with leather straps. There were two spare tires and a rifle rack above the back of the front seat.

Isaiah said the vehicle had belonged to an American missionary but did not explain why it no longer did. Bedford didn't ask. There were still a few cloth-covered Bibles in the rear.

Stopping at a small general store at a crossroads near Oltepesi, Bedford acquired a hat and rode with it pulled down low over his face, letting Isaiah drive. When they reached a curve in the road by a grove of trees at the edge of the Ralls plantation, he bade the African to stop.

Then he and Mzizi walked up the road a bit, until the

hilltop house was distantly in view. "You said she threw the pistol under a bush?" Bedford asked.

"Yes. Under a bush."

"Could you find it again?"

"Now?" Mzizi asked.

Bedford nodded. "It's one of the reasons we've come."

The African looked up at the bright sky. "Maybe it will be gone."

"You said the woman you saw on the veranda that night had dark hair and was wearing clothes."

"Yes."

"If the gun is still there, that will tell me something. If it is no longer there, that will tell me something, too."

Mzizi looked toward the hilltop. "What will it tell you?"

"That I know less about all this than I think."

The tracker studied the approach, as might an advancing general. "What will it tell you if I find the pistol?"

He thought upon this. "That I should think better of someone than I do."

THEY parked the truck behind a thickness of trees just off the Rallses' property line. Leaving Isaiah to keep watch, Bedford lay down on the ground on his back, propping his hat over his face. He would have to take sleep as occasion permitted.

A long while later, Mzizi shook him. Removing the hat, Bedford saw first the gun—a small revolver of possibly .32 caliber, which Mzizi held with the barrel aimed at Bedford's face.

"You found it."

Mzizi nodded. "Under the bush. Where I saw it go."

"What took you so long?"

"The lady was on the veranda."

Bedford gingerly took the weapon from the man's hand and held it before his own eyes, shaking out the cylinder. All but one round had been fired.

He sat up. "Did she see you?"

"No one saw me."

Bedford put the revolver in his pocket. "We'll go into Nairobi."

"Now?"

Bedford lay down again. "No. When it's dark."

THERE was an Indian restaurant of sorts in Nairobi—in a mud-walled building with a corrugated iron roof like so many in the town. The neighborhood was uncomfortably near the Central Police Station, but Bedford figured that was to his advantage.

Having left Isaiah with the truck and having sent Mzizi off to find Mr. Asif, he took a table in a dark, rear corner and waited. As the establishment did not serve alcohol, he drank tea.

Three cups of tea later, Asif entered in a sweaty rush, looking furtively over both shoulders before pulling out a chair and seating himself.

"All of Nairobi is talking about you, Captain Green. They say you took Mr. Finch-Hatton's airplane at gunpoint and flew off into the Serengeti. They have military planes out looking for you."

"What military planes?"

"Mr. Van Gelder's and Miss Markham's—with military officers on board."

"Mrs. Markham is flying?"

"Yes."

"And they went south to the Serengeti?"

"Yes."

Bedford smiled. She was still on his side—after a fashion. "Mr. Asif, I shall need you to perform some more good offices. First of all, I should like you to ascertain the whereabouts of Captain Owen and his associate, Mr. Grubb."

"How am I to do that?"

"Go to the Muthaiga Club where Owen resides and inquire. Tell them it's court business."

Asif took a dirty envelope from his coat pocket and wrote down the instruction. "Anything else?"

"Meet me about midnight at Mr. Sim's bank."

"But it will be closed."

"Precisely."

"What are you going to do, Captain Green?"

"Break in."

"But that's a crime."

"I'm a wanted criminal."

"But I am not, Captain Green. I am a barrister. I would be removed from the bar."

"Very well. I'll rely on Mzizi and Isaiah."

"As what?"

"A lookout and a wheel man."

Asif became exceedingly furtive. "May I go now?"

"Certainly. And, if you could, would you meet me by the cattle yards in the morning?"

"Will you be dressed like this?"

"I'll find you."

"I may have cases in the morning."

"Really. Do you have any cases pending?"

"Not many."

"Why is that?"

"I don't know. Not many crimes being committed of late—except for yours, Captain Green."

"Perhaps they're just not being prosecuted."

"Whatever do you mean?"

"Let's have dinner, Mr. Asif."

THE curry had been generously served and was excessively spicy. Two hours after leaving the restaurant Bedford could still taste every particle of his meal. A splash of whiskey would help. There would be an abundance of that at his next destination.

Dixon was not in the bar of the Old Stanley. At so late an hour, Bedford did not expect him to be wandering the streets of so dangerous a city. He guessed the Chicagoan would most likely be drinking in his room, or perhaps just sleeping.

Bedford stood outside, studying the hotel's facade. There were lights on in only seven rooms. Sloane had told him Dixon had a suite on the second floor. He noted illuminated windows at the corner.

He went into the Stanley's large, airy lobby, taking a seat and picking up a day-old newspaper, pausing to look at his watch before starting to read in earnest.

The desk clerk observed him for a minute or two, then returned to his duties. After a time, Bedford asked for directions to the gentleman's toilet. When he was done, he turned up the stairs.

Smith took his time coming to the door. His appearance was worse than when he'd been in his cell.

"Have you been in this room all day?" Bedford asked.

"No," said Smith, closing the door after Bedford had stepped inside. "I went down once to eat."

"Not the Casino Club."

"No sirree." Smith returned to his armchair, nodding to the bottle of scotch on the table. "Why are you still in Nairobi?"

"Doing what you asked me to do." He took a seat on a wicker divan opposite, reaching to pour himself a drink.

"How did you escape?"

"Your niece, I think, had a hand in it—along with half of British East Africa."

Dixon sipped. "They want you out of here."

"Well, things didn't go according to plan."

There was only one lamp on in the room. Bedford wondered if he could be seen from the street, and moved to the other end of the divan, turning his back to the window.

"Were you unable to get away from Nairobi?" Smith asked.

"No. I came back. Unfinished business."

"So you have escaped twice," Smith said. "Once from your captors, and once from your rescuers."

"The former was easier than the latter."

"But you are still in Kenya. You said you'd help me so you could get out of jail. Now you're out of jail. You had a chance to be out of Africa. Why are you still here?"

"Overactive curiosity. It's one of my faults."

"You're going to help me no matter what."

"I'm going to see this through—for a variety of reasons, but your concerns are among them. You can help me—if you don't mind talking about recent unpleasantnesses."

Dixon waved his hand. "Anything."

"When did Lord Ralls first take a romantic interest in your, uh, late wife?"

An unhappy smile. "The night before the murder."

"Do you have any idea what prompted this sudden yearning?"

A shake of the head. "It took me by surprise. He spent a long time with the Prince of Wales, then came out of the tent and took Georgia away."

"Why do you suppose that was?"

"I think she was beginning to annoy the prince. She was too—attentive, perhaps." He struggled with a thought. "You're not suggesting that Ralls was carrying out some royal order?"

"That sort of thing went out with Queen Victoria." Bedford took out a piece of paper, and carefully printed out a message, as though on a telegram form. "I'd like you to send this as a cable to London." He handed it over.

"Lady Furness?"

"She's a good friend."

"You move in high circles for an art dealer, Mr. Green."

"The relationship dates back to my time as a newspaper columnist. Newsies move in all circles."

This seemed to strike Smith as an absurdity and an affront to his provincial Midwestern social sensibilities, but he didn't press the issue. "I'll do it. Is there anything else?"

"I was going to ask you to help me break into a bank, but—no offense—I fear you've been enjoying your refreshment to the point where you're usefulness as an accomplice has been seriously compromised."

"I won't argue with you about that. But I wouldn't assist you in anything like that, anyway."

A bank robbery charge might get one tossed out of the Casino Club.

Bedford finished his drink and stood up, keeping his back to the window. "There's one more thing. You must get Sloane and your ex-wife out of British East Africa as soon as possible."

Smith shook his head. "I can't find Sloane. But it doesn't matter. They said they won't leave until I do."

"Precisely."

"You want me to leave Africa?"

"As fast as you can. We're dealing with murderers here, Mr. Smith. I daresay people as ruthless as your charming Mr. Capone. You were useful as a scapegoat to be blamed for everything, but now I've assumed that role. It's going to be a bit dangerous here—at least around me."

"I'm not going to run out on this."

"That's very noble. But what about Sloane and Kate? They've gone a long extra mile for you."

Smith stared sorrowfully at the floor. "I know."

"You care for Sloane. That's clear. What about Kate?"

"It's complicated. I'm very fond of her. But . . . not like Georgia."

Bedford started toward the door. "Think of Sloane, Mr. Smith. Please. Book passage. Get out of here. I'll take care of the rest."

"I'll talk to Sloane. That's all I can promise you."

BEDFORD left Isaiah with the truck, which he had parked by a church a block from Sim's bank. "Wait for me, no matter what."

"Yes sir, Captain Green."

"You know the police are looking for me?"

"Yes sir. Mzizi tell me this."

"That doesn't bother you?"

"You are paying me five pounds. The police are not paying me anything."

Bedford shook his hand. "Thank you. I'll try not to take long."

He and Mzizi came up on the bank building from the rear, turning into a narrow alley that ran beside it. He was certain there would be an alarm at the vault and other areas where cash and securities were kept. But he was hopeful that the doors and windows had no such protection. If they did, he'd have to beat a hasty retreat.

His police detective friends in New York had taught him a number of interesting skills, and one of these was the ability to pick locks. He had no doubt he could manage the bank's front door, but that faced a well-lit street and a public square beyond. A high side window offered a much better prospect.

"Can you bark like a dog?" Bedford asked Mzizi.

The question did not faze the man. "I can make many sounds."

"I just need barks. Very sharp and very loud. Many of them. I'll tell you when."

"I will bark."

"Thank you. Very good. Now, sir, if you would please lend me your spear."

He got a grip on the windowsill with his left hand, taking Mzizi's weapon with the other. After a look up and down the alley, he decided to get on with it. "Okay. Bark now."

Mzizi was remarkably good at this bestial mimicry. Bedford had shattered two panes before the noise ceased. For a moment, he thought there were incredible echoes, until he realized that Mzizi had set all the dogs in the neighborhood to barking in response.

Bedford locked his hands together. "Can you do this? I need a boost up."

Mzizi linked his fingers and held both hands out like a stirrup. "Okay?"

"Okay."

"You do not want me to come inside, too?"

"No. Go up by the street. If you see anyone coming, start barking again—even louder."

Mzizi responded with a single bark.

THE sash slid up without setting off anything. Crawling through it, Bedford landed on the hard wooden floor of a small office, knocking over a chair. Getting to his feet, he rubbed the pain from his elbow and took out a small electric torch, playing its light over the desk that sat in the center of the room.

It belonged to Sim, but yielded little of interest except for a small ledger book, which proved to be Sim's personal accounting of a variety of loans, mortgages, and notes. He was distressed to see that the baroness was quite deeply in debt.

He was wasting time. What he needed to see would be found in one of the long row of filing cabinets along the wall of the main room of the bank.

Happily, the drawers were merely locked, and not linked to any alarm. The files were arranged alphabetically. There was one for Victoria Ralls's account, its contents reflecting regular transfers from a London bank of small sums—her trust fund, no doubt. If Lord Ralls had an account here, there was no sign of it.

A motor vehicle of some sort came chuffing by. Bedford ducked down, clicking off the torch, until it had passed.

He went through the drawer again, thinking the file might have been misplaced. But there was nothing. Unless Dickie Ralls had an account elsewhere, he was keeping all his cash in that interesting box at his house.

Or his file had been taken from this drawer.

Bedford's appetite had been whetted. He started moving down the row of cabinets but abruptly halted at the sound of frantic barking coming from the alley. He had to calculate all time now in seconds. Moving down to the next cabinet he sought, he quickly opened it and plucked out a file, clutching it tight.

Another round of barking.

He'd waited too long. There was a light playing about the front door. Crouching down, he hurried back to Sim's office. As he prepared to drop from the window, he heard voices behind him. He twisted his ankle upon hitting the ground, but kept moving.

CHAPTER 24

MR. Asif was not at the cattle yard. Bedford, dressed in khaki, lingered in the area as long as he dared, but one of the African workers there began to take note of him, and so he beat a retreat to the back of the Model T, which he'd left by a warehouse near the railway station. He returned to the yard perhaps half an hour later, and then one more time after that, all with the same result. The Indian barrister was not to be found.

"Shall we go to his house, Captain Green?"

"Not yet, Mzizi. We go to Alice de Janze's house."

BEDFORD drove right up to the front door of the place. A small horde of servants quickly surrounded the truck, opening both doors and generally treating Bedford and his associates as a conquered land might a conquering general.

Alice was not so well disposed. It was well into a hot afternoon but she appeared to have only just arisen. Her eyes kept blinking as she looked upon him, as though he were an apparition.

"I'm looking for Sloane," Bedford said. "It's time for us all to leave Kenya, but I can't find her."

"She's gone."

"Where?"

"Hunting."

"She wouldn't go hunting. That's crazy."

"They've both gone hunting. Her Aunt Kate has gone hunting, and Sloane has gone with her."

Alice was wearing a dressing gown. She clasped hands at her front, and kept clenching them. She looked about— as though she had allies at hand who would come to help her.

Mzizi, short spear in hand, took a step forward.

"What do you want of me?" Alice said, retreating. "Did you come here to kill me? Lions. People. Lions. You are a beast, Bedford Green."

"Where did Sloane go?"

"Into the Rift Valley. Kate wanted to see Kilimanjaro."

"Kilimanjaro is east of the Rift Valley."

"Well, that's where they went. Go away."

"Sloane didn't say when she'd return?"

"Soon. That's all I know."

"With whom did she go?"

"Captain Owen. And his Africans."

"Was Grubb with them?"

"I don't know any Grubb."

Alice appeared now to be as uncomfortable as she might be if she were crawling with ants. Bedford's reservoir of sympathy for her was low. He took the small revolver from his pocket.

"Here," he said, watching her sharply. "You left this."

She let it drop from her hand, and then screamed.

Bedford hurried away from the house, loping for the truck.

"We need to get away from here," he said.

"Okay. Jolly good," said Isaiah.

"And we must acquire a different vehicle than this truck."

BEDFORD sent Isaiah into Nairobi to get rid of the truck while he and Mzizi waited in some woods behind the racetrack. They'd no idea when Isaiah would return, if at all.

"How did you come to work for Owen?" Bedford asked. "You said you were a sergeant in the German army."

"The English became the bosses. Owen is English."

"But why did he want to hire you—a German?"

"I am the best tracker in East Africa."

Bedford certainly had no reason to doubt that. "And why are you sticking with me?"

"You pay well. And you are different. You treat me like a man, not a tracker."

A small group of Africans was walking toward Nairobi along the road below. "Are those Masai?" Bedford asked.

"Yes. Not Kikiyu."

"That robe the woman is wearing. Do you suppose you could get me one of those?"

"*Ja. Ich kann.* But not hers. They would fight me, those two men with her."

Bedford dug six shillings out of his pocket. "Try these. Buy it."

"What will you do with it?"

"Wear it—when the times comes."

"What time is that?"

"We're going to the Muthaiga Club. As soon as it gets dark."

THEY loitered near the kitchen entrance to the club until the Africans working within had quieted down—signifying, Bedford hoped, that they were done with the evening servings of supper. When it was clear that the chatter and bustle was not going to resume, Bedford motioned to Mzizi and they crept forward.

Most of the members Bedford had encountered here had the English habit of ignoring their servants unless they had committed some transgression. Except for the baroness and Beryl, they seldom looked the Africans in the face. He counted on that now as they slipped inside.

There was the usual revelry going on in what Bedford assumed was the main lounge, but that was far down the central corridor. He and Mzizi were bound elsewhere. Taking up a bucket and mop from the kitchen pantry, pulling the cowl of the robe far over his head, Bedford started toward his goal.

Turning a corner and going up a short flight of stairs, they encountered a drunken man and woman in evening clothes, pawing at each other in a clumsy embrace against the wall. Bedford moved quickly past them. As he had hoped, he and Mzizi were completely ignored.

He went on past Owen's room, turning another corner. Peering around it, he watched as the drunken man bared one of his lady friend's breasts and pressed his face against it. A few minutes later, they noisily entered one of the rooms.

Bedford quickly returned to Owen's door, handing Mzizi the bucket and mop.

"You pretend to be working here. I'm going to look inside."

"What are you looking for?"

"Whatever I can find."

"How can you go in? It is locked. It will make great noise to break in."

Bedford took out his small pocketknife. "Not if you have certain magical powers."

OWEN kept an orderly place. Like his hunting camps, everything was where it belonged. This was true of his desk drawers, and the business records he kept therein.

He had account books with entries for payments and expenses relating to every safari. The one for the safaris that year was on top. Bedford thumbed through it, finding a listing for the Smiths and himself and the cost they had run up. Sloane's uncle had spent a fortune on their tragic adventure.

After looking through a few more pages, Bedford set the book aside. The rest of his search produced nothing of interest.

MZIZI appeared quite distressed, as Bedford had never seen him before. "You don't like it in here, do you?" Bedford asked.

"We must leave now. Two Englishmen came by when you were in there. They gave me bad look."

"Did you pretend to be cleaning?"

"I stood by the bucket."

"All right. Let's go." Bedford pulled the cowl over his head again.

"What do you find in Captain Owen's room?" Mzizi asked when they were outside in the shadows again.

"Just account books."

"Account books?"

"Showing how much money came in and how much Owen spent on each hunt. He had quite a few."

"Did you take them?"

"One. He didn't pay you very much, did he?"

"Half what you pay me. I am grateful, Captain Green."

"I don't intend to remain in Kenya forever, Mzizi. You will have to find yourself other employment."

"Maybe I will go back to Tanganyika."

"Not yet."

"Where do we go now?"

"We go to Mr. Asif's house."

T HE door was unlocked, and opened to the touch. Bedford was about to call out Mr. Asif's name when an unaccustomed sound compelled him to keep his silence.

Flies—buzzing in the darkness in the middle of the night.

He put a finger to his lips for Mzizi to see—perhaps unnecessarily, for the Masai always moved in silence—then pushed the door open all the way.

The lawyer was sprawled on his sofa, one arm flung to the side. There was little light, but it appeared to Bedford that the man was widely grinning—until he realized it was a second mouth he was looking at, one that had been cut across the Indian's throat. A dark stain had spread across his shirt and the lapels of his white suit.

Mzizi went quietly past him to the next room, his short spear in hand. Bedford stood unable to move, gripped by the inescapable conviction that Mr. Asif's death was entirely his fault. What was not clear was what it was supposed to have achieved.

There was a muffled sound from the next room, and then an anguished cry. Bedford still had the revolver that had been provided him for his escape and brought it to hand. He took a step forward.

"Mzizi?"

It was a white man who appeared at the doorway, clutching at his chest.

"Grubb!"

The other made a horrible gurgling sound, then collapsed. Mzizi emerged from the gloom and stood over him, as he might a kill in the bush. Satisfied that Grubb had left this life, he reached down and pulled out his spear.

Bedford tried to calm his rapid breathing.

"He was waiting," Mzizi said. "He was going to kill you." He wiped the blade clean on Grubb's shirt.

"Perhaps he was."

There was a noise at the front door. Bedford turned around, aiming the revolver without waiting to see who the intruder might be. The fellow took note of the two living and the two dead men and leapt back, pulling the door after him.

Bedford moved now, catching the edge of the door before it closed and flinging it open as he rushed out into the courtyard. His visitor was crashing through bushes on the other side of the wall.

"It was Truscott," Mzizi said.

CHAPTER 25

BEDFORD had no more idea where Truscott would go than he might where a startled rat might skitter in the back alley on the waterfront. Unable to think of anywhere else, he decided to head for the airfield, waking up a taxi driver parked in front of the Old Stanley.

There was absolutely no activity of any kind when they got to the field. Bedford decided he'd made a very bad guess. Then he heard the faint drone of an airplane engine off to the southwest. Squinting, Bedford thought he could make out the tiny pinpoint of light of the exhaust against the night sky.

"Is that Truscott?" Mzizi asked.

"I don't know who else would be up there at this moment."

"How can he fly if he cannot see the ground? How can he land?"

"Someone could light flares for him." Bedford looked to the paler sky to the east. "It'll likely be daylight by the time he gets where he's going."

"Going where?"

"Down toward Kilimanjaro, I expect. As Alice de Janze' said."

Mzizi considered this. "Where will you go?"

"Down toward Kilimanjaro."

"How?"

"I will fly."

Bedford looked down the line of aircraft. Beryl's was there, but he did not want to impose upon her any more than he so egregiously already had.

He would take Van Gelder's machine. The man had it coming, if only for the near miss he'd been responsible for the day Bedford had flown an inside loop. "Come along, if you would, Mzizi."

"I don't want to fly."

"If you're coming with me, you will have to."

"I do not fly."

"If you stay here, the police will come after you. They have trackers, too, you know. They'll find you. By flying with me, you can go far, far away without their being able to track you."

"It is not safe."

"Of course it's safe. I flew airplanes all through the war, and here I am before you."

"You never fell down?"

"Only once or twice."

The Masai stood implacably.

"I was a warrior," Bedford continued. "I fought as a warrior in the sky. You are a warrior, Mzizi. You were a sergeant in the German army, a brave man. Surely so brave a man would have no fear about flying in the sky with a fellow warrior—however less than formidable I may appear to you now."

Mzizi looked up at the sky, then back to Bedford. "I will go with you."

"Splendid." Bedford started toward Van Gelder's red machine.

"Why are you going down toward Kilimanjaro?"
"To find some friends."

THERE was just enough light to discern the boundaries of the big field next to the baroness's house. Bedford could not tell the direction of the wind. It had been from the southeast in Nairobi, but the baroness's farm was at a much higher elevation.

He'd been drifting a little to the left on the short flight from the airfield. He guessed the wind was blowing from the northeast. Reducing power to begin his descent, he aimed the aircraft for an approach toward the western edge of the field.

As it turned out, the wind was changeable, shifting around to northwesterly just as Bedford was about to touch down. Blowing strong for a moment, it lifted the left wing.

Bedford threw the stick over and kicked in the left rudder. This made the airplane drop like a rock and bounce, but the threatened ground loop was averted.

"You make the airplane fall," Mzizi said, after the prop had stopped.

"Only a little."

The baroness's dogs had come bounding out of the house. As he climbed out of the cockpit, Bedford hoped their memories of him would be friendly ones.

They remained excited. One nearly knocked him down as it stood on hind legs and put paws on his chest. But otherwise he and Mzizi were not molested.

The other residents of the place were less amiable. The baroness and Finch-Hatton were on the veranda, the latter cradling a hunting rifle in his right arm. Beryl, wearing pajamas, appeared a moment later.

"Good morning," said Bedford, as cheerily as he could manage.

Finch-Hatton studied the aircraft in the dim early light. "Van Gelder's?"

"Yes."

"Has stealing airplanes become your new profession?"

"The main reason I stopped by was to tell you where you can find yours."

"I'm already in possession of that knowledge, Captain Green. Beryl found it. You unfortunately cracked one of the landing gear struts. We were going back today to repair it."

"My apologies. I'll see you're compensated."

"The courts will see to it as well. I'm afraid I've filed a criminal complaint. Didn't know how else to get my airplane back, old boy. The Nairobi police are doubtless looking for you."

"I'm sure they are." Bedford came a step closer. "There's trouble. There've been more killings."

"Where?" the baroness asked.

"In Nairobi. Mr. Asif the lawyer. And Grubb, Owen's man."

"What happened?" said Beryl.

"I'm not altogether certain. But whoever did it seemed to be acting from a pressing need." Bedford kept his eyes from Mzizi.

"This is just bloody amazing," said Beryl. "Why have you come back? I think the good people of Nairobi would rather have von Lettow-Vorbeck return."

"I'm on my way to find Owen's camp. He's taken Sloane and her aunt down to see Kilimanjaro. I need to talk to them. And him."

"Kilimanjaro's down in Tanganyika," Beryl said. "Just across the border. Have you petrol enough?"

"I've no idea."

"Perhaps we can help you out with that," the baroness said.

"That's very kind of you. And unexpected."

"Come in and let us give you something to eat," she said. "And coffee."

"I was hoping you might be able to give me some idea where Owen might be."

Beryl let her irritation drop. "That's easy enough. I'm sure he's somewhere down by Lake Amboseli. It's a big salt lake just on the Kenyan side of the border—and due south of Nairobi. A lot of white hunters take their clients there. Wizard views of Kilimanjaro."

They all sat down at the baroness's table, except Mzizi, who stood quietly in a corner. The baroness nodded to her servant to feed him as well.

Bedford ate quickly. "I suggest you report my visit to Inspector Jellicoe. With my escape and two more corpses on his blotter, he'll be compelled to act a little more resolutely. You don't want him throwing you in one of his cells as accomplices."

"That's not necessary," said the baroness. "We can let the good inspector bumble about here without our help. After you conclude your business, you'll need to get out of the colony—which I strongly recommend you do this time."

"Actually," said Bedford, finishing his coffee, "I'd be grateful if you would summon the inspector—and tell him where I've gone."

"But why?"

"It's time for the end of the story." He stood up. At the door, he paused. "If it's no imposition, I'd be very appreciative if you would inform Lord Delamere as well—and tell him I'd like an audience with him, when I return to Nairobi, doubtless in the company of the police."

"You can't mean that," Beryl said.

"It's for the best," Bedford said.

He flew back over Nairobi to be sure of his bearings, then headed due south, crossing the three tributaries of the Athi River and then over the Kaputiei Plains beyond, steering for the Maparasha Hills. Once he reached them, he bore left, following the ridge to the Olkeju Adu River, as Beryl had instructed, and from that watercourse to the Amboseli. It was the dry season, and there was less to the lake than there might have been. But it was an extraordinarily beautiful place, nonetheless—its northern shallows crowded with flamingos, and all manner of other creatures gathered along its shoreline.

In the distance, the great snow-capped mountain rose as an almost mystical splendor.

He flew toward it for a few minutes, as though drawn by a magic spell. Then he dropped low and began a slow aerial perambulation of the lake, following the western edge. He passed over two hunting camps but neither had an airplane in sight. Turning over the narrows at the south end of the lake, he headed east and came upon Truscott's airplane shortly thereafter. It had been hauled into some brush, but the blue was brightly visible.

Bedford continued in the same direction. Something more than a mile or two farther, he spotted tents. Flying low over the camp, he saw a few dark-skinned figures and at least one white man, but no women.

Bedford landed a mile or more to the north, on salt flats left by the retreating waters of the drying lake. It was as gentle a touchdown as he'd made as a pilot, in marked contrast to the clumsy one that had injured Finch-Hatton's landing gear.

"Now what we do?" Mzizi said.

"We go off into the trees over there and eat a little and sleep."

"You don't go to Captain Owen's camp?"

"When it's dark."

"Can you find your way?"

"You'll come with me, Mzizi."

THE baroness had loaned Bedford a Remington .375 just before they'd left her farm and he had found another hunting rifle in Van Gelder's plane. He had his own revolver as well, and Mzizi still carried the short spear. Whatever awaited them at Owen's camp, they would face it well armed.

Before starting out at sunset, Bedford divided the water and provisions and gave Mzizi Van Gelder's weapon, a Mannlicher-Schonauer big game rifle, which, like Bedford's, had a sling.

"What must I do with this?" he asked.

"Prepare for a sudden need to use it. But with a care not to injure Miss Smith or her aunt."

"This could mean much trouble for me."

"That didn't bother you when you took on Grubb."

"No, but now I fear trouble."

"I'll take care of it."

"You are in trouble, too, Captain Green."

"Just have that rifle handy when we go in there. You carried a rifle when you were a sergeant in the German army, didn't you?"

"Yes. I killed many English."

"We'll hope that won't be necessary."

They followed the shoreline south—an easy trail with the water level so low. Animals were coming down to drink, some of them large, making fearful noises, but nothing so dangerous as a lion. Bedford was relying on Mzizi to warn him if one approached, but the African seemed much preoccupied. He walked somewhat less than ramrod straight now, staring ahead, speaking little.

CHAPTER 26

OWEN'S campfire was visible at a great distance, lying just inland from the lake. They continued along the shoreline until Bedford could make out individual figures. Then he moved into the brush, motioning to Mzizi to follow.

"Do you remember doing flanking movements in the German army?" he said, speaking softly, as the Masai knelt beside him.

"What we did most they call 'retrograde' movement. But when von Lettow-Vorbeck attacked, it was always flanking movements."

"We're going to perform one now," Bedford said. "I'd like you to circle around to the other side of the camp and wait just outside the firelight."

"Wait for what?"

"I'm going to walk into the camp. When I call out your name, I'd like you to come in from the other side, holding that rifle ready to fire."

"I worked for Captain Owen."

"Yes, but he sacked you. And sent you to work for me. I'm paying you now."

"I don't want to kill Captain Owen because he sacked me."

Bedford put his hand on the man's hard shoulder. It was like touching leather-covered rock. "I don't want you to kill Owen for any reason. It's my hope that your fearsome presence will prevent any such violence."

Mzizi looked to the campfire. "Why do you not now go back, Captain Green? Then nobody get hurt."

"I can't leave Miss Smith and her aunt here. I fear they may get hurt."

"Take them with you."

"I can't do that just yet. Truscott must be turned over to the police. And I wish to talk to Captain Owen about the murder of Lord Ralls. I don't intend to leave British East Africa as a fugitive."

The African's gaze continued fixed on the camp. All at once, he removed Bedford's hand from his shoulder and stood up, disappearing soundlessly into the bushes. Bedford waited several minutes, then rose and began a careful walk toward the campfire. He kept his rifle slung over his shoulder, but put his revolver in his belt where he could reach it easily.

Someone was playing a phonograph record—a jazz tune—muffling the sound of his approach. When he stepped into the circle of light, he took everyone by surprise.

Sloane and her Aunt Kate were seated side by side in canvas chairs. Owen was nearby, cleaning a rifle next to a camp table. He was the first to take note of Bedford's presence.

"Good God! Green, can that be you?"

"Captain Owen, I presume."

Sloane was as stunned as he'd ever seen her. "Bedford!

You're supposed to be out of the country! On your way to New York. Why are you here?"

There wasn't an available chair, so Bedford seated himself on a wooden crate that was lying nearby, laying the Remington on it with the barrel pointing toward the fire—and Owen.

He could see three of Owen's African assistants hunkered down by one of the tents. Owen's car and truck were just behind.

"I've come to fetch you back," Bedford said to Sloane, "so we can all leave Kenya—together."

"But Uncle Dixon won't go," Sloane said.

"He's been very stubborn about it," said Aunt Kate. "We gave up waiting on him and came down here. I wanted to see Kilimanjaro before we left."

"Took them partway up," said Owen.

"I'm obliged to you then."

"For what, sir?"

"For bringing them down again."

Owen undid a button of his jacket and scratched his chest. "What do you mean by that, Green? How did you get here?"

"By airplane."

"That was you?"

"Yes."

"You flew down here—found this place—all by yourself?"

"A skill I picked up in the war."

Owen took out his pipe and filled it with tobacco. Striking a match, he lighted it with three puffs, the smoke obscuring his expression. "And all you want is to take these ladies home? We're leaving for Nairobi in the morning, you know."

"We are, Bedford," said Sloane. "You can come with us."

"Yes," said Kate, gracious as ever. "I should like that very much."

He smiled politely in return. "Unfortunately there's the little matter of murder to be cleared up. Otherwise, I can count on being clapped back into prison the moment we return."

"What about that airplane?" Owen asked. "You're not leaving that here, are you?"

"It belongs to Mr. Van Gelder. I'll let him know where it is."

"Hell, Green, you're going to prison no matter what."

"Maybe, but I'll deal with the murderer first."

Bedford wondered if Mzizi was growing impatient out there in the darkness. The man was a hunter, who might spend hours waiting motionless for his prey to appear. But Mzizi had been most unhappy about coming here.

"The last I heard, the police were quite convinced they had jolly well cleared up Lord Ralls's murder," Owen said, "when they arrested you."

"They're in error, as I intend to show them. Where is Mr. Grubb? How are you managing without him?"

"Don't know where in hell he's gone to. Didn't show up when it came time to depart."

"That's odd. He wasn't killed until last night."

"Killed?" Owen set down his whiskey glass. "Grubb is dead?"

Bedford decided to gloss over a few details, leaving them to Owen to guess at. "We found him at Mr. Asif's house. You remember my lawyer? The Indian gentleman?"

"He came around the club, asking about me."

"The poor man's throat was cut."

"What are you talking about?"

"And his legal files were tossed. Including my file."

"Tossed?"

"Gone through. Searched. Someone has taken a considerable interest in my case."

"Now you'll be charged with four killings."

"I don't think so, Owen. We also found the pilot Truscott on the premises. He is not dead. He ran off, and flew down here."

"How would you know that?"

"His aircraft is on the ground not far from here."

"Well, he's not come around us—has he ladies?"

Aunt Kate's face had gone blank. Sloane appeared stricken. "Mr. Asif is dead?"

"As dead as the dead in the war."

"I don't understand," she said. Her eyes were glistening. "Why? Who could he have harmed?"

"He was a criminal lawyer. He'd become aware of some criminal activity. My guess is that his assailant thought Mr. Asif might have acquired some evidence of it."

"And had he?" Owen asked. "He was your barrister, as I recall."

"He had not," Bedford said, bringing forth his words slowly and carefully. "But he'd been in contact with someone who's accumulated quite a lot."

"And that person would be?"

"Me," Bedford said.

They stared at each other like animals fixed on the same prey, only they were each other's prey. He moved his hand a few inches closer on the crate to the rifle. He had put a bullet into the chamber before entering Owen's camp.

He was feeling fairly stupid now. His fellow Royal Flying Corps pilot from the war, Liam O'Bannion, would have handled this situation much differently—by his light, much more sensibly. He'd have moved on the camp on the quiet, identified everyone who might be a threat to him, and shot them all dead.

Liam, logically, had become a bootlegging New York gangster. Bedford had avoided that path.

And would again.

"Mzizi!" he called.

Owen snapped his head around. A moment later, Mzizi emerged from the shadows, holding his rifle at the ready, but with the barrel pointed down. His spear was in a sling on his back.

The white hunter returned his attention to Bedford—as if Mzizi were of no more interest to him than a wild bird that had happened by. "I think I'd like you to be a bit more direct."

"I think you know precisely what this is about."

Owen had somehow gotten a revolver into his hand. He held it next to his leg, but without aiming it.

"Well then," Owen said, "why don't you tell me what you intend to do about this criminal information you've acquired."

The heat from the campfire now seemed quite intense. Sweat was running down Bedford's neck into his shirt collar. Mzizi was absolutely motionless, somehow watching both Owen and Bedford, his rifle still pointed down.

"The police have by now been informed of where I've gone to. I intend to wait for them."

"Bedford, what're you talking about? What's going on?" Sloane stood up.

"Sit down!" Owen barked. He brought his revolver up, aiming it toward the two women. Kate reached and gripped Sloane's arm, pulling her back down.

Bedford looked to Mzizi, but the African ignored him. Sloane's eyes were silently imploring Bedford to put an end to this.

He should have simply sent Mzizi into the camp with a message for Sloane to wait until everyone had retired for the night, and then flee with her aunt and run to Bedford on the lakeshore.

But there was no guarantee she would have done that.

Owen's three Africans had gotten to their feet. They did

not appear to be armed, but they undoubtedly knew where arms could quickly be found.

"We don't have to conclude matters this way," Bedford said. He was still sweating, but his skin now had turned cold.

"I think we do," said Owen, the revolver still pointed at the women. "I think it's best."

Bedford had his hand around the rifle, his index finger inside the trigger guard. It was quite a heavy weapon. He would need both hands on it to fire.

"Mzizi?" he said.

The Masai neither spoke nor moved.

"Jezt, mein freund! Wir brauchen sein Hilfe," Bedford said. A plea for help.

It went ignored. Owen smiled. "All right, Mzizi," he said. "The time has come to end the charade and do what I pay you for."

This drew no response.

"Did you hear me?" Owen continued. "Get him!"

Mzizi now looked directly at Bedford, his rifle swinging Bedford's way.

"Damn Kaffir!" Owen said. "Do what I say."

Mzizi's eyes shifted. The rifle came up quickly. The crack of the shot seemed to slice the night air. Bedford dropped to the ground. Sloane and Aunt Kate did the same.

CHAPTER 27

BEDFORD was immobilized by the sudden multiplicity of possibilities. His impression was that Mzizi had not fired at him but at something behind him, but there was no time to turn and look to see at what. Owen had his pistol in his hand and had fired a shot at the women, but was turning now toward Bedford. Sloane and her Aunt Kate were down on the ground, one of them screaming. Owen's three Africans were running into the brush. Mzizi had his rifle still pointed in Bedford's direction, and was bolting a new round into the chamber. Everything was moving very slowly, as it had sometimes in aerial combat over Belgium, but Bedford knew he had just instants in which to act, that death was reaching for all of them.

He would charge Owen. There was no time to raise and fire his rifle. He pulled out his revolver and lunged forward. If Mzizi were foe and not friend, he was a dead man, but Owen had less of a shot with the campfire in the way, and was using a pistol as well.

He fired. Something stung the inside of Bedford's leg, and he went sprawling, his arm going into the campfire and knocking down a log in a sudden blizzard of sparks. He rolled away, clutching at his burned flesh, trying not to cry out.

Another shot, very loud. He'd dropped his revolver. Clenching his teeth, Bedford rolled one more time, then looked up.

Aunt Kate was standing near him, a hunting rifle, which she had snatched up from Owen's table, in her hands. On the ground at her feet was a writhing form in khaki— Owen leaving this life like the myriad animals he had slaughtered.

Gathering his strength, Bedford stood. Dizzy, he staggered back to his chair to steady himself. Sloane was standing, too, apparently unhurt.

"Where did you learn to shoot?" he asked Kate.

"I haven't," she said. "I didn't know what else to do." She let the weapon fall from her hands in a clatter.

Mzizi had come up to Owen as might a hunter examining his kill. The Englishman was still moving about and moaning. Sick of the bloodshed, Bedford had no wish to look upon him. Mzizi spoke a few words to him that Bedford could not understand. After a moment, the movement stopped.

The African turned and, without a word to Bedford, walked past him into the bush, where he stopped to examine another body. It wasn't moving at all. Mzizi knelt beside it, probing it here and there, then fetched up a rifle lying nearby on the ground and returned to the others.

"Truscott," he said. *"Tot. Kaput."*

"What did Owen say?"

"He said bad things about Americans."

Sloane had been a statue, but now she came fully to her senses, as though from a trance. Eyeing Owen's body with distaste, and then her aunt with a sort of wonder, she finally turned her attention to Bedford, who was holding his injured arm.

"My God, Bedford, have you been shot?"

"Singed."

She rushed to him, taking hold of his arm tenderly and turning the burned area toward the light. "I was a Girl Guide during the war," she said. "They taught us first aid. I know what to do."

"I'll presume he has a medical kit."

Mzizi nodded and went off to the truck. Sloane gently pushed Bedford back down onto the crate and sat down beside him, cradling his arm.

"What a stupid, beastly idea this was," she was.

"It wasn't yours. It was your uncle's."

"I shall join a movement to have safaris banned."

"I'm sure some of our socialist friends in Chumley's would be happy to join—if only for the novelty."

Mzizi returned with the medical kit, setting it before Sloane and opening the lid. "You want whiskey?" he said to Bedford.

"Champion idea. Whiskey all around. Aunt Kate looks like she could use a couple."

The woman had gone back to her chair and was staring into the campfire.

"Very good. Captain Owen always keep plenty."

"Mzizi." The African stopped. "I'm not urging it upon you, but if you'd like a nip yourself, please feel free."

"General von Lettow-Vorbeck's soldiers did not drink."

"The war is over."

"I never leave the German army."

L**IKE** dogs returning to the hearth, Owen's three Africans came back, viewing the body of their former employer with great excitement, and then offering themselves to Bedford and Mzizi. The king is dead; long live the king.

Bedford put them to work wrapping both corpses

tightly in the canvas segments of Owen's tent, and then had them place the unwieldy packages in the back of the truck. The job was completed by pulling a rubberized tarpaulin over both and setting some crates and other heavy objects on top. Lastly, he ordered the three of them to guard the bodies against nocturnal scavengers—in whose company, he supposed, there might be lions.

"You should get some sleep," Bedford said to Sloane, who was sitting with her aunt, who was still staring into the fire vacantly.

"How can I do that?" she asked.

"Have another whiskey."

"That's your solution to everything."

"It is tonight."

Nevertheless, she complied with his suggestion. Aunt Kate was reluctant at first, but ended up having three. Sloane had to help her back to their tent, after first securing a promise from Bedford that someone would stand watch over them until morning.

"Mzizi and I will take turns," he said.

"You should get some sleep yourself," Sloane said, pausing at the opening to her tent.

"At the appropriate time," he said.

The fire was diminishing. With his good arm, he threw some more wood on it, then hauled one of the folding chairs to the other side, asking Mzizi to do the same.

They sat side by side, Bedford finishing what he promised would be his very last whiskey of the night; Mzizi chewing on a piece of roasted bush meat he had found on a platter.

"You're very good with a rifle," Bedford said. "You dropped the unfortunate Mr. Truscott without aiming."

"I aimed. I looked where the bullet should go."

"You didn't give him much of a chance."

"He was coming right for you. He had a knife. Maybe same one he use on Mr. Asif."

"You gave Owen a hell of a chance."

"Who do you mean, Captain Green?"

"You let him fire a shot at the ladies, and then turn his gun on me."

"I deal with Truscott. Then I look to Captain Owen." He finished his meat, and threw the bone into the fire.

"But that woman beat you to it."

Bedford sipped. The scotch was making him woozy. But his arm was still hurting and he had more to say.

"Mzizi, I don't believe you quit working for Owen when you said you did."

"I work for you."

"You've taken our money, and I daresay you performed some valuable services. But you were working for Owen all the time, weren't you?"

The African put his hand to his chin, obscuring part of his expression, what there was of one. Bedford could not tell if he was searching for words or calculating Bedford's response—and his own to that.

"He wanted to know what you were doing," Mzizi said, finally, lowering his hand. "What you were learning."

"And what did you tell him?"

"I told him I thought you found out who killed Lord Ralls."

"He didn't ask you to do something about that? Maybe stick that short spear of yours into my back?"

"No. He wanted to keep knowing what you do."

Bedford finished his whiskey and set down the glass. There was some growling out in the darkness, but nothing he associated with a big cat.

"Mzizi. I know you and Owen left camp early that morning, and that you went to the clearing where the bodies were found."

"How can you know that, Captain Green?"

"Because you led the way when we all went back there. Because you had a fair idea where to look in the trees for the bullet I found. And because Dixon Smith told me he heard someone following him for a while, until said someone—or someones—turned off in another direction, toward the clearing with the bodies. He said he went that way himself—after he heard two gunshots. That's when he found his wife and Lord Ralls."

For the first time in their acquaintance, Mzizi began to look tired. "I go from camp with Captain Owen. He heard Mr. Smith go off alone. Owen was afraid he would get hurt."

"Or perhaps he heard Lord Ralls go off with Mrs. Smith and wanted to see where they went."

"He say it was Mr. Smith. He ask me to help track him."

"And you found his tracks?"

"I found the fresh tracks of a man, yes."

"And a woman's?"

"Yes."

"And they led to the clearing?"

"Yes."

"And then Owen shot them?"

"I don't know. He went ahead, then came back and told me to go back to the camp. He say there were things a black man shouldn't see."

"And then what?"

"I go back to camp and later Captain Owen come back and wake you."

Bedford yawned. Coherency was draining away.

"Would you be willing to tell this to the police?"

Mzizi shook his head. "I don't want to go to jail. Maybe they hang me."

"If what you say is true, you've done nothing wrong. You won't go to jail."

"I kill Grubb. I kill Truscott."

"Self-defense. My defense. My women friends are witnesses."

Bedford thought of the men he had killed in the war—

machine-gunning them from the air as they marched along a road. The presumption was that, if he hadn't, they would have killed his fellow soldiers. In the end, that was the only reason men killed in war.

He gestured toward the truck. "Anyway, the two men who have the most to say about all this now have nothing more to say."

Shakily, he got to his feet, and took a blanket from a small stack of supplies. Spreading it out near the fire, he lay down—the hard ground now as good as a feather mattress. "Wake me in two hours."

"Jawohl, Haumptmann Green."

THE airplane first flew over at some altitude, coming across the lake. It kept going, its engine noise diminishing, then came by again much lower, barely above the tree-tops. It was Beryl's Gypsy Moth, and there were two people aboard.

Bedford and his companions were waiting for them. The camp had been struck and packed aboard the two vehicles. They'd eaten, and were drinking the remains of tea. Kate was anxious to be going. She seemed still much rattled by the previous night's events.

Bedford listened to Beryl's landing, which sounded very smooth. She had picked the same crumbly mud shoreline where Truscott had set down. It was some twenty minutes after the machine shut down before she and her passenger trudged into view.

"I brought the company you asked for," she said.

JELLICOE, annoyed to be without assistants, spent the better part of an hour examining everything, though giving short shrift to the bodies, lifting the canvas only to note the identities and the number and place of the bullet wounds.

"This is a bizarre tale, Captain Green," he said, putting away his notebook.

"As I am confined to the truth, I make no apologies."

"I do wish you had not disturbed the scene of the crime. That will count against you."

"If I had not packed up the bodies, they would be extremely disturbed—by the local wildlife."

"We'll sort it all out in Nairobi. I dispatched a team of constables. They should be here this afternoon. Certainly by nightfall."

"The longer we tarry, the more these remains are going to ripen. May I suggest we start now and meet with your constables on the road? Sloane can drive the car and you the truck."

"I'll decide what arrangements will be made. And I most definitely do not intend to allow myself to be taken into the wilds so outnumbered by you and your cohorts."

"We're already in the wilds," Bedford said. "And I'd hardly describe Sloane and her dear Aunt Kate as 'cohorts.'"

"Well, I shan't be here to augment your numbers, Inspector," said Beryl. "I've done my duty now, haven't I? If someone will be so kind as to help me start my airplane. I need to be back with my horses."

Bedford raised his injured arm. "I'll do my best."

"Let me look at that."

"A slight burn. I'll explain it all in my statement."

"Slight burn?" Beryl said, stepping close to look. "You deserve to be in hospital. I think you'd better come back with me."

"Out of the question," said Jellicoe. "He's under arrest."

"What for?" Beryl asked. "He summoned you here. It's

dead cert now Owen was the real murderer of Lord Ralls. Let him go."

"Can't. If nothing else, I must hold him for the theft of Van Gelder's airplane."

"Theft is one way of looking at it," Bedford said. "Another might be that I took possession of it to hold for the police—as it has been used in the commission of a crime."

"Are we back to this 'murder from the air' nonsense now?"

"No sir. But if you'll examine it, you'll find in the rear compartment a considerable quantity of a substance called cocaine, which Mr. Van Gelder has been transporting in direct violation of the Dangerous Drugs Act of 1920. Doesn't that interest you?"

CHAPTER 28

"THIS is not an official judicial proceeding," said Sir Ian Mercer, the Crown prosecutor, from behind the great oaken desk that dominated one end of the large room. "This is a continuation of a police inquiry. Statements will be taken down and may be used as evidence in the event of a trial, but this is not a trial."

"At the moment, I see bloody few grounds to hold one," proclaimed Lord Delamere, seated in an armchair to Mercer's right.

There were several of them in that office, a gloomy chamber with the ubiquitous small windows testifying to the colonials' dread of daytime heat and sunlight and a desultory ceiling fan that would occasionally stir the papers on the desk—a compilation of the charges and particulars brought against Bedford.

Police Superintendent Ramsey Haynes was on hand, with Inspector Jellicoe seated circumspectly beside him. If Bedford failed in this enterprise, there was little doubt he'd be marched directly over to the Central Police Station and back to his cell.

"Let me begin by saying that we have taken statements from Miss Sloane Smith and Mrs. Katherine Smith, and they corroborate Captain Green's account of the deaths of Captain Owen and Mr. Truscott, as his does theirs. I see no need for any charges to be brought in that regard."

Delamere nodded his approval of this pronouncement.

"This is, however, an inquiry into the deaths of Lord Richard Ralls and Mrs. Georgia Smith," Mercer said, "a matter as yet unresolved."

"But let us do our damnedest to do that," Delamere said, in punctuation.

Bedford was no lawyer, but held to the notion that, if he could convince Delamere of the truth of this sordid matter, all the rest that he sought would follow—including the swift departure of all the Smiths from Kenya as well as his own deliverance from the threat of the rope. The enormously wealthy Delamere had been the universally acknowledged leader of the white settlers of the colony almost from the day he had first bought land there in 1901. It was a prominence owing less to his money and title than to his courage, honesty, and powerful personality—traits strongly in evidence when he'd led a powerful settlers' revolt some years past that compelled the Colonial Office to quickly end a policy of transplanting the Empire's excess population of Indians and other Asians to British East Africa. A man who'd stand up to His Majesty's Government was certainly equal to the likes of Jellicoe.

Jellicoe had been surprisingly decent about matters, taking custody of the evidence Bedford had acquired and obtaining several items Bedford requested. No one could credibly accuse him of obstruction.

"What have you to show us first, Captain Green?" Mercer said.

"Three packages," said Bedford, taking them from the table at his side and placing them on the desk before His Lordship. "One was taken from a compartment in the fuselage of an aircraft owned by the white hunter Per Van Gelder—discovered there by Inspector Jellicoe himself."

"That's correct," said Jellicoe.

"The second," Bedford continued, "was obtained by the Nairobi police from the residence of Mrs. Mimi Chisholm, an American lady known to most people here, currently visiting friends in the United States. The third package was confiscated from a ship bound for Mombasa from Port Said. You will note that the packages are essentially identical and that they all contain cocaine—a substance prohibited under the Dangerous Drugs Act."

Delamere examined one diffidently, passing it on to the chief prosecutor. "Yes, very well. And next?"

"Inspector Jellicoe, the bullets, if you please."

Jellicoe handed over the three rounds.

"This one," Bedford said, "contains an expended round fired into a giraffe. Mr. Dixon Smith said he had been hunting the morning Lord Ralls and Mrs. Smith were killed and had shot this giraffe. I have a statement from Mrs. Beryl Markham affirming the recovery of the bullet from the giraffe."

He set the misshapen round on the desk. "This next was taken from the ground beneath the bodies, and briefly gave rise to the theory that the two were murdered with a single shot fired from an aircraft. The third here is a bullet the tracker Mzizi and I dug out of a tree at the other end of the clearing where the bodies were found. I believe this is the bullet that actually killed the victims."

"I can't make head or tails of this," said Delamere, holding one of the spent projectiles close to his eye.

"The first round is a .416 caliber and according to the ballistics expert was fired by Mr. Dixon Smith's Rigby rifle," said Jellicoe. "The second is a .375 caliber round that was fired by Captain Owen's Merkel. The third round is also of .375 caliber, but the weapon it came from has not yet been identified."

"There's a fourth round," said Bedford, taking it from his pocket. "It was fired into a railway carriage from the bush a bit east of here. I think you will find that it matches the one taken from the tree, and that they were both fired by a Winchester .375 in the possession of the late Mr. Grubb, a hunter in Captain Owen's employ."

"That's correct, sir," said Jellicoe. "We test fired it this morning."

"Very well," said Delamere. "You have something else there. What's that?"

"This is Captain Owen's private account book." Bedford handed it to the Crown prosecutor. "You will note a number of entries over the past two years of payments to 'L.R.,' which I suggest stands for Lord Ralls."

The prosecutor frowned, went through the pages one by one, then passed it to Delamere, who examined it as carefully.

"There's an entry here *from* 'L.R.,' " he said.

"Perhaps there was an overpayment, and that's his change," Bedford said. There was laughter, though not from the Crown prosecutor.

"May we get on with this, please," Mercer said—a command, not a question. "How did you obtain this?"

"A method perhaps similar to Inspector Jellicoe's."

"Lacking, however, the nicety of a court warrant."

Bedford bowed slightly. "With all respect, sir, what's of note here is what this book contains."

"Does this exhaust your evidence?" the prosecutor asked.

"No sir." Bedford took up the last item on his table, a sheaf of notepaper with sets of figures on the pages. "For this I am obliged to my barrister, Mr. Asif, who obtained this information through proper channels, before he himself was cruelly murdered."

"And what information is this?" Mercer asked, seeming genuinely puzzled.

"Information with which the chief prosecutor is perhaps familiar. Among Lord Ralls's military responsibilities was the colony's border security. He was the officer chiefly concerned with combating smuggling. This is a comparison of arrests for smuggling before he assumed his post and after. You'll note a sharp reduction that continued until his death."

"Ralls was doing splendid work," Mercer said. "A dramatic decline in smuggling traffic was the result. That's all this means."

Bedford coughed, then reached into his shirt pocket, unfolding a cable message and placing it with everything else. "My very last submission, sir."

Mercer held it up to the light, and read, aloud: " 'Lord in Waiting.' " It's signed, " 'T.' Who in blazes is 'T'?"

"This cable is a response to an inquiry I made to a friend in London—a very highly placed friend whose identity discretion forbids me to reveal but with whom some of you may be familiar."

"What in blazes are you talking about?"

"Shall I say, a friend intimately familiar with royal affairs?"

This produced dead silence, then a cautious titter from, of all people, Jellicoe.

"What does this mean, 'Lord in Waiting?' " Delamere asked.

"It's a royal household office, sir."

"I know that! But what does it mean?"

"Lord Ralls was a very good friend of His Royal Highness, the Prince of Wales. During his visit here, you may recall, there were reports that the king was ill, which occasioned the prince's early return. I have reason to believe the prince told Lord Ralls that, if he was indeed to assume the throne, there would be a position in the household for him. I inquired of my friend what that position might be. This was the reply."

The prosecutor looked at his watch. "I'd like to conclude this business, Dee. I'm meeting someone at the
club."

"Please, Captain Green. Sum all this up."

"Yes sir. I believe that Captain Owen, Per Van Gelder,
and Ernest Truscott were all engaged in smuggling of
some sort or another—including substances in violation of
the 1920 Dangerous Drugs Act. I also believe that they
were all paying regular inducements to Lord Ralls to look
the other way. He was famously in debt and short of cash.
His farm had failed. He had no other income besides his
army pay."

"Agreed," said Delamere. "Why should any of them
want to kill him then?"

"I believe he wanted to put an end to this nefarious
business. Conduct himself as an honorable gentleman—in
light of the prince's visit and the possibility of advance-
ment and a future high position. I think Captain Owen and
his colleagues feared that, to demonstrate his newfound
probity, he'd clean up the smuggling in British East
Africa."

"Please," said Mercer. "Conclude."

Bedford gestured to the bullets on the desk. "Shots were
fired at our railway train on the way up from Mombasa, as
that rifle round attests. The weapon used was a Remington
normally in the possession of Owen's assistant Grubb. I
suggest to you that Grubb was the shooter. He was an extremely good shot. And he wasn't with Owen in Mobasa or
aboard the train. He didn't join us until we went on safari."

"Those shots fired at the train served to remove Owen
from suspicion," said Jellicoe.

"But you're saying it was Owen who shot Lord Ralls
and Mrs. Smith in the clearing?" Delamere asked.

"Yes."

"Why wouldn't he have done that earlier?" Mercer

asked. "During one of the hunts? He could have claimed it an accident."

"White hunters don't have accidents. Owen needed a better opportunity, one that would cast guilt on somebody else. Lord Ralls provided him with it by going off into the bush with Mrs. Smith at the same time Mr. Smith had gone off on his dawn hunt."

"Why that business of a shot fired into the ground, then?" Superintendent Haynes asked.

"I've no idea, though I've tried hard to think of one. Maybe Owen was just trying to muddy the waters. An aircraft had flown over the area shortly before. Perhaps he thought someone actually might speculate the shooting had been done from the air. Van Gelder had that reputation. I was persuaded of it for a time—recalling how we used to do just that sort of thing during the war."

"Have you located this man Van Gelder?" Superintendent Haynes said to Jellicoe.

"He appears to have fled the colony," Jellicoe said. "A group of traders saw him crossing the border into Somalia."

"By airplane?"

"In a car. We have his airplane."

"Where Van Gelder has gone doesn't matter," said Bedford. "What matters is that Owen left camp shortly after Mr. Smith did and came upon Lord Ralls and Mrs. Smith in that clearing."

"How can you say that for a fact?" said Mercer.

"I have a witness. Owen's tracker. Mzizi. He accompanied Owen to the clearing."

"Where is he?"

"Out on the lawn. They wouldn't let him in."

Delamere turned to Jellicoe. "Have that man brought here at once!"

Mzizi entered the room between two constables looking like a conquering general come to grant an audience to those he'd vanquished. They didn't offer him a chair. Bedford started to, then realized that the African would refuse it.

Someone had taken his spear. He seemed odd without it, but no less dignified.

Mercer's stern demeanor did not faze Mzizi, nor worry Bedford. Except for the Baroness Blixen, Delamere was probably the black man's best friend in British East Africa.

"You are the tracker Mzizi?" the prosecutor asked him.

"I kann nicht Englisch sprechen," said the African.

"What in hell is this?" said Mercer.

"He's from Tanganyika," Bedford said. "He doesn't speak English."

"Tanganyika's been British since 1919," said Delamere. "How does he manage?"

"He speaks Swahili."

One of the African constables was brought forth to act as an interpreter. What followed was very direct and to the point. Mzizi said Owen had ordered him to come along and track Dixon Smith. They had crossed the fresh trail of Ralls and Mrs. Smith, and, hearing the couple, had followed them. Nearing the clearing, Mzizi said Owen had told him to return to camp. A short time later, on his way back, he heard two gunshots—the one following the other after a long interval.

"But you didn't actually see the shooting?" Mercer asked.

Mzizi waited for the translation. *"Nein."*

"So it could have been anyone? Including Captain Green, here?"

The African started to speak, then caught himself and waited. When he'd heard the question in Swahili, he turned to look at Bedford. *"Nein. Er was schlaffen mit eine Frau."*

"What's that?" Mercer demanded.

Mzizi repeated his statement in Swahili. The translation lifted Delamere's considerable eyebrows.

"What woman was that?"

After the translation, Mzizi looked to Bedford again, and received a nod.

"Frau Ralls," Mzizi said.

Up went the eyebrows again—Mercer's and Haynes's, too.

"You may go," said Delamere. "Thank you." He waited until the African had left the room. "How do you converse with him?"

"I speak German," Bedford said. "I learned it during the war."

Mercer leaned forward. "Is he your only witness?"

"Yes sir. I should have thought he'd suffice."

"He's an African," said Mercer. "And he works for you—for considerably more than the going wage for trackers, I understand. He's hardly a credible witness, especially as concerns eliminating you as a suspect."

"Perhaps we should talk to Lady Ralls," suggested Superintendent Haynes.

"I just now saw her at the Muthaiga Club," said Delamere. "She was lunching with Alice de Janze'."

"I hardly think we need to subject the poor woman to such embarrassment and unpleasantness so soon after her husband's death," Mercer protested.

"Well, I do," declared Delamere. "Inspector, would you please have Lady Ralls brought here."

Jellicoe stood, then hesitated. "You said this was not an official court proceeding. If she does not choose to come, what am I to do?"

The chief prosecutor pointed belligerently at Bedford. "If she declines to join us, then march this fugitive right back to the Central Police Station and a cell. Then we'll set a date for a court appearance."

VICTORIA entered the room primly. She might well have been some elderly lady arriving late to church—except that she had never looked more radiantly beautiful, not withstanding her black dress and hat and the melancholy in her eyes.

The men all rose at her entrance, Delamere offering her an armchair that had been pulled up close to his. She seated herself quickly, not looking at Bedford.

"We shall endeavor to make this as painless as possible," said Delamere, gently.

"Thank you, Dee."

"But, unfortunately, some of our questions will be of a delicate nature," Mercer added.

"I understand."

"At the time of the murder," said Mercer, "you were at Captain Owen's camp, rather than Denys Finch-Hatton's, where you were guests of the Prince of Wales."

"Yes. That's correct." She kept her hands in her lap, perfectly still.

"When did you go there?"

"I'm not sure. Very late. Everyone was asleep. Sometime before dawn."

"Why did you go there, Lady Ralls?"

She made no reply.

"Was it to visit Captain Green?" Mercer asked.

"No. I was looking for my husband. I'd awakened, and he was gone."

"What made you think he had gone to Owen's camp?"

"That's where Mr. and Mrs. Smith were staying. He had become friendly with the Smiths—with one of them."

"Wasn't that a bit dangerous?" Delamere asked. "Walking through the bush in that country in the dark?"

"It wasn't far—perhaps a half mile. We'd been going back and forth. There was a path. And I had an electric torch. We'd been drinking. I wasn't concerned with any danger."

"Did you find your husband at Owen's camp?"

She shook her head emphatically. "No. He wasn't there, and she wasn't there."

"Did you go looking for them elsewhere?"

Another shake of the head. She brushed away a tear. "No. I was very unhappy. I suddenly felt very weary. I was angry and frustrated."

"So what did you do?"

"I saw Captain Green sleeping by the campfire. I got under the blanket with him."

An awkward silence intruded, broken finally by Delamere. "Sorry to ask you this, Victoria, but—well, was this any sort of romantic rendezvous on your part?"

"Certainly not. We were in the middle of a hunting camp. I was cold. Truth to tell, Dee. I got under the blanket because that's where I wanted my husband to come upon me on his return. Captain Green had become a friend. I didn't think he'd mind."

Bedford watched her intently—admiringly.

Mercer consulted the papers before him, then leaned toward her. "Lady Ralls, in your initial statement, you said you and Captain Green were together all that time. You subsequently recanted, saying Green was gone part of that time, and didn't appear until morning." He leaned closer still. "Which of these statements is correct?"

All eyes were upon her. Victoria's were fixed on Jellicoe.

"I am sure Inspector Jellicoe was only doing his job," she said. "But he subjected me to relentless questioning. I was quite distraught—confused. What I meant to say was that I was asleep some of the time. I—"

"Which statement is correct, Lady Ralls?"

Bedford looked at her now. To his surprise, her bright blue eyes were fully on him.

"The first one. I awoke several times while I was there. Captain Green was always beside me."

$\int$ HE departed as circumspectly as she had come. The men she'd left behind sat uncomfortably and uncertainly a long moment. Finally, Lord Delamere rose.

"Well, Green, I'm satisfied. Damn well satisfied. I don't know what more we need to hear. It was Owen."

"We have a motive," said Superintendent Haynes. "A weapon. Ballistics matches. Opportunity. And a witness placing him at the scene."

"And his attempt to kill Captain Green and the Smith ladies," said Delamere.

"That conclusion is agreeable with me," said Jellicoe. "I see no need to detain any of the Americans any further. We can close this matter and wish them bon voyage."

"Hold on here," said Mercer. "What about Grubb? And the Indian lawyer?"

"That's a very nasty neighborhood—the Indian quarter," said Jellicoe. "Asif had a lot of rough customers for clients. The Smiths were paying him quite a larger retainer. It might have drawn some of the cutthroats he'd represented."

"But the bodies were found by the ubiquitous Captain Green here," said Mercer.

"He was Asif's client," countered Jellicoe. "He was in trouble. Nothing at all odd about his turning up there. And he did report the killings, mind."

"By means of the Baroness Blixen," noted Superintendent Haynes.

"Grubb was Owen's accomplice," Delamere added. "Perhaps a falling out among thieves . . ."

"Owen's the logical answer," said Jellicoe. "Now we

can close this case—these cases—and everything will be all tickety boo."

BEDFORD was late to the railway station, and he arrived without luggage. The three Smiths were in the station bar, looking every inch the family group, though Aunt Kate and Uncle Dixon were seated to either side of Sloane, who was not pleased.

"Bedford! Where are your bags? The train leaves in twenty minutes!"

He nodded to the older Smiths, then took Sloane by the arm, urging her toward the door.

"What are you doing?" she demanded.

He caught himself. "Just a brief, private conversation—about a personal matter." He nodded to Dixon and Kate again. "If you'll excuse us. We'll only be a minute."

The waiting area was crowded, acrawl with every class and caste to be found in Nairobi and as noisy as a metalworks. Bedford steered Sloane out to the platform. She turned to face him as soon as they were out the door.

"Explain yourself, Bedford. Aren't you coming with us?"

"I'm going to linger on for a day or two."

"Are you mad? You've only just escaped a hangman's noose. We all need to be aboard a ship steaming for home as soon as possible. And you must get away from this place before these 'white man's burden' types change their imperial minds about you."

"And so I will, probably tomorrow. But I've unfinished business still."

"What can that be? We've said our good-byes. Beryl promised to come see us in New York. The baroness said she'll write. Denys Finch-Hatton gave you a bottle of very good Scotch. And Lord Delamere gave you souvenir

Kikuyu bracelets for your lady friends Tatty Chase and Claire Pell. Alice has even forgiven you. There's no reason to stay."

"I'll be along directly. I may even find a fast ship that'll beat you back to New York."

"Is it that African gentleman? Is he still in trouble?"

Bedford shook his head. "I've enough in my pockets for railway and steamship tickets, a night in the Norfolk Hotel, and the price of a round of drinks at Chumley's as soon as I hit the New York docks. The rest I gave to Mzizi, and sent him back to Tanganyika."

"How much is that?"

"A bit shy of five hundred pounds."

"Good lord, Bedford."

"Consider me a socialist." He smiled, then reminded himself of his purpose. He took Sloane by the shoulders. "There's something more to be done, and I think I must leave it entirely up to you."

She looked unhappily into his eyes. "You suddenly sound very serious."

He wanted very much then to drop the whole matter and try to put it out of his mind. But of course he could not. He reached into his pocket and took out Owen's small account book, placing it carefully in her right hand.

"One of the tricks I've learned from hanging about Detective Lieutenant Joseph D'Alessandro is how to palm things," he said. "I lifted this from the chief prosecutor's desk when we were all standing around and they weren't looking. It's Owen's private account book."

"Why are you giving it to me?"

He looked back toward the waiting area and the bar. "I've no doubt whatsoever that it was Owen who fired the shot that killed Lord Ralls and your unfortunate step-aunt. But there's a complicating factor."

She stepped back. "Complicating how?"

Bedford took a deep breath. "I'm not sure Lord Ralls was his main target."

A confused, then angry look. "What do you mean?"

He opened the account book to a now familiar page. "These are Owen's receipts for the past year and a half."

She looked at the column of figures, then back at him, not comprehending. "So?"

He placed a finger at one entry. "This notes the receipt of one thousand pounds from a person named Smith."

Sloane glanced at the writing. "That's my uncle's payment for the safari."

"No," said Bedford, turning to the next page. "That's over here. The full amount." He went back to where his finger marked his earlier place. "This is a quite different payment. You'll note it actually says, 'Mrs. Smith.' "

She pushed the book away. "Yes, well. Georgia—"

"No, Sloane. Georgia didn't become Mrs. Smith for another three months." He took hold of Sloane's purse and pushed the account book inside. "This entry was made between the time of Dixon's divorce from your Aunt Kate and his marriage to his new and now departed bride. It's a payment of a very large sum that has nothing to do with the safari charges. Made by your Aunt Kate."

Sloane slumped a little. "That can't be."

"But it is. You see it right before your eyes."

"Aunt Kate? That's ridiculous. This is some cruel joke you're playing."

"Just look at the account book, Sloane. That writing is far more persuasive than I could ever be."

She rubbed her eyes. "Why didn't you tell me before?"

"I wasn't that certain."

"How could you be? My Aunt Kate? It's impossible!"

"Sloane, now I am certain."

She seemed about to cry, but somehow managed to keep control of herself, biting down hard on her lip. She looked off down the railway tracks, as though they offered some escape from her dilemma.

"What do I do?" she said, finally, sounding like a lost little girl.

"Whatever you want. It's entirely up to you. The authorities here paid no attention to this entry, and I didn't say a word to them about it. They were much more interested in the entries concerning Lord Ralls. At this point, they have absolutely no interest in reopening the case. Owen's their man—and rightly so."

"But whatever shall I do?"

"I'd give you advice, but if you took it, and then became unhappy with your choice—you'd never forgive me."

"Uncle Dixon. Maybe he could explain. But if I tell him . . ."

"It's your family, Sloane. I am not a police officer. I'm not going to intrude."

"You won't come with me?"

"I'm just going to stay on a day or two. I'll be along directly. You'll want to give this some long, hard thought. On your own. The trip back will certainly provide time for that."

She shook her head, slowly, sadly, then turned away. At that instant, he realized he would likely not see her on the premises of his art gallery ever again. Whatever happened, she would blame him. Whatever happened, she would likely now disappear into the Chicago life from which she had come.

But a moment later, she was in his arms, burying her face against his neck. He felt the moistness of her tears, but there was no sobbing. Finally, she kissed him, then cast her eyes aside and walked slowly away.

Bedford didn't rejoin the Smiths, but lingered in an out-of-the-way corner of the waiting room until he saw them board the train. When it had rolled off out of the station, he walked out to the busy street, where a long-hooded road-ster awaited at the curb.

"That, my darling, was a very, very long 'back in a minute.'"

"I'm sorry," he said, getting in beside her. "Couldn't be helped."

She squeezed his hand, then started the automobile. "I don't mind. I'm too happy to mind."

"Where did you get this car?"

"It was Dickie's. He kept it hidden away. Thought it would rouse suspicion."

"And now?"

"Now I don't give a damn."

They whizzed along the street, dodging cattle, people, and other vehicles. When they reached the screen of trees at the top of Nairobi Hill and turned onto the Ngong Road, she pulled off to the side, putting the shift in neutral.

"I can't wait," she said. "Kiss me."

CHAPTER 29

SHE found the deep scar on his side where a German tracer bullet had torn through his fuselage and flesh—touching it gingerly, as if the old wound still hurt. In memory, it did.

"Is this from the war?"

"Yes. My last aerial combat. I lost."

They were again on her veranda chaise longue, and again without clothes, though the evening was cool. She'd fetched brandy. After all the unpleasantnesses of his African visit, Bedford supposed this was its nicest moment—or would have been, were not Victoria so involved in the worst of them.

"Did I tell you my brother was an aviator?" she asked.

"No."

"He flew as an observer in a two-seater."

"I don't think I knew him."

"He was killed in 1916. Laurence was several years older than I."

"I'm sorry."

"I was engaged to be married to his pilot—Tommy

Allerton. He and Laurence went down to Oxford together. They joined the Royal Flying Corps together. And then they died together in the same crash."

Bedford stroked her hair gently, then kissed her brow. "That must have been very, very hard."

"I was so devastated. I used to have a lovely memory of them, taking off from a flying field in Devon—waving to me. I thought them both gods. But then they crashed, and though I didn't see it, I have this other memory. Flames and screams. And so I married Dickie."

"Are you serious?"

"Yes. He was immensely diverting. He was so handsome—very dashing in his uniform—and a merry fellow. Always trying to cheer me up. And he was from a good enough family. But I wouldn't have married him, were it not for the war. And what happened. I shouldn't have married him."

"He was in the British army?"

"A staff officer. That's how he first met Mr. P."

"Mr. P?"

"That's what the Prince of Wales likes his friends to call him. 'P' for prince. When he made his famous royal visit to the front, Dickie was assigned to his entourage. They hit it off from the start."

"Almost 'Lord in Waiting.' "

She stretched out her lovely arms, reminding Bedford of one of the big cats in repose.

"He didn't want that job."

"I thought he did. The income and all."

"He was making quite a lot of money here, as the world now knows." She snuggled warmly against Bedford's side, prompting him to put his arm around her. "He didn't want to leave British East Africa. He liked it here. I daresay he adored it here. He had his own little kingdom—the Prince of Kenya, he was; as much if not more a prince here than His Royal Highness is back in England. He could do whatever he wanted here—and did. They all do. It's all they do here. Simply what they want."

She had finished her brandy, and now took a sip of his. "He would have hated it back in England. He'd have been rather nothing."

"But he's an English lord."

"Dickie was merely a baron, Bedford. It rates the address of 'Lord,' but it's the bottom rung. Do you know your peerage?"

"It's not something we sat around the kitchen talking about in Cross River, New York, when I was growing up."

"Dukes are on top. Then marquess, earl, viscount, and baron. Baronets and knights don't count. Dickie was merely baron. Lord Delamere? He's God here in Kenya. But in England he's merely a baron. Almost below the salt. It was the same with Dickie. My father never forgave me for marrying him."

"I don't understand."

"My father is the Marquess of Belvoir. He owns thousands of acres of some of the best land in England. When he dies, I shall inherit it all—and the title 'Marchioness.' As Dickie's wife, I've been 'Lady,' but only 'by courtesy.' I shall be Marchioness 'suo jure'—by law. And all that that means."

He had seen a few of England's vast, castled country estates, and could well imagine the magnitude of change her life would undergo.

She sat forward, lifting her head a little. "Do you see? There's still light in the sky. You can see the Ngong Hills."

"Beautiful even now."

"Yes, beautiful. I could never deny that. It's intoxicating in its way—I daresay addictive. There are people here who are madly passionate about this country. Baroness Blixen—"

"Beryl Markham."

"Beryl, yes. She's spent her whole life here."

"Alice."

"Alice is quite mad. But perhaps her especially. Not me though."

"That was Alice, wasn't it—who fired those shots through your window?"

"I don't know who it was—as I wasn't out there."

"But it wasn't you?"

He felt her stiffen. "Bedford, please. You were there. You saw where I was."

"Yes I did."

"And now I'm feeling chill. I think we should advance to the bed."

He hesitated.

"Bedford?"

"You want me to stay the night?"

"Dear boy, I've wanted you to stay the night every night since the night we first met."

"It was late afternoon, actually."

"Afternoons, too." She swung her slender legs over the side of the chaise, and then took his hand.

AN hour and more later, passion drained and further refreshment consumed, they lay staring up at the high ceiling, as though they could see each other's thoughts up there.

"I intend to depart for England within the month," she said. "I'm keeping the car. I'll sell everything else."

"I would certainly keep the car."

"I would like to keep you."

"Victoria?"

"I want you to come with me. We could have a bit of fun."

"I hadn't thought beyond today."

"You could meet Father."

Bedford pondered this. "I'm not even a baronet."

"Of course not. That doesn't matter. The husband of a marchioness does not become a marquess. The title does not convey by marriage. Dickie would have remained a baron. You would remain Captain Green."

"Which suits me just fine."

"Me too." She kissed him, then rolled over, pressing her back and soft bottom against him.

"Are you really, actually talking about marriage?" he asked.

"No," she murmured. "I'm talking about keeping you with me. What happens later . . ."

"But you know so little about me."

"I know that you are different than the others. That you are an actual gentleman, and not one simply by virtue of title, family, or school. And you are an aviator."

"Van Gelder is an aviator."

"No. Not like you. This will sound silly, Bedford, but you are the god that didn't crash."

He had absolutely no reply to that, and lay silent. After a bit, her breathing gentled, and then could scarcely be heard.

He slept as well, but awakened not long after to a hard, sharp thought. He stared at the darkness of the ceiling again, his mind fixed on something quite different. Then, carefully, he eased himself off the bed.

The study looked little different from when he had last visited it. The shattered window had been replaced. The objects on the desk appeared not to have been moved at all.

Bedford opened the drawer. There was still money in the cashbox, though he could not tell if there was more than before or less. This time, he looked beneath the hundred-pound notes and found a small notebook. Opening it, he bent close, holding it near the light.

"Bedford? What are you doing?"

She was more distraught than angry—at least for the moment.

"I'm sorry," he said. "I've been nagged by a question. About your husband—"

"That's my desk! How dare you?"

"Owen's had an account book. There were entries for all the money he paid your husband. But there was another, for nearly a thousand pounds. It was from your husband. I didn't think about it at the time, but the date of the entry— I believe it was after your husband was killed."

Victoria was calm now. "What is it you wanted to know?"

"I was looking to see if there was an account book here that would show a corresponding entry of payment made. And the date."

"Please close the drawer, Bedford."

She was carrying no weapon—and certainly not concealing one. But he did as she asked.

"Did you make that payment, Victoria?"

Victoria leaned against the doorway. "Dickie was not a nice man, Bedford. Not in any way a good one."

"I understand that."

"I'm not sure you do."

He stepped away from the desk. "I'm afraid I must go."

He returned to the bedroom and began to get dressed. She followed.

"Is that why you came here tonight? Just to find that notebook. Is that all we—"

"No, Victoria. I came because of you."

"But why . . . are you going to the police?"

He paused. "No. No I'm not. I want no more entanglements with them."

Bedford was ready. He felt a great sense of urgency now, but he didn't want to simply walk out. He didn't really want to leave.

"I wish I could stay, Victoria. I really do. But I cannot. I've made a big mistake, and I must correct it."

"A mistake with me."

"No. Not with you." He had an impulse to say she was her husband's mistake, but a gentleman would do no such thing.

CHAPTER 30

DROPPING his bags at his flat, Bedford started for his Eighth Street art gallery feeling as disoriented and displaced as he had when he'd first stepped off the boat in Mombasa. Crossing Seventh Avenue, he was almost clipped by a taxi that for a moment seemed to be on the wrong side of the street.

His art gallery appeared unmolested, the "Closed" sign in the street window still hanging askew, the artworks still on display, with nothing purloined—at least so far as he could determine peering through the dusty glass.

The post office would be holding his mail. There was no sign of Sloane inside the shop. There was no reason to enter—unless he simply wanted to be depressed.

Leaving his keys in his pocket, he turned back up the street, stopping in front of the imposing structure that was his friend Gertrude Vanderbilt Whitney's studio and Manhattan pied a terre. A servant answered his ring, saying Mrs. Whitney was on Long Island. Sloane had not been by.

He tried Sloane's Grove Street apartment, with similar lack of result. Chumley's—his favorite speakeasy—was just around the corner. It was early morning, but it would be open. It was always open.

The proprietor, Leland Stanford Chumley, was at the bar, reading a newspaper. His bartender was not in view.

"Help yourself," he said. "Pour me one, too."

Bedford went behind the bar and produced a bottle of bourbon, deciding something that American would taste very good at this juncture.

"I'm looking for Sloane," he said, setting out the glasses.

Chumley looked up from his reading. "She's been looking for you."

"Yes?"

"Yes."

"When?"

"Quite recently." Chumley returned to his newspaper. Bedford heard the women's room door open.

They both froze in place, fixed by the look in each other's eyes. Then Sloane, chic in a very fashionable traveling suit and black velvet cloche, went to the other end of the bar. He poured a third whiskey.

She took his hand, not for any display of affection, but to examine his ring finger. She then released him.

"There was a rumor you'd married her."

"Can you imagine me the lord of a castle?"

"That's what I've been trying to do. But it's too hilarious."

She wasn't smiling.

"You've no idea how close I came," he said.

"An infatuation, Bedford."

"A powerful one."

"What if she was a shopgirl."

"Wouldn't have mattered."

"Rot." She lighted a cigarette, striking the match on the box with one hand, a small trick that always fascinated him.

"I sent cables to you," he said.

"I received one of them. Just as I was going to board the *Berengaria* in Southhampton."

"Was I too late?"

"Everything was too late." She looked to the short flight of wooden stairs that led to Chumley's unmarked street entrance, as though fearful of who might come in.

"Well?"

"Well, what?"

"What did you do about the item in Owen's book of receipts?"

"Do you mean, did I confront Aunt Kate? Did I tell Uncle Dixon?"

"Or go to the police?"

She shook her head, the bangs of her bobbed dark hair falling over her eyes. "I did none of those things." Sloane tossed her hair back. "You said you were reluctant to intrude on what was a family matter? I found I felt precisely the same way. It's their marriage—or was. I still have that horrible image burning in my mind of Kate standing there with that hunting rifle. If he can live with that, if she can live with what she's done—well, I want no part of it."

He waited, wondering how much he wanted to say. "Where are they?"

"They've both gone back to Chicago. They went separately, but there they'll be. I leave it in their hands."

A flicker of a smile, quickly gone.

"There's reasonable doubt, Sloane. Your Aunt Kate wasn't the only one who made a large payment to Owen. He received another from someone else. I won't say from whom, but it was equally as generous. The only difference is that it had nothing to do with Georgia."

"I know. I saw it in the account book you gave me. I wondered about it, since the Rallses were supposed to be stone broke. And it was almost a thousand pounds."

"Where is the book now?"

She gave him a sideways glance through a veil of cigarette smoke. "Somewhere in the North Atlantic. It seemed the best place for it."

He pondered the amber fluid in his glass, looking deep to the bottom. "Perhaps it is. We're stuck with the fact that it could have been either of them who paid for the murders."

Sloane exhaled a whisp of smoke. "Bedford, we're damn well stuck with the knowledge that it was probably both."

"And only one shot."

They drank. Imbibing this early was a Happy Valley habit Bedford was going to have to break.

The next day.

"Bedford, can we just leave it like this?"

"The police examined Owen's account book. They had their chance. Now that it's at the bottom of the Atlantic, I don't think Inspector Jellicoe would be much of a mind to stir the matter up again. It was Owen who pulled the trigger, after all. As far as he's concerned, everything is all tickety boo."

"All tickety boo." She sighed.

"Murders happen every day without our doing anything about them, I suppose. The difference with this one is that it involves two people we care for a great deal."

"I didn't like Africa."

"I did."

She drank. He followed suit.

"It's too early for another," he said.

"I'll buy you lunch. At the Riviera Café."

"What shall we do after that? I don't feel like opening up the gallery just yet."

She didn't reply. On the way out, Bedford set a dollar bill on the bar beside Chumley, nodding farewell.

Sloane took his arm as they stepped out onto the street.

"You could go back to her. You could become Sir Bedford or something."

He put his free hand on hers. "No thank you."

An artist Bedford knew passed on the opposite side of the street, a large paint box dangling from one hand, a leash leading a basset hound from the other. Seeing Bedford and Sloane, he beamed and waved gaily, almost insanely, then resumed his course and his grim expression. Bedford felt at home.

"We failed to rescue Alice," he said.

"I fear Alice is beyond rescue. Always was."

They rounded the corner onto Christopher Street. Bedford turned her toward him. "I just had a wonderful idea."

"A different restaurant?"

"Will you marry me?"

She smiled, as though he had said something very amusing. "You keep asking me that."

"Yes."

"The answer is no, Bedford."

"Why?"

"I'm much too fond of you for that."

AUTHOR'S NOTE

THIS is a work of fiction. Bedford Green, Sloane Smith, Lord and Lady Ralls, Mzizi, Mr. Asif, Inspector Jellicoe, and others are fictional characters created to serve the purposes of this mystery novel. But it's also the author's intent to have the book serve as a form of time travel for its readers, back to the magical if somewhat depraved world that was Kenya's "Happy Valley" in the 1920s. Thus Karen Blixen (Isaak Dinesen), Denys Finch-Harron, Beryl Markham, Alice de Janze', the Prince of Wales (Edward VIII), Thelma Furness, and other actual persons appear in the story as authentically as an author's research can make possible. I hope the reader enjoys the result.